The CAUSAL ANGEL

Novels by Hannu Rajaniemi

The Quantum Thief

The Fractal Prince

The Causal Angel

The CAUSAL ANGEL

Hannu Rajaniemi

TOR®

A Tom Doherty Associates Book

New York

THE CAUSAL ANGEL

A Tor Book
Published by Tom Doherty Associates, LLC
175 Fifth Avenue
New York, NY 10010

www.tor-forge.com

Tor® is a registered trademark of Tom Doherty Associates, LLC.

Library of Congress Cataloging-in-Publication Data

Rajaniemi, Hannu.
    The causal angel / Hannu Rajaniemi.
        p. cm.—(Jean le Flambeur ; 3)
    "A Tom Doherty Associates book."
    ISBN 978-0-7653-2951-6 (hardcover)
    ISBN 978-1-4299-5610-9 (e-book)
I. Title.
    PR9170.F563R33 2014
    823'.92—dc23

                                                                2014014649

Tor books may be purchased for educational, business, or promotional use. For information on bulk purchases, please contact Macmillan Corporate and Premium Sales Department at 1-800-221-7945, extension 5442, or write specialmarkets@macmillan.com.

Published simultaneously in Great Britain by Gollancz, an imprint of the Orion Publishing Group, an Hachette UK Company

First U.S. Edition: July 2014

Printed in the United States of America

0 9 8 7 6 5 4 3 2 1

This is for Zuzana.

He interrupted himself and stamped his foot on the ground:

'You confounded Lupin! Will you never change, will you always remain hateful and cynical to the last moment of your existence? Be serious, hang it all! The time has come, now or never, to be serious!'

– Maurice Leblanc, *813*

Imagining the end of things, when you are a child, is perhaps impossible. The thin child, despite the war that was raging, was more afraid of eternal boredom, of doing nothing that mattered, of day after day of going nowhere, than she was of death or the end of things.

– A.S. Byatt, *Ragnarok, The End of the Gods*

Seaton did grin then. 'Well, you've always known that making things bigger and better is the fondest thing I am of.'

– E. E. 'Doc' Smith, *Skylark DuQuesne*

Prologue

Alone on the timeless beach, Joséphine Pellegrini finds herself disappointed by the end of the world.

The sun is almost down, an orange flare just beyond the edge of the calm expanse of the sea. The globe of Earth hangs in the sky. There are dark tendrils chasing each other in the white and blue, spreading like spilled ink. Matjek Chen's Dragons, turning matter and energy and information into themselves. Soon, they will burrow into the crust of the dying world to swallow the remnants of the subterranean bacterial biosphere. When that last bastion of life is gone, they will devour each other, and only a dead globe of dust and rock will remain.

As Ragnaröks go, she has seen better. The last one was the glorious birth of something new. This is merely the final withering of an ancient placenta, long since overdue.

Still, she watches, for Matjek's sake: it was the last thing he made before the All-Defector took him. Beautiful, brilliant, dangerous Matjek. It's the kind of grand gesture she loved him for, a bit childish but larger than worlds. She allows herself to miss him for a moment, his fierce gaze, his calm smile.

She even forgives him for trapping her inside this mind-shell. It is *old*, like the cocoon of flesh she hatched from, centuries ago. The fine white sand is cold beneath her veiny bare feet. When she hugs herself against the chill, the goose-pimpled flesh of her arms sags in her grip. A sharp pain scuttles up and down in her lower back like a crab. *Age is the cruellest of prisons.*

She would have been merciful in victory. She only wanted to show Matjek how to rule the Universe. And she would have spared him, in the end.

But her tools failed her. Traitorous, ungrateful Mieli, rebelling at the crucial moment, throwing away the glorious destiny Joséphine had planned for her.

And then there is her Jean.

The thief betrayed her. The Kaminari jewel, the key to Planck locks, the one Joséphine brought him back from hell to steal – it was a fake he made decades ago, to mock her. He will pay for that, dearly. Being eaten by wildcode inside Mieli's ship is not nearly punishment enough.

Tools always break. She should have remembered that.

And now she is here, imprisoned by the All-Defector. It left her here after it saw the message inside the jewel.

I'm going to take everything, in the end, it said. *But I still need you.*

As if *she* was a tool to be used and discarded, when she gave that abomination everything. It was Joséphine who sent Mieli to retrieve the All-Defector from the Dilemma Prison, made sure it was hidden in the thief's mind, ready to be unleashed if Jean was caught. A purpose it fulfilled admirably, until it ate Matjek and began to have delusions of grandeur.

It needs to be educated.

She takes a deep breath of the sea-scented air to fan the spark of incandescent rage in her chest.

She will not be caged by a twisted thing bred wrong in one of Sasha's gogol hothouses. She will break this little prison, this tawdry childhood memory of Matjek's, like he broke the Earth.

The All-Defector was a fool to leave her here alone.

Slowly, she sits down, ignoring the complaints of her bones. She digs her hands deep into the sand. It retains an echo of the imaginary day's heat. She lets it run between her fingers. The grains catch the last rays of the sun. She looks closer, tries to see the shapes of the sand particles, all their jagged detail.

No vir, no sandbox, is ever perfect: she learned as much from Jean. And this one is a dream-vir, facsimile of an ancient jannah, not something made to cage a Founder. There will be demiurge gogols here, world-makers that fill the gaps when she looks too closely.

Just so. Under her gaze, the fabric of the vir wavers for an instant. She pushes her Founder code into the crack: *the little red thing and the bed and the vow.* The veil of reality opens just a bit, lets her feel the firmament, the hard edges beneath the softness of the sand. It is locked with Matjek's code, of course. But she can hear whispers.

Who? Founder! Xiao! Fear! they say. The demiurges shudder and flee at her touch, but she speaks to them, coaxes them. *Wait. Stay. Play!*

She knows this copyclan. They are industrious and childlike, and very, very lonely.

They listen to her, suddenly curious. She smiles. She may be caged in a decrepit mindshell, she does not have her

Prime aspect, but she is still Joséphine Pellegrini, ancient beyond reckoning, and she knows how gogols are tamed. *She may be trapped here, but if she can command the demiurges, perhaps she can make a partial, a lesser shadow of herself that can slip through the cracks.*

First, a test.

Paint the sky for me, she tells them. *Paint far and wide. Paint the System.*

Joyfully, they rush to obey. This is what they were told to do by their master, to shape the vir as if it was a dream, fill it with the stories other gogols gather from the distant outside world, and with stories told within.

The sky comes alive with fire and war.

Joséphine watches the System boil with motion like a nest of disturbed ants.

The demiurges show it to her as a swirling galaxy where each star is a ship. The Highway, the gravitational artery of the System, is flooding with refugees – the lesser civilisations of the Belt that have so long huddled close to the brilliance of the Sobornost, hoping to catch a spark. They flee, thinking the great reaping of their mind-wheat has finally come. Joséphine sneers: they should be so lucky as to serve the Great Common Task.

It is shadows on a cave wall compared to seeing through the billion eyes of her Prime aspect, but she is sure to glow with pleasure at the demiurges. *Well done. Now show me my sisters.*

The sky expands, shows the Sun girdled with Sobornost sunlifting machines and smartmatter factories, unfolds into a high-dimensional map of the raions and oblasts and *guberniyas*, and the many-faceted virs within, countless gogols

4

as signals in the neurons of the vast brain of the Sobornost, a cosmic web of thought. A brain at war with itself.

Her sisters are fighting the vasilevs and the hsien-kus. It is a confrontation that is long overdue, after baseline centuries and subjective aeons of scheming and backstabbing. She knows the pellegrini copyclan will lose. The Founders' warminds and weapons are equal, and only numbers matter.

Still, it is not too late. A scheme is already unfolding in her mind. Something to unite all the Founders, that's what she wanted in the first place. The All-Defector can still be her tool, an enemy that will force even the vasilevs and the hsien-kus to join her. Sasha will follow her, and the rest of them will fall in line—

Joséphine frowns. There is something wrong in the weave of the battle. The reflection of her myriad selves in the sky is skewed, like an image in a funhouse mirror.

Suddenly, she sees the pattern emerge, sees the hand of the All-Defector at work. She gazes into the face of an apocalypse, greater than any Matjek ever dreamt, woven out of orbits and battles and thoughtwisps.

She watches the war for a long time. It is like staring into the barrel of a gun, seeing the cylinder turning, inevitable and mechanical, the hammer coming down before the thunder and the white and the black.

It is then that she understands what the All-Defector truly is.

Finally, she closes her eyes, lies down on the cold sand, arms at her sides, in corpse pose. She listens to the white sound of the sea.

It wanted me to see that, she thinks. *It knew what I was going to do. That's why it left me here.*

For the first time in centuries, a void grows inside her, a temptation to end things at last.

Are you sad? the demiurges ask. *We will show you more! We are sky-painters, world-makers, singers, shapers!*

She squeezes her hands into fists. Her knuckles ache. She sits up and looks down at the darkening beach. Her footprints follow the curve of the sea in an orderly row, one after another.

She stands up.

It is my turn to show you something, she says. *If you help me, we can make you a friend.*

We listen! We make! We shape! says the chorus of the demiurges.

She starts walking, stepping into her own sandy impressions with slow, tired strides. Cold waves lap at her feet.

In the sky, the true end of the world begins. Joséphine ignores it. She is busy making a last hope, out of memories and sand.

1

THE THIEF AND THE LAST BATTLE

We are barely past the orbit of Mars when Matjek figures out the truth about Narnia and helps me find Mieli's trail.

'That can't be the end!' he says, holding up a book. It is a big, battered purple volume, with a circular window-like cover image that shows clashing armies. He has to lift it with both of his four-year-old hands. He struggles with its weight and finally slams it down onto the table in front of me.

The Last Battle, by C.S. Lewis, I note with a sigh. *That means difficult questions.*

For the past few subjective days, the tiny main vir of our ship, the *Wardrobe*, has been a calm place. I created it based on a dream Matjek told me about. It is an incense-scented labyrinth of high bookshelves full of haphazardly stacked books of all sizes and colours. Matjek and I usually sit at a rough wooden table in the small café area in the front, brightly lit by diffuse sunlight through the display windows.

Outside – painted on the imaginary glass for us by the vir – is the turbulent flow of the Highway, thousands of lightwisps, rockships, calmships, beamriders and other craft of every kind, reflected from the *Wardrobe*'s solar sails in a myriad glinting fragments. And somewhere in the back, in the shadows, the blue and silver books that hold the fractally compressed minds of the people and jinni and gods of Sirr whisper to each other with papery voices.

Until now, Matjek has been reading his books quietly, leaning his chin on his fists. Which has suited me fine: I have been busy looking for Mieli in the death cries of Earth.

'They can't just all die! It's not fair!' Matjek says.

I look at him and make my sole Highway-zoku jewel – an emerald crystal disc with a tracery of milky veins inside, a gift from a friendly cetamorph – spin between my fingers.

'Listen, Matjek,' I say. 'Would you like to see a trick?'

The boy answers with a disapproving stare. His eyes are earnest and intense, a piercing blue gaze that is at odds with his soft round face. It brings back uncomfortable memories from the time his older self caught me and took my brain apart, neuron by neuron.

He folds his arms across his chest imperiously. 'No. I want to know if there is a different ending. I don't like it.'

I roll my eyes.

'Usually, there is only one ending, Matjek. Why don't you find another book to read if you didn't like that one?'

I really don't want to have this conversation right now. My minions – a swarm of open-source cognitive agents distantly descended from rats and nematode worms – are scouring the System public spimescapes for public data on Earth's destruction. There is a steady stream of qupts in my head, cold raindrops of information from the storm of ships beyond our ancient vessel's walls.

And each of them is like the stroke of a clock, counting down time that Mieli has left.

*

A lifestream from a Ceresian vacuumhawk. A grainy feed recorded by photosensitive bacterial film on the solar sail wings of a fragile non-sentient space organism that was following a female of its species past Earth. Not nearly detailed enough. *Next.*

A <SPIME> from a Sagan-Zoku synthetic aperture array on Ganymede, public feed.

My heart jumps. *Not bad.* A hyperspectral dataset from a few days ago flashes past my eyes, like flying through aurora borealis, multicoloured sheets of light that show both Earth's surface and the surrounding space in intricate detail. The Dragons are dark gashes in every layer, but I don't care about them. With a thought, I zoom into the L2 Lagrange point and the cloud of technological debris where *Perhonen* should be. *Come on.*

'But I want to know,' says a distant, insistent voice. 'Who was the Emperor? What was beyond the sea? Why was Aslan no longer a lion?'

The spime view is detailed enough to show the space-time trail and history of every synthbio fragment and dead nanosat in that little Sargasso Sea of space – except that Mieli's ship *Perhonen* is supposed to be there, too, and it isn't. I swear under my breath.

'You said a bad word!' Somewhere far away, Matjek is tugging at my sleeve.

It is frustrating. All the public data I can find is subtly corrupt, even data with supposedly unforgeable quantum watermarks from zoku sensors. It makes no sense, unless there is a major spoofing operation going on. It makes me wonder if it's already too late.

Where the hell is she?

I rub my eyes, send the minions to scour the ad hoc

networks of the Highway to see if anyone else has noticed the phenomenon. Then I let their qupts fade into distant background noise. Suddenly, I miss *Perhonen*'s intel gogols very badly, although not as much as I miss the ship itself.

'Why did they have to look at his face in the end?'

In a situation like this, it would know exactly what to say.

'Look, Matjek. I am very, very busy now. I have to work.'

'I can help you. I am good at working.'

'It's grown-up stuff,' I say carefully. 'I think you would find it boring.'

He does not look impressed.

'That's what Mum always says but once I went with her to her work, and it was fun. I crashed a quantum derivatives market.'

'My work is not nearly as exciting as your mum's.' I know it's a mistake the moment I say it.

'I don't believe you. I want to try!' He reaches for my zoku jewel. I hold it up, spin it in my fingers and make it disappear.

'Matjek, it is rude to take other people's toys without asking permission. Do you remember what I told you? What are we doing here?'

He looks at the floor.

'We are saving Mieli,' he mutters.

'That's right. The nice lady with wings who came to visit you. That's why I came back to you. I needed your help. That's why we are in the *Wardrobe*. I let you name her, didn't I?'

He nods.

'And who are we saving Mieli from?'

'Everybody,' Matjek says.

Look after her. For me. Promise, Perhonen said.

When a Sobornost Hunter attacked us, the ship tried to

save Mieli by shooting her into space. I'm sure it seemed like a good idea at the time.

The problem is that Mieli served the Sobornost for two decades and carries a Founder gogol in her head. There are too many forces in the System that want access to that kind of information, especially now. For example, the Great Game Zoku, the zoku intelligence arm. They might be *nice* about it, but when they find her, they are going to peel her mind open like an orange. The pellegrinis, the vasilevs, the hsien-kus or the chens will be less polite. Let alone the mercenary company she infiltrated and betrayed on Earth.

We have to find her, before someone else does. And several baseline days have already passed.

Even if I knew where she was, getting to her would not be easy. Our good ship, the *Wardrobe*, is little more than a tangle of carbon nanotubes inside a cherry-sized blob of primitive smartmatter, tugged along a Belt branch of the Highway towards Saturn by kitelike solar sails. It hatched from a 3000-ton Wang bullet. I lit a 150-kiloton nuclear explosive under it to escape a dying Earth. Fragments of the shell that protected the ship still float around us, a three-dimensional puzzle of steel and boron, and a wispy mess of used anti-acceleration gel that trails the ship like a stream of toilet paper from a car window. It's not the vessel I would choose for a high-speed System-wide chase.

And if I do find Mieli and she finds out what happened to *Perhonen*, there will be blood. Mostly mine.

I take Matjek by the shoulders gently. 'That's right. Everybody.'

'I want to help Mieli, too.'

'I know. But right now, you will help her best by being quiet and reading a little bit more. Can you do that?'

He pouts.

'The Princess said we were going to have an adventure. She didn't say anything about you having to work so much.'

'Well, the Princess does not know everything.'

'I *know*. That's why I wanted to talk to you. I thought you were my friend.'

There is a sudden, hollow feeling in my chest.

I hate to admit it, but my motives for bringing Matjek along were selfish: his jannah was the only place that Chen's Dragons were forbidden to touch.

And then there is a fact that not too long ago, I was ready to steal his soul.

'Of course I am your friend, Matjek. What was it about the book that that upset you so much?'

He hops from one foot to another. Then he looks at me with those clear eyes.

'Is this place like Narnia?' he asks. 'Are we both really dead?'

I stare at him.

'Why do you say that?'

'It makes sense, when you think about it. I remember going to Mr Perenna's white room. I was really ill. There was a bed, and then I was on the beach, and felt fine again.

'I never thought about it when I was there. I just kept playing. Mum and Dad said I could play a little longer. They were going to come back, but they never did. It was like I was dreaming. But Mieli came and woke me up.

'So maybe I was ill and died in the real world and the beach is Narnia and you're Reepecheep the mouse.'

Matjek was four years old when his mind was copied into the jannah. The last real thing he remembers is going to the upload insurance company with his parents: the rest is a never-ending afternoon on the beach. As far as he knows, one of his imaginary friends, the one he calls the Flower Prince, came back and took him on an adventure. I can't bring myself to tell him that his parents have been dead for centuries and that the world he knew was eaten by Dragons that his future self made.

'Matjek—'

For a split second, I consider my options. I could roll his gogol back a few days, make him forget all about me and *The Last Battle*. I could recreate his beach. He could keep playing forever.

I take a deep breath. For once, Mieli was right. There are lines that have to be drawn. I'm not going to turn Matjek into an edited gogol like me. And there is no way I am building a prison for the boy.

I take Matjek's small hand in my own. I squeeze his fingers gently, looking for words.

'You are not dead, Matjek. Being dead is different. Believe me, I know. But things can be real in different ways. Your parents never believed in us, did they? In me, the Princess, the Soldier and the Kraken?'

It takes some effort to speak the names in a steady voice. Matjek's imaginary friends – or their distant descendants, the Aun – make me uncomfortable. They claim I'm one of them, and saved me from being eaten by wildcode in Earth's atmosphere. But they did not save *Perhonen*.

Matjek shakes his head.

'That's because we live in a world they can't see, the world of stories. Once we find Mieli, I promise I will take you back to the real world. But I need you to help me first. Okay?'

'Okay.' He sniffs. I suppress a sigh of relief.

Then he looks at me again.

'Prince?'

'Yes?'

'I always forget the stories in my dreams. The children always forget Narnia. Will I remember you when I go back?'

'Of course you'll remember.'

The word echoes in my mind like thunder. *Remember. That's it!* Grinning manically, I lift Matjek and hug him tight.

'Matjek, you are a genius!'

I have been looking for Mieli's trail in public data sources that have been compromised by unknown forces. But there is one place in the Solar System where they remember *everything*. And keep secrets better than anyone else.

Setting up an anonymous quptlink to speak to the King of Mars is not easy, but I work feverishly now that I finally have a plan. I've encouraged Matjek to tackle an algorithmically generated, neuroadaptive fantasy book from the late twenty-first century next: I'm hoping it will keep him busy for a while.

We are several light-minutes away from Mars, and so I slow down my subjective clockspeed to simulate a real-time conversation. I create a slowtime sub-vir and step inside: nothing fancy, just a fragment from my visit to the hsien-kus' ancestor simulation of old Earth, a basement bar in Paris, full of calm, friendly expatriate bustle.

I pause for a moment, savouring a screwdriver cocktail. Technically, the detective and I were adversaries, and I would hate to ask for his help even if he wasn't my ex-lover Raymonde's son. I make a last-minute effort to think of other options, conclude there are none, and send the first qupt, making sure to attach a grin.

How are you, my King?

Don't call me that, the answer comes. You have no idea what it's like. The qupt carries the gritted teeth feel of frustration, and I smile.

It's a title you earned, Isidore. You should embrace it.

What do you want, Jean? I did not expect to hear from you again. Don't tell me you want your Watch back.

Clearly, the boy is growing teeth.

You can keep the Watch. I seem to recall you had trouble with keeping appointments, or so Pixil said. I would like to let him ponder that for a while, but time is short. I need something else, though. Your help. It's urgent.

What happened on Earth? There is a hunger in his query. Did you have something to do with it?

It's better that you don't know the details. As for what happened – that's what I'm trying to find out.

I send him a quick summary of my efforts to find Mieli, adapted to the Martian co-memory protocols.

Isidore, someone has been tampering with all the public data I can find. The Oubliette exomemory may have slipped past them: if your encryption schemes are too much trouble for the Sobornost, they will give anyone pause. I need all the Earth and Highway observation data you have from this period.

Isidore's reply is full of feverish enthusiasm. This is almost like the Kingdom, forging the past, but on a much larger scale! I'll have to use the Cryptarch Key to get all this. Why would anyone go to so much trouble?

Perhaps someone is really afraid of a Dragon infection. That is the best idea my minions found amongst Highway

chatter. *Or to keep anyone else from finding Mieli*, I think to myself. Although why anyone would deploy such resources to hide one Oortian, even a servant of Joséphine Pellegrini, I have no idea.

Please hurry, Isidore. And stay out of this. You have a planet to rule. There is a Sobornost civil war going on: the usual courtesies do not apply anymore. If they find out you have the Key, they will come after you. You don't need distractions.

Like I said. You have no idea, Isidore qupts. **There you go.** A dense, compressed collection of co-memories floods the quptlink. I file it away for detailed analysis, thankful that I kept the vasilev-made exomemory emulation and hacking tools I used during my brief but eventful visit to the Oubliette.

Thank you, Isidore. I am in your debt. I pause. **Please say hello to Raymonde for me.** I try to hide the bittersweet emotion with vodka and lemon, sending the tart taste of my drink with the qupt.

I will. But Jean, why are you trying to find Mieli? She fought side by side with Raymonde, her ship saved us from the phoboi, we are all grateful for that, but what do *you* owe her? It sounds like you are free now. You can go anywhere you want. This time the hint of bitterness is his. **From what I know about her, Mieli can look after herself. Why are you trying so hard to save her?**

The question takes me by surprise. I let time flow at its usual pace so I have time to think. Isidore is right. I could go anywhere. I could be anyone. I could go to Saturn or beyond, find someone to take care of Matjek, and then be Jean le Flambeur again.

Perhonen once asked me what I was going to do when our mission was over. When I think about it now, it is like peeking over a sheer cliff. It makes my gut wrench with fear. So little of me came out of the Prison intact. What do I have left, except promises?

Besides, Mieli still has a chance. She has spent her entire life chasing after a lost love, and it has all been for nothing. That's what happens to those whom Joséphine Pellegrini touches, I know that far too well.

Because it's the kind of thing that Jean le Flambeur would do, I whisper down the quptlink. **Stay out of trouble, Isidore.**

Then I cut the link and lose myself in the data, and finally find Mieli in the memories of flowers.

The data is from a Quiet-built distributed telescope. Like much of Oubliette technology, it is more like an art project than engineering: synthbio flowers with photosensitive petals that collectively form a vast imaging device, seeded in the city's footsteps across Mars. They spend their lives watching the Martian sky like a vast compound eye, until the phoboi eat them.

The data is from the Oubliette exomemory, and so accessing it is like remembering. Suddenly, I recall seeing a tiny dot in the sky. But unlike with a normal memory, the more I focus on it, the clearer the image becomes, until I see *Perhonen*'s winged spiderweb form. A thought brings me to the right moment. There is a flash, and then a smaller shape detaches from the ship, hurtling through the void.

There she is. I follow her with the flowers' eyes.

Mieli floats in the nothingness, a woman in a dark robe, turning and tumbling, until a ship comes for her, a zoku ship, shaped like a glass clockwork orrery. Zoku trueforms – foglet clouds around human faces with jewel haloes – pour out and surround her. Then she is gone, and the ship accelerates at a solid G, towards the Highway.

I summon my minions. It only takes them moments to identify Mieli's rescuer in the public Highway spimescapes. *Bob Howard*, a Rainbow Table Zoku vessel – one of the sysadmin ships that the zoku use to maintain their router network. Uncharacteristically, it is currently on its way to Saturn, riding one of the expensive kiloklick beams, and will reach Supra City in approximately seventeen days. Not very efficient use of resources for a sysadmin zoku, especially given the chaotic situation in the Inner System.

I steeple my fingers and think. The Great Game Zoku has Mieli, there is no doubt about it now. One of their sleepers in the Rainbow Table must have spotted an intel gathering opportunity and has been ordered to deliver Mieli to Saturn. Of course, they could have decided to shove her through a Realmgate instead, turned her into quantum information and used the router network to get her there nearly at the speed of light – but Mieli has military-grade Sobornost implants that could have self-destructed her when passing through a Realmgate. No, they are trying to get her there with all her atoms intact.

I empty my glass, lean back and let the mutter of the bar wash over me. *There is still time.* The seeds of a plan are already taking root in my head. Unfortunately, the *Wardrobe* will never get to Saturn that fast. My issues with the jannah ship are not merely aesthetic.

But Isidore had a point. I *do* have my freedom now: apart from annoyingly persistent copy protection, the cognitive locks that Joséphine caged me with are almost completely gone. Ever since we left Earth, I have been thinking about my *other* ship, my *real* ship, the *Leblanc*, and its hiding place in the Gun Club's Arsenal on Iapetos. If I could just get to it in time—

Or if I could slow things down.

All the uncertainty is gone. I feel like myself again. I lose myself in the plan. I'm going to need tools. *A quantum pyramid scheme. A pair of physical bodies, a nugget of computronium, a bunch of entangled EPR pairs and a few very special hydrogen bombs ...*

I'm going to take her away from you, Joséphine. I'm going to steal her back.

To my surprise, the pyramid scheme turns out to be the easy part.

You are now a Level 4 Navigator! I receive a satisfying jolt of entanglement from the Highway-zoku with the qupt, a reward for discovering a new coordination equilibrium that unravelled a conflict over trajectories through a Jovian Lagrange point. Of course, they don't have to know that I used a botnet to create the conflict in the first place.

Bid for your mass stream herding contract: gathering fragments specified by <SPIME> and guiding them to Iapetos. Offer: a combinatorial auction for Iapetos corridor access or equivalent Highway entanglement. A cetamorph ship – a huge bubble of water held together by a synthbio membrane and crewed by hominid-whale hybrids – wants to take up my job offer to collect the Wang bullet fragments and take them to Saturn. I set up a mental alert to review it later: I can't afford it just yet.

Expressing. Desire. Collective. Join. A qupt that echoes with a thousand collective voices. A big punter, this one: a Venusian floating city jury-rigged into a spacecraft, the *Vepaja*, carrying Sobornost-grade computronium. I devote a few milliseconds of attention to reel it in and send it a quantum contract. The city does not read the fine print. It's hard – NP-hard, to be precise – when verifying the contract structure is computationally intractable within the lifetime of the Universe.

Earth's destruction convinced the Beltworlds that the Sobornost has finally started a campaign of active assimilation. The Highway is overloaded, with every refugee competing for rapid low-energy orbits out of the Inner System. I am one of many entrepreneurial minds to propose a collective computational effort to nearby ships to look for better corridors out of the Inner System, and to win Highway-zoku entanglement. The trick is to embed a simple quantum program in the contract that allows me to skim a small amount off the top of whatever the collective members receive – and to make algorithmic bids for certain trajectories, making them *very* desirable.

Ursomorph rockship Yogi-14 attacking Ceresian ships *Featherlight* and *Honesty*.

I cringe. That was an unfortunate side effect of my scheme. An ursomorph rockship – shaped like a flint axe, kilometres long, sculpted by synthbio and fusion flame – refuses to admit that it lost a trajectory bid. The wispy medusa ships of the Ceresians descend upon it. The Highway-zoku struggles to contain the destruction, sends in their own q-ships, relocates lightmills to route traffic around the expanding bubble of the battlefield.

Mass stream disruption in the Saturn corridor. Streamship *Bubble Bobble* buying mass stream queue positions.

Lightmill in Martian orbit unavailable.

Requesting Poincaré invariant surface access for Saturn kiloclick beam.

Buying derivatives on future access rights to Saturn kilo-klick beam.

I hold my breath. That's the great thing about the zoku: their jewels force them to follow the zoku volition. I watch with satisfaction as the Highway-zoku routes the *Bob Howard* to a slower beam. It does not buy me much – perhaps an extra week – but that is just enough for me to get to Saturn right behind the Rainbow Table Zoku ship. Hopefully that won't be enough time for the Great Game to break Mieli completely.

And of course, I now also have enough entanglement to trade for the tools I need for the Iapetos job.

Smiling to myself, I step back into the *Wardrobe*'s main vir.

It is snowing in the bookshop. Large white flakes drift down from the shadows in the ceiling. The bookshelves look like snow-covered trees, and the café table has been replaced by a tall lamppost, with a cast-iron gas lantern on top that casts yellow, fluttering light. My breath steams. It is cold. Matjek is nowhere to be seen.

Somewhere, far away, there is the sound of tiny bells. A set of small footprints leads into the shadows between the shelves. There is a discarded candy wrapper on the ground, silver and purple against the snow. *Turkish Delight.*

'Matjek!' I shout, in a snow-muffled voice. There is no reply. *How the hell did he do this to the vir?*

I stick my hands into my armpits for warmth and fumble at my Founder code to repair the damage done by the future god-emperor of the Solar System.

A snowball hits me in the back of the head.

I blink at the stinging wetness that slides down my neck.

Matjek laughs somewhere in the darkness. I'm still rubbing my head when the qupt comes. It's Isidore.

Jean! You can't believe what I found! I struggle to receive an exomemory fragment, flashes of flying in the Martian sky, a bright star between a man's fingers. **It's not just Earth, it's the Spike, and the Collapse, you have to see this—**

The detective's voice is lost in a flood of images. Phobos falling from the sky. A pillar of light in the horizon. An earthquake, the whole planet ringing like a bell, the Oubliette losing its balance.

And then, silence.

2

MIELI AND THE MOUNTAIN

You have come to the mountain to find the witch.

The steep slopes and the white, bowl-shaped peak are shrouded in lacelike clouds. The mountain stands alone, perfect within itself, not caring for the narrow human path that zigzags up before you, like a stitch in a wound.

You think back at the journey, at the choices. Beads on a string, jewels in a necklace, one after another.

You adjust your katana and start climbing. The wind brings a whiff of smoke. Somewhere, behind you, a white pillar rises to the sky.

Your village is still burning.

The gaki attack when you make it up to the mountain's shoulder ridge in the early evening.

You are above the clouds now, and the last rays of the sun turn the cloudtops into a mixture of blue and pink. A chilly wind comes down the white slope of the mountain, bringing tiny snowflakes. The breath of Yuki-Onna, the white witch. She knows you are coming.

There are pits in the mountainside above. The gaki emerge

from them slowly, like pale tongues from dark mouths.

They are emaciated, withered creatures, except for their swollen bellies, filled with dark blood. They sniff the air, and come down the mountain path, hesitantly at first, then in a loping run.

Your katana comes out of its scabbard of its own volition, a sliver of bright silver.

The first gaki hisses and swings a scythelike arm at you. Its smell makes you gag: excrement, wet earth and decay. Your katana draws a lightning arc in the air. Ash-coloured liquid spurts out from the stump of the gaki's outstretched paw. It backs off, clacking its teeth together angrily, yellow eyes burning.

Then you see two of its comrades going up the slope to the right. They scamper back down towards your flank.

There is an outcropping not that far below, with a large standing boulder that would protect your back. But getting there requires risking the steep, snowy slope.

A gaki makes the decision for you. It hurls itself straight at you, looking to impale itself on your blade. You dance lightly to one side, slice at its legs; it rolls down the slope, and you follow it, making crazy leaps as rocks rattle and roll beneath your feet, praying that your ankle won't catch and twist.

You nearly fall close to the bottom, but catch yourself in a half-roll, come back up, and turn around, breathing hard. Your back is now protected, but a half-circle of gaki is coming at you, clawing and hissing and clacking and spitting. You wait. The wind picks up. It feels like a good place to die. Your only regret is that the Yuki-Onna will escape your vengeance and keep your lover's soul. You grip the katana lightly, like a calligrapher's brush, and prepare to write a haiku of death.

A feathered arrow sprouts from the neck of the gaki in the middle. More come arcing down at the others, in rapid succession. You advance with rapid, shuffling steps, and strike left and right. A gaki head rolls down the mountainside.

Then another ronin appears behind the gaki. He – or *she*, judging by her light frame – wields a naginata and wears an usagi mask, the cross-marked white face of a demon rabbit. She spins her weapon in an arc and clears a space around her, then lunges forward to pierce a gaki's chest. She stops to look at you. Her eyes flash behind the mask.

The battle goes quickly after that. You coordinate your movements, swift sword and reaching naginata. It feels like you were back in the dojo, and even on the uneven ground of the mountain, difficult strokes become easy, and the gaki fall before you like wheat. Soon they flee, leaving dismembered bodies behind. The rocks are slick with their gore.

Afterwards, you are the first to bow.

'Honoured ronin,' you say. 'You have saved my life.'

She bows back and removes her mask. Her face is dark-skinned, and her long jet-black hair is tangled with sweat.

'The honour is mine,' she says, with a soft voice that is like the whisper of silk wiping blood off a blade. 'Without you, I would have fallen prey to the gaki myself.'

You bow again.

'What is it that you seek, usagi-sama?'

'The witch Yuki-Onna, who has done me a wrong,' she says.

The wind picks up.

'An ill-spoken name. I seek her also,' you answer.

'Shall we join in a common purpose, to seek our vengeance together?'

You hesitate.

'My path is my own,' you say. 'And so are the dangers of the mountain.'

'I understand. But we have both travelled far. Let us guard each other's sleep tonight, and then go our separate ways.'

You nod. You return to the path together and continue the climb, with the usagi-ronin leading the way. You try to ignore a whispering voice in your head, a voice that tastes like fire and sulphur, of a bite of metal against your cheek.

Mieli, you fool, it says. *Mieli, wake up.*

You make camp in a cluster of pitiful, low pine trees. For a long time, you sit quietly and eat your meagre fare of rice cakes.

'Would you honour me by allowing me to accept the first watch?' the usagi-ronin says, after you have finished eating.

To accept the offer would be an admission of weakness, and thus you just shake your head. Could she be a creature of the witch, sent to lead you astray? It is said that everything on the slopes of the mountain belongs to her. But of course, in her eyes, *you* could equally well be one. So perhaps she is honouring you with her offer. You look at each other for a while, but eventually she averts her eyes and opens her sleeping pallet. You nod, rest your katana on your knees, and watch the fire as she falls asleep.

The night mountain whispers around you. The cries of birds and the wind and the distant cries of other, darker creatures blend together into a voice that speaks to you.

Do not trust her, Mieli. She is one of them.

You brush it aside. Surely, it is the voice of a baku, a dream-eater, another servant of Yuki-Onna.

But there is an absence in your chest that the sleeping form of the ronin fills, somehow. The flames dance like the fan of a geisha, colourful and bright. They make shapes that remind you of the wings of a butterfly. Or a heart, perhaps.

After a while, you become aware that the usagi-ronin is sitting up, watching you. 'You look weary,' she says. 'It is your turn to rest. I will rouse you at first light.'

Watching her, you drift to sleep.

In the dream, Yuki-Onna comes to you. She looks different from what the stories say, but then, it is also said she takes many forms. To you, she appears as a gai-jin devil woman in a strange white dress, auburn hair, wearing a necklace of diamonds.

'I don't have a lot of time, Mieli,' she says. 'They are trying to find me. Do not trust the rabbit. This is a zoku Realm, a game. If it was a vir, I could help you, but I have no power here. They are trying to play you. They create mechanics to manipulate your behaviour, to create trust. My Founder brother learned it from them.

'No matter what they tell you, they are the Great Game Zoku. You fought them for me, in the Protocol War. They have not forgotten. You have to get out of this Realm as soon as possible, before they find me.'

Her face is stern.

'You betrayed me, but I have not betrayed you. I could self-destruct and leave you to them. Remember that. Remember.'

Then she dissolves into the rest of the dream. There is a giant butterfly that flies through the void. There is a weaselly man with a grin like the Monkey King. Feverish illusions, woven by the witch.

You wake with the usagi-ronin watching over you. She offers you water: the fire has died, and the sky is pale again. You shiver in the cold, hold the tepid liquid in your mouth and look at her. Surely, it is the mountain witch who is the mistress of many faces and lies, not this ronin who fought with honour by your side?

There is a strange, bitter taste in your mouth from the dream. As if you had just eaten a peach.

'I have decided,' you say. 'We shall climb the mountain together.'

Winds blow down the side of the mountain. They drive raindrops that bite like shards of glass. The usagi-ronin uncoils silk rope from her waist, and you scale a sheer cliff together. Once, a rock crumples beneath your sandal, and you hang above an abyss by the thread. The usagi pulls you up. The thin cord cuts wounds in her hands, but she does not complain.

After the climb, there is little need for words. Your destinies are bound together now, with silk and with blood.

The alien presence in you grows stronger as you climb, perhaps strengthened by the ill wind and the ever-shifting, desolate landscape. It fears the *weight* of the mountain, yearning for flight. It whispers that every action you take is resolved not by nature, but by a Book of Changes, a roll of the dice; that the things you and the ronin did together should not be possible, that you should be wounded and broken. You try to ignore it, but it is becoming hard to shut it out.

At noon, the sky is grey. A fierce snowstorm starts, forcing you to seek shelter in the ruins of an old shinto temple.

A flight of tengu attacks. Bird-men, black wings like shadows in the snow, powdered faces and beak-like noses, curvy iron swords. Their bones are hollow, their bodies light, and your blows toss them around like rag dolls. But there are many of them, forcing you to retreat further into the temple.

While the usagi-ronin holds them off, you discover a scroll

at the feet of a Buddha statue, a holy text whose power drives the tengu off when you speak it aloud. The ronin takes a wound, a tengu claw along her ribs. You bandage it the best you can, but from then on she leans on her naginata as she walks.

At nightfall, you arrive at the crater's edge, and see Yuki-Onna's palace.

They say it changes shape, and it does not look like any fortress built by human hands. It clings to the edge of the crater with stone claws. Its walls are as white as bone. There are three ascending baileys, resting on grey stone bases. Ragged, bare trees grow on top of the bailey platforms, and dark arrow slits glare at you. Low gatehouses cluster around them. It reminds you of the nest of some giant, malevolent bird.

You enter through an iron gate that stands open, waiting for you. You feel exposed, walking the long corridor that takes you through the first bailey, up a narrow, steep staircase, through small courtyards and deserted towers. There are faces watching you as you pass, and you think you recognise dead enemies.

There is a huge mansion at the heart of the third bailey. Dark samurai with rusty swords guard it, but they let you pass.

The throne room is lit with pale blue torches. And there, finally, is Yuki-Onna, white and beautiful and deadly. A young girl sits at the witch's feet, clad in silk, face in shadow, her hair hanging down. There is a pile of grains next to her. She is counting them. Your heart jumps when you see her.

'You should not have come here,' Yuki-Onna says with a cold voice. The bitter taste is back in your mouth.

'I will grant you this honour, sister,' the usagi-ronin says.

'Your courage has earned you the right to take her life.'

There is something in your mouth: a peach-stone. Its contours are rough on your tongue.

You draw your katana in one fluid movement and plunge it into the usagi-ronin's belly.

As the light dims in her eyes, you feel a stab of regret. 'I did not come to take her life,' you say, 'but to offer her my sword. I wished the mountain would take you first, or that I could have died for you. But it is too late.'

'Well done, child,' the witch says. 'Now come to me and accept your reward.'

She gestures and the figure at her feet stands up unsteadily. You rush to her side and embrace her. She rustles in your grip. She has no flesh or bones.

She is a doll, made of cloth.

The laughter of Yuki-Onna is high and cold and blue like sunlight on snow. You let go of the doll image of your lover and fall to your knees.

Your katana claims your flesh just as hungrily as it enters your body. To your surprise, the blade is not cold but hot, burning iron just below your heart. Gripping the hilt with both hands, you twist it upwards.

The witch disappears, and so does the world. And then you are Mieli, the daughter of Karhu. And Mieli is standing on a balcony. Below her is a blue canal. It goes on forever, a thread that vanishes into a haze somewhere impossibly far. The wind is warm and gentle on her face. And above her spreads the vast, vast sky of Saturn, cut in two by the blade of a ring.

3

THE DETECTIVE AND
THE FIREFLIES

The King of Mars can see everything, but there are times when he prefers not to be seen.

Invisible, hidden in a cloak of gevulot, he walks the streets of the Moving City of the Oubliette. As usual, he is late: this time, it has taken a while to elude his tzaddikim bodyguards. The Martian sky is pale, Phobos just a bright promise beyond the jagged teeth of Hellas Planitia. There is a chill in the air. Heaters are lit in the shadows of the tall grand buildings along the wide avenues of the Edge, and diners and drinkers are starting to come out. The city sways softly as it walks, and the distant boom of its steps is a constant, reassuring heartbeat. On the surface, everything is as it always has been.

But the King – Isidore Beautrelet – knows better. He tastes the tangy, bitter undercurrent of fear, sees the excessive formality in the steps of the people who no longer trust their anonymity to gevulot. A smiling couple walks past, hand in hand. The woman is tall, mahogany-skinned, and catches Isidore's eye. By accident, he brushes her memories, remembers being Jacqi the tailor, tears running down her cheeks when she gathered with the crowd on the Permanent

Avenue to watch the death of Earth in the sky, the world she had come from.

Isidore shakes his head. He can hear and *remember* every conversation, every thought in the Oubliette. It is a double-edged gift given to him by his father the cryptarch, the thief Jean le Flambeur's twisted copy, now imprisoned in the needle of the Prison, doomed to play endless games. The only way Isidore can think and breathe is by hiding and, even then, the Oubliette is always with him, just a thought away. He knows how afraid his people are. Giants are moving beyond the sky, and the soft light is not as soothing as it used to be.

His destination is near the southern rim of the city, a small house surrounded by a fenced garden. It is a curious design, round windows and soft amber concrete, almost disappearing into the dense foliage of white sword-shaped Thoris roses that grow wild and thick all about it.

As he approaches the gate, a co-memory message reaches him, as if the rich smell of the roses reminded him of the stern gaze of his mother, Raymonde. He remembers that he is supposed to be at a meeting with her, the other tzaddikim – the city's technological vigilantes – and the zoku Elders, to discuss how to deal with the refugees. He remembers the efforts of the Oubliette's orbital Quiet, overwhelmed by the flux of immigrants from the Inner System. He remembers the Loyalists, a new political party who insist that the Kingdom was real and that all claims to the contrary have been engineered by the zoku – and that Isidore is their tool. He remembers that his mother is going to have strong words with him, afterwards, and that he is not yet too old for a spanking.

He sighs and brushes the memory aside. There have been

endless meetings in the last few months. He finds them frustrating: no solutions, just people pulling in different directions. None of the cold beauty of crimes and puzzles and architecture. And even those are lost to him now: he can find the most cunning criminal with a 'blink.

And then Jean le Flambeur's qupt arrived three hours ago, bearing a true mystery.

He sends a small, polite co-memory to the house's occupant, walks to the door and waits. He squeezes the thief's Watch in his pocket.

A young-looking black man opens the door. At a first glance, he looks like a Time-miser, someone who has saved the Oubliette's intangible currency for extending his life in a Noble body, rather than using it for self-modification or opulence. But his skin has a fresh, almost glowing look, which means that he has only recently come back from the Quiet, passing through the halls of the Resurrection Men.

'Ah,' the man – Marcel Iseult – says. 'Isidore Beautrelet. The famous detective. What an honour.' There is a note of irony in his voice. He gives Isidore a weary look.

Isidore clears his throat. Even before recent events, he was featured far too often in the Oubliette's illicit analog newspapers, but now it's impossible to go anywhere without being recognised unless he masks his features with impolitely thick gevulot.

'I know it's late, but I was wondering if I could—'

The man closes the door. Isidore sighs and knocks again, sending the man a small co-memory. Slowly, the door opens again.

'I am sorry to disturb you, but I was hoping you could help me find some answers,' Isidore says.

'There are no answers here. Only silence.'

'In my experience, that's where answers are often found.'

A spark of curiosity lights up in Marcel's brown eyes.

'Fine,' he says slowly. 'I suppose you had better come in.'

It looks like the apartment used to belong to an artist, but now it feels more like a tomb. There are sculptures covered by dusty tarpaulins, a bright working area that is covered in the clutter of decades, full of old claytronic models and sketches and found objects. The only pieces of art that are prominently displayed are paintings that have small, fleeting co-memories attached to them. They give Isidore flashes of two young men together.

'It was time for a nightcap, anyway,' Marcel says. 'Can I offer you something? You look like you could use one. No wonder: you must be very busy, trying to fix the world.'

'It sounds like you disapprove.'

'Oh, I think your efforts are admirable, it's just that they make little difference. We are about to be eaten, and we must enjoy the time we have left. Such as it is.'

Marcel opens a mahogany cupboard and takes out a bottle of cognac and two classes. He fills them to the brim with the dark amber liquid and offers one to Isidore. Mournful ares nova starts to play in the background, gently amelodic tones.

'That is a very bleak view of things,' Isidore says. 'But I will drink to saving the world.'

Marcel lifts his glass without a word and smiles. Isidore coughs at the sting of the drink, and only sips a little. So far, he has resisted trying to numb the constant tickle of exomemory with drugs. Besides, alcohol has a way of making him talkative, and that might be counterproductive under the present circumstances.

'It's a realistic view,' Marcel says. 'Ever since the Collapse, we have not *mattered* very much. I was not at all surprised by what you discovered – that our precious Kingdom was a zoku lie. If anything, I don't think you went far enough. I believe we have always been playthings, simulations in some Omega Point where Sobornost has won.'

'They haven't. Not yet. That's why I'm here.'

'Ah. Idealism. Heroics. Very well. What can I do for you, to help you save the world?'

'Earlier today, someone … asked for my help. It seems that at least in one instance, information about a major event outside the Oubliette that has been lost elsewhere has been preserved in the exomemory. I am trying to find out if there are other examples of unique information that cannot be found anywhere else.'

'I see.' Marcel touches his lips with a forefinger.

'Paul Sernine used to visit you, did he not? He gave you a Watch.'

The words come out more rapidly than they should. When the thief asked for his help, Isidore felt something click into a gap in an old unsolved puzzle. *What did Paul Sernine find on Mars?* Even the thief himself failed to find out, and Isidore very badly wants to see le Flambeur's face when he tells him the answer.

Marcel slams his glass down on a table. The cognac wobbles sluggishly in Martian gravity.

'Yes. Yes, he did. And then he took my Time away, just because it amused him to do so, just because it was a part of his scheme. He pretended friendship because it suited him.'

Isidore sighs. Le Flambeur – posing as a man called Paul Sernine – hid something in the memories of his friends, twenty years ago, and came to reclaim it recently. As a result, nine people were sent to the Oubliette's afterlife prematurely:

after considerable effort, Raymonde and Isidore convinced the Resurrection Men to allow them to return.

'So be careful when you talk to me about Paul Sernine,' Marcel says. He narrows his eyes. 'I've never noticed it before, but you *look* like him. Don't tell me this is another one of his games.'

'It's not, I promise,' Isidore says. 'Quite the opposite. I'm trying to figure out why he did what he did. It's important to know why he visited you. Would he have had access to your partner's memories?'

'Owl's? What does he have to do with this?'

'That's what I'm trying to find out. Please. It's important. Not just to me, but to all of Mars.'

'I see.' Marcel runs a hand along his shaved scalp. 'I suppose it's possible. Not with my permission, but then he did give me that damned Watch. The tzaddikim told me that he hid things in my memories, somehow. And Owl and I shared everything: he had no secrets from me. So Paul could have accessed Owl's memories through my gevulot. What good that would have done him, I do not know.'

Isidore takes a deep breath. 'With your permission, I would like to take a look at those memories. The night of the Spike in particular. I have been trying to understand why the person you knew as Paul Sernine came back here, what he was looking for. There is a pattern, I can feel it, and it's related to the Sobornost civil war, the Spike, what happened to the Earth – to everything. We need to understand it if Mars is to survive this.'

'Hm.' Marcel smiles a sad smile. 'So you really think it's worth it? Saving our world, even if it is built on a lie?'

'Yes, I do,' Isidore says. 'Not all illusions are bad. Sometimes they are necessary. My father – my adoptive father – taught me that.'

Marcel looks at Isidore. Then he picks up his glass.

'Very well. Please come and meet my love. His name is Owl Boy.'

Owl Boy sits by the window wrapped in a medfoam cocoon, looking out. There are fresh flowers in the room, and a faint lavender smell from scented candles. It is clearly the cleanest room in the house. The view is directly over the Martian desert. The city is passing through Hellas Planitia, and tendrils of orange dust worm along the rough surface behind it.

Owl Boy makes hollow metallic sounds in his throat, like a fingernail tapping a tin can. His Noble body is still young, but he has the face of an old man, slack-jawed and worn. His eyes are blank. The gevulot around him feels foggy, broken.

Marcel kisses his cheek. 'I take it you know about his condition?'

'I 'blinked it. His brain was altered by the Spike in ways that the Resurrection Men do not understand: there is a quantum condensate in his microtubules, something like the ancient theories of consciousness, but artificial. He can't go to the Quiet, or the condensate might collapse, and they do not know what would happen then.'

'Twenty years, he's been like this.' Marcel sighs. 'I live in hope. Quantum states do not live forever. Perhaps he will come out of it. When he does, I will be waiting. So I live modestly, stretch out my days.'

'Perhaps the zoku can help him. I could talk to—'
Marcel smiles sadly.

'I do not put my trust in gods anymore,' he says. 'Please. Do what you came to do. It will be his bedtime soon.'

Isidore nods, holds the thief's Watch in a tight grip and takes out the Key in his mind, the one that opens the doors of all memory.

Owl Boy's exomemory unfolds before him, but Isidore closes his eyes to most of it, 'blinking for a night in a glider, over Noctis Labyrinthus. The night of the Spike.

And then he remembers being there, above Ius Chasma, laughing at Marcel's fear at the aerial acrobatics.

Owl Boy thinks Marcel can be such a *girl* sometimes. To pacify him he takes the glider higher, to see the stars. It has been a good night. Sometimes he does not understand Marcel, his obsession with his work, his need to be alone. But up in the night sky, it feels like they are meant to be together.

And of course, that's exactly when Marcel has to drop the bomb.

'I've been thinking about going away,' Marcel says.

'Leaving?' Owl Boy says. Somewhere, far away, Isidore tastes his disappointment, the bitter sting that pierces his chest. 'Where would you go?'

Marcel gestures. 'You know. Up. Out there.' He presses his palm against the smooth, transparent skin of the glider.

'It's a stupid cycle here, don't you think? And it doesn't feel *real* here anymore.'

Owl Boy is angry now. *Is that what I am, after all? A part of the stupid cycle. A diversion, something that you could play with before you go to do bigger and better things?* He lets it come out in his words.

'Isn't that supposed to be your job? Feeling unreal?'

'No,' Marcel says. 'It's about making unreal things real, or real things more real. It would be easier, up there. The zokus have machines that turn thoughts into things. The Sobornost say that they are going to preserve every thought ever thought. But here—'

Here it comes, thinks Isidore, clinging onto his self, trained by his Kingship to sustain the flow of his own consciousness in the river of memory, looking at Owl Boy's frozen thoughts one by one. *Is this why Marcel clings to him? Because the last thing he told him was about going away?*

The time in the memory slows down. Marcel's fingers are pressed against the glass. A bright Jupiter winks between his fingers. And then there is another memory, a sudden discontinuity, a knife-cut through the thread of Owl Boy's thoughts.

Marcel can be such a girl sometimes. Jupiter is bright between his fingers. A sudden discontinuity—

Isidore remembers remembering, is caught in a memory of the memory itself, an infinite mirror tunnel that draws him in. Marcel's fingers move more and more slowly. Time flows sluggish and cold, as if he was swimming against an icy current.

Of course. The thief would have left a trap for anyone who tried to follow. A memory pit that traps you in the infinite moment.

But Isidore is not anyone. He is everyone. He is the King of Mars, and exomemory holds no secrets for him.

Struggling against the memory flow, he takes out the Key again, and reluctantly summons its *other* function: accessing the back doors of memory that allows them to be edited, changed and manipulated. It burns red-hot against the ice of the memory trap and melts it away. Time leaps forward like a dog from a snapped leash.

Jupiter explodes in Marcel's hand and turns his fingers into red glowing pillars. There is a rain of stars in Owl Boy's eyes. And then the quantum gods speak to Isidore.

The first voice belongs to a child. A tiny hand holds his own, by two fingers.

You live on an island called causality, the voice says. *A small place, where effect follows cause like a train on rails. Walking forward, step by step, in the footprints of a god on a beach. Why do that when you could run straight into the waves and splash water around?*

Laughter. He feels the joy of water droplets flying up, glittering in the sun, toes digging into the sandy bottom, and he knows that he could leap up and fall and all it would do is create a big splash.

Causality. It's a lens through which we see things. An ordering of events. In a quantum spacetime, it is not unique. It's just one story among many.

Listen. We'll explain.

You have to understand before you can be us.

A different voice, an older male voice, a tone that sounds like Pixil's tanglemother the Eldest, with the same hint of ancient weariness.

It was an idea they already thought of in the twentieth century, that spacetime could compute. They tested it, in the last days of the Large Hadron Collider, when they learned how to make tiny black holes. Encode computations into their event horizons, then probe the information paradox by smashing them together, see if quantum gravity is more powerful than Turing Machines or their quantum cousins. Something to do for the humming LHC, still warm from finding the first Higgs.

Fragments of lifestreams come, images of blackboards and huge humming machines in tunnels, distraught faces pointing at screens. The frustration he knows all too well when two shapes do not fit together, when there is no pattern.

No one expected to find something wrong *in the starbursts of the collisions. At first, what came out seemed like noise. It took many experiments, but the data was clear. The answers were there, but they were* encrypted. *Spacetime was not just a computer, it was a trusted quantum computer. To run anything on it, you needed a key, to open Planck-scale locks.*

It was thought it was another law of nature, another speed limit, another second law of thermodynamics. It was forgotten for a long time. Until we were born.

Who are we and how did we come to be?

A third voice joins in, a female voice, warm and rich like Marcel's cognac. It makes Isidore feel safe.

We are the Kaminari: the fireflies, the short-lived, those drawn to light.

When the Collapse came and no one could afford to live on Earth anymore, we took care of our own. We piled our fleshbodies into the cargo holds of asteroid-mining ships hastily augmented with life support, moved our minds and early jewels – clumsy ion traps or diamonds that held slow light – strapped them to rockets that we launched to Jupiter and Saturn like little glittering Kal-Els as the world tore itself apart around us.

And that's when the adventure really began.

We grew and we fragmented and became many. We forged jewels to house those things that defined us, our relationships to each other, those things that could not be copied, only given or stolen. We built Realms to play in. We covered the great planets in smartmatter. We fought wars with the Sobornost. We made little suns to warm the Oortians.

And now we are old. The game of being Kaminari has lost its thrill. But the Planck locks remain, teasing us. We think we know what lies beyond.

The voices become a chorus, speaking in unison.

A dreamtime. The infinite, sunlit sea.

We have done most of the work. We found a solution in the most unlikely place: in the Collapse, in our own genesis. A beginning hidden inside an ending.

We just need your help to make it real.

If you want to leave the island, give us your hand. Accept our entanglement. Join your volition to ours.

So we can be you. So we can all swim out to the sea.

Isidore sees three figures standing in the light, reaching out to him, stars shining in the palms of their open hands. He opens his arms to embrace them, to accept the bright thought they are offering him. His fingers entwine with theirs and then it is like he is not one but many, a node in a web of light stretching across the System, a part of something that he does not understand but which he can touch through the light of Jupiter in the sky, between Marcel's fingers.

The entangled web grows at the speed of light, stretches from Mars to Earth to Saturn and beyond, as billions of minds accept the Kaminari's offer. He does not understand how, but on Jupiter, their shared brightness is used to make a key, and it is turning in the lock.

No. Stop. The Kaminari chorus cries out. Isidore feels it, too, a wrongness in the weave, a hidden thread in the web that tightens, suddenly, like a noose. A trap. A betrayal.

The web unravels and catches fire. Far away, the Kaminari struggle to contain it. For Isidore/Owl Boy it is too late. The light consumes him as Jupiter dies in the sky.

*

Isidore opens his eyes and blinks at the light, but it is only Phobos that shines on his face, in the zenith of its rapid journey across the sky, casting golden beams through the dust curtains of Hellas Planitia. He is back in Owl Boy's room. The mystery of the Spike flows through his thoughts like an inverted avalanche, pieces assembling themselves into something larger than he could have ever imagined.

He grabs his zoku qupter and sends a dense thought to the thief. **Jean! You can't believe what I found!** He wraps the vision of the Kaminari in the qupt as a co-memory. **It's not just Earth, it's the Spike, and the Collapse, you have to look at this!**

The link breaks. Something is wrong. The room is too silent. There is a faint smell of ozone in the air. Marcel stands still next to him, eyes wide, mouth half-open, frozen.

And Isidore's connection to the exomemory is gone.

The silence is so overwhelming that it takes him a moment to notice the fourth person in the room – or more like a person-shaped disturbance, a black and faceless shadow that does not catch the light properly. There is a silver rocket-shaped q-gun floating in the air above its left shoulder. The weapon's sharp end glimmers dangerously, tracking Isidore's every movement.

'I apologise for any inconvenience caused,' the shadow says. Its voice is vaguely male, but metallic and distorted. 'Did I say that right?'

Isidore does a quick calculation in his head. He is not sure how much time has passed – only a few minutes, perhaps – and it should only take his bodyguard of the night, the Futurist, a few more to find him. He probes the exomemory to see if he could get a message out, but there is simply nothing there, the same empty feeling he has only experienced

43

before while visiting the zoku colony in the Dust District.

'You should have left things alone,' the shadow says. 'But it is not too late to make it right. Just give me the Cryptarch Key, and I'll help you forget.'

'Why?'

'What you found is dangerous. It's much better for all of us if I erase it for good, both from the exomemory and your mind.'

'You are too late. I already sent it out.'

'Ah. Well. That situation is already being dealt with, I'm told. Above my paygrade, in any case. It does not concern you. Please, I am asking nicely. Give me the exomemory key. I know you don't want it anyway.'

'It is not mine to give,' Isidore says. *I need to buy time.* 'Not many people know about the Key. You are somebody from Pixil's zoku, aren't you?'

'Yes and no. We have sleepers in every zoku.'

'But why are you doing this?'

The shadow fidgets with its hands. 'Because we have to protect you. We keep things stable. We keep things sane.'

Isidore stares at him. 'It was *you*, whoever you are. You caused the Spike. You interfered with what the Kaminari were doing. *That's* what destroyed Jupiter. That's what broke this poor man's mind. And you have been covering your tracks ever since. Why would you tamper with data from Chen's attack on Earth? Who are you?'

'It doesn't matter. Look, Isidore, if you don't cooperate, we will have to take more drastic measures. If we can't edit the exomemory, we'll have to … erase it. The situation in the System is too unstable to risk the information you have falling into the wrong hands. Please, it's just a few edits for the greater good, you won't even notice it.'

'No.' Suddenly, Isidore is full of a righteous fury. 'The Cryptarch deceived us long enough, with the zoku's help, no less. We are not doing that again.'

'You don't understand.' The shadow's metallic voice is almost desperate. The q-gun brightens. 'I don't want to do this, you understand, but I have to follow the zoku volition, I don't have a choice. I'm going to take the Key from your mind, Isidore. I'll try to make this painless.'

'Pixil said you always have a choice, that you are always free to leave.'

The shadow sighs. 'She is too young, not entangled enough. She'll learn. It's no use trying to distract me, Isidore. Your tzaddikim won't make it here in time. We built their technology, remember? I can control what they see. And afterwards, their memories will change, too.'

Isidore blinks. One more piece falls into place. 'You're one of the Elders. You're Sagewyn.'

The shadow explodes into a zoku trueform, a swirling mandala of foglets and jewels, with Sagewyn's face in the middle, still wearing a lopsided, pointy-eared mask. 'One more thing for you to forget,' he says.

Isidore takes the thief's Watch from his pocket. It is cold and heavy in his hand.

'Wait.'

'You can't flee into the Quiet, Isidore,' Sagewyn says. 'I have blocked your access to the exomemory. Just close your eyes. It will be over soon.'

'It's not my Watch,' Isidore says, 'although it was Justin the Watchmaker who modified it for me. We of the Oubliette are not zoku or Sobornost, but we have our own crafts. I have known for a long time that someone would come for the Cryptarch Key, so I took precautions.' There is a knot in his belly, and his hand shakes, but he holds the blazing trueform's gaze. 'It has a Mach-Zehnder trigger, coupled to my brain. And a microgram of antimatter. It should be enough to take out us both. Certainly enough to burn the Key.'

Sagewyn swirls back into the form in which Isidore first met him, a heavyset man in a blue cape with a ragged edge. His shoulders sag, and he looks tired. He smells faintly of stale sweat.

'I was worried there would be something like that. I like you, Isidore. I like all of you. I wanted to give you a chance.'

'We'll stop you,' Isidore says. 'Whatever you are planning, it won't work.'

Sagewyn sighs and clasps his hands behind his back, rocking back and forth on his heels.

'We already did it, thirty-five minutes ago.'

The zoku Elder smiles wistfully. 'I've always wanted to say that.' He turns to look at the sky. 'They'll blame the Sobornost for it, of course. It's all part of the game. Nothing is without purpose.'

Sagewyn becomes a black ragged silhouette against a white light outside. The silence disappears, and the exomemory is back in Isidore's head. Phobos arcs down towards Hellas Planitia, a sharp, sudden sunset. A chorus of panic and fear echoes through the exomemory, rushing into Isidore like a tsunami. A white pillar rises in the horizon. Everything shakes. The city stumbles.

The last thing Isidore sees is Marcel, a hand squeezing Owl Boy's shoulder, looking at the light, a sad look in his eyes, as if he knew he was right all along.

Like a drowning man, Isidore reaches out to the exomemory. His mother, in the Gentleman's guise, floating far above the city's rooftops. Pixil, walking through an agora of the Permanent Avenue with her friend Cyndra. His Quiet foster father, toiling in the footsteps of the city, looking up from the wall he is building as the light grows brighter. There is no time for words. Their minds meet, and for a moment, they fit together like the pieces of a puzzle. Pixil's rage, her hand on her sword; Raymonde's futile attempt to create a foglet shield around the city, his father's Quiet calm as he places a final regolith brick on top of the unfinished wall and turns to face the light, and suddenly, he is not alone in the maelstrom of fear anymore.

As Isidore erases the last of the gevulot between himself and his loved ones and their courage and love fills him, he/they suddenly know what must be done.

The Cryptarch Key turns in all the mind-locks of the Oubliette. The boundaries of memory dissolve, as if they had never existed. All the privacy trees of gevulot collapse into a single point. All secrets are revealed. All memory is one. Centuries, millennia of life, shared in an instant.

As the Phobos singularity consumes the planet and becomes incandescent, the mind called the Oubliette opens its million eyes and looks straight into it, no longer afraid.

4

THE THIEF AND THE GUN CLUB

Just before the Iapetus job starts to go south, Barbicane the Gun Club Elder and I watch zoku children play global thermonuclear war.

We drink dark tea in the mahogany-panelled drawing room of the Gun Club Zoku's copper-and-brass sky-train. It rides smoothly along the bright golden curve of the Club's orbital ring around Iapetus, fast enough to create a cosy half a g of artificial gravity. Our view of the Saturnian moon's surface through the large, circular viewports is spectacular. We are above the Cassini Regio, a reddish-brown birthmark that stains the white of the icy surface. It makes Iapetus look like a giant yin-yang symbol. And inside the Turgis Crater, five hundred kilometres in diameter, directly below us, is a miniature Earth. A disc of green and blue, its continents and seas circumscribed by a glowing silver line.

'The Cold War Re-Enactment Society, they call it,' Barbicane says in his bassoon voice. He gestures at the view flamboyantly with the gleaming fractal foliage of his manipulator arm. It makes a tinkling sound against the viewport glass.

The amber halo of zoku jewels orbiting his stovepipe hat like a miniature Solar System makes Barbicane look like a melancholy saint. In contrast to most members of his zoku, the Elder's primary body actually has biological components left. His head belongs to a fifty-something man with impressive red sideburns, a prominent nose and a fierce blue-eyed gaze. But the rest of him is artificial: a rounded, cast-iron torso, a bushbot manipulator arm and a heavier, cylindrical gun limb. His legs are brass stumps – exhaust ports for small ion engines. He smells faintly of machine grease, metal polish and an old man's aftershave.

'Too modern for me, dear Raoul, far too modern! But I applaud their enthusiasm. They even made the warheads by hand, the old-fashioned way. Synchrotrons and plutonium! Aah!' Barbicane makes a rumbling sound of pleasure.

In fact, they had a little help this time. I smile, recalling my dealings with the zoku youths a few days ago, in a different guise from my current persona of Raoul d'Andrezy, an emigré and antique dealer from Ceres. *Give children matches and they will start fires. Nothing ever changes.*

The silver ring running along the crater's steep edge is a zoku Magic Circle that defines the boundary of the playground and the rules of reality within. The North American continent inside is dark, perforated by pinpoints of city lights. Every now and then, it is lit for a second by the dazzling wink of a hydrogen bomb.

'Delightful,' I say, as the East Coast goes up in a shower of nuclear sparks. The response is already on its way. White parabolic arcs of ballistic missiles reach for Moscow and Leningrad like skeletal, clawed fingers.

Suddenly, I wonder what they saw in the Oubliette, when the rain of fire started.

Maybe it was the Sobornost, as the System chatter would have us believe. Maybe it was Joséphine covering her tracks. Maybe the chens did not want an active zoku presence so close to the Inner System, without Earth as a buffer zone. Maybe the vasilevs and the hsien-kus just wanted to stop anyone else from getting the Oubliette minds they had been pirating for years.

I want to believe one of those things is true. At least that way, there would be a chance that the Oubliette citizens survived as gogols, somewhere. But deep down, I know the truth is worse.

I told him not to get involved. I told him.

Mars is gone, collapsed into a single point, eaten by the artificial singularity of Phobos, and with it, nearly everyone alive I could call friends and lovers and sparring partners. Raymonde. Isaac. Gilbertine. Xuexue. The foolish, brilliant Isidore. What was left of my other self, Jean le Roi, and his Prison. The Quiet and the phoboi. Gone. Locked behind an event horizon together.

They were never yours. They belonged to the other Jean, the one who betrayed them, the one who left them. You don't need to miss them.

Perhonen was right when she told me I'm a good liar. But the best lies I save for myself: they are perfectly crafted, indestructible and glittering, like zoku jewels.

My eyes sting. Without thinking, I pinch the bridge of my nose. Then I feel Barbicane's eyes on me.

'Raoul? Would you like more tea?'

I smile, giving myself a mental kick. I need to stay sharp. Barbicane is not really a steampunk cyborg gentleman, he's a quantum-brained posthuman *playing* one. Of course, for the zoku, the two are close to the same thing. Everything is a game. The tobacco smell in the room, the mahogany tables and armchairs, the gas lamp candelabras made of revolvers, the lemony taste of the Labsang Souchong tea – all of it is defined by the train's Circle, a game in which we bargain like civilised gentlemen in a nineteenth-century club room.

'No, thank you. I was just thinking that you start them off in the trade early.'

Barbicane sighs.

'It's the zoku volition, dear boy, impossible to resist. We are all made for a purpose! Well, except us old clankers, of course. The young ones make me feel positively ancient, growing up so fast! Tomorrow, they will make Realms and Circles and guns that I can't even imagine.' He frowns. 'Better than this one, I hope!'

'But you are not a fan of the atompunk aesthetic?'

'Ha! Indeed not! There is no beauty in an *uncontrolled* nuclear explosion! *Your* item, on the other hand—' He winks.

Now we are in business. I suppress a sigh of relief. Barbicane likes to talk, and during the last hour, I've heard more about guns than I ever wanted to know – especially after the intimate lessons my stay in the Dilemma Prison of the Sobornost taught me about their effects. But now it is clear that he wants to buy what I have to sell.

'I take it you are interested?'

'Raoul, you know very well that I cannot pass up on a genuine Wang bullet from a 150-kiloton Verne cannon.'

'I can personally guarantee that it has.'

'Capital!'

'Of course, there is still the small matter of the price …' I set my teacup down and fold my hands.

He raises his eyebrows. 'Well, we'll just have to see how

the Club feels about that.' There is a mischievous glint in his eyes. 'If you will allow me to step outside for a moment?'

I incline my head politely. The boundary of the Circle appears, a silver line on the floor around us. Barbicane hovers up from his chair and crosses it: his appearance wavers slightly. Then he raises his bushbot arm. It fans out into a golden tree that touches a number of the gems in his halo gently, weaving his wish into the zoku's volition.

I am certain it is mostly for show. Barbicane is an Elder, someone who has achieved the maximum level of advancement in his zoku, by performing actions in accordance with its goals and values – in this case, building bigger and better guns and blowing things up. He won't have any problems using his entanglement with the rest of the zoku to acquire the paltry item I am asking for: a high-level jewel for a Supra City infrastructure zoku, enough to instantiate a personal Circle in one of the more fashionable zones of the zokus' Saturnian capital.

What Barbicane doesn't know is that the real stakes are much bigger than that.

After a second, he smiles and returns to his seat.

'All good! The shell has been transferred to the Arsenal. And now for the celebratory drink! Stronger than tea! Would you care for a—'

A Realmgate pops into being on the other side of the room with a rush of displaced air and a whiff of ozone, a glowing blue circle two metres in diameter. A zoku trueform pours through it: a shimmering utility fog cloud with a haughty face in the middle, surrounded by a swirling mandala of zoku jewels. The newcomer enters the Circle and the Schroeder tech locks kick in. The foglets hiss and rasp with waste heat as they coalesce into a tall woman, first sketching her as a crystal statue, and then as flesh. Even before she is fully formed, she strides forward towards Barbicane, a pine-scented warm breeze behind her.

'What in Verne's name do you think you are doing?' she says.

She is a honey blonde wearing a rather skimpy version of a pilot's outfit: a short tan flying jacket that leaves her midriff bare, heavy boots, a cap, a scarf and a fighter pilot's goggles. Her black eyebrows accentuate the cold beauty of her triangular face. Her ruby mouth is a tight line.

'What am I doing? What am I doing? Acquiring an important historical artefact!' Barbicane looks at her incredulously. 'Chekhova dear, this is most irregular! You are offending our guest! Raoul here is a gentleman!'

'I know who he is, Elder,' Chekhova says. 'The real question is, do you?'

I became Raoul d'Andrezy a subjective week earlier, in the *Wardrobe*'s vir, four days before the *Bob Howard* reached Saturn.

I sit at our usual table, a thought-mirror in front of me, a floating glass disc that is actually a vir construct, plugged into my dorsal stream. My face in it morphs from the slightly greying man with pencil eyebrows, hollow temples and Peter Lorre eyes into something darker, younger, more rough-hewn. The face alone is not enough, of course – my minions are also laying down a carefully designed data trail – but it's a start.

'What are you doing?' Matjek asks.

I frown at him. It took a long time to clean up the vir. During my brief absence, Matjek recreated large swathes of Narnia faithfully, stretching the meagre computational capabilities of the *Wardrobe* to its limits. I have spent a lot of valuable time erasing islands inhabited by one-legged people and chasing down centaurs and talking mice with swords. I'm still not sure I got them all, nor do I fully understand how the boy did it. But given that his future self was the architect of Sobornost's firmament, I should not be surprised that he cracked the Sobornost-style vir I built on top of the ship's ancient hardware. And I suspect he had help from the Aun.

I have done my best to lock him in a sandbox, and since then he has been sulking quietly, watching the blue-tinted landscape outside our virtual window, the craggy, multi-coloured shapes of the zero-g coral reefs that drift past us and the smooth-skinned, whale-tailed humanoids that dart between them, leaving trails of silvery bubbles. The Wang bullet and the *Wardrobe* are now safely in the watery belly of *The Rorqual's Revenge*, a cetamorph ship, en route to Iapetos.

'I'm getting ready to be someone else,' I say. My voice is colder than I intended, but Matjek does not seem to care.

'Why?'

I run my fingers along the surface of the mirror. My mind feels as smooth and blank. I had to use my metaself to calm down after Isidore's qupt came. I haven't been able to analyse the data he sent attached to his final message: it was a mess of quantum information, and the *Wardrobe* does not have the hardware to untangle it.

'Everybody does it sometimes.'

Somewhere, deep underneath, I want to get drunk. I want to scream. I want to smash the thought-mirror into a million pieces. I want to tear the vir itself all the way down to firmament. My temples hurt.

'I don't,' Matjek says. 'I like being me.'

54

'Even when you play war with the Green Soldier?' I ask softly. 'Or when you wanted to be the Silence?'

'That's just pretending.'

'Well, this is the same. You just have to pretend hard enough.'

I adjust the shape of the nose a bit. I have met Barbicane before, and so I need to pitch my disguise carefully, close enough to my self-image to avoid cognitive dissonance

'So, who are you going to be?' Matjek asks.

I tell the vir to change my mindshell. Broader shoulders, a more military bearing, a swarthier complexion, a flashy suit and a vest with golden chains. I used to be rather pleased with Raoul. He is based on an identity I previously used on Mars.

Matjek's eyes widen.

'This is Raoul d'Andrezy,' I say with a new voice. 'An antiques dealer.'

A matchstick smell comes to me, unbidden. Thaddeus's breath. The first glass of wine I drank with Raymonde. *Damn these old dream virs. Not enough detail to have a real drink, just memories.*

I shake my head. *Pretend harder, Jean.*

'He looks *boring*,' Matjek says. 'Why would you want to be him?'

'Being boring is the point. He has to look trustworthy. A bit weary. Experienced. Somebody competent. Somebody who has seen things. Somebody who is tired and just wants a comfortable life, who is ready to bend the rules a little bit to get it.'

'That *is* boring. But I liked how you changed. Show me how.'

'No. I think you have played with virs enough for a while.' I restore my mindshell to normal and put the mirror on the table. 'Why don't you—' Fatally, I pause, trying to think of something for the boy to do.

'It's boring here. You are boring. The fish-men are boring. I want to change, too.'

'I told you, that's not going to—'

'I want to I want to I want to!'

The structure of the vir ripples. Matjek starts changing. His features flow into the first face in the mirror, a caricature me.

'Look!' he shouts with glee. 'I did it all by myself!'

The pain in my temples turns into white noise. Something dark and scaly opens its claws in my chest. I raise my hand. There is a flash of fear in Matjek's eyes. I bring my fist down onto the mirror, roaring the bloody Founder code of Sumanguru the warlord in my mind – *rust and fire and blood and dead children.*

The vir time stops. Matjek freezes, his normal mindshell restored. The mirror fragments float in the air, glittering and sharp and myriad, like the Highway ships.

The rage drains from me. The echoes of Sumanguru's Code in my mind die. The look of terror on the boy's face makes me turn away.

Almost immediately, the firmament software running the vir does something unexpected. It accesses a hidden cache and executes a complex command that I don't entirely follow. I take a deep breath.

He has already been there.

Matjek starts moving again, faster and faster. In an instant, he is darting between the shelves and around the table faster than I can follow, a flickering grey blur.

'Matjek, wait!' I match our clockspeeds.

He stands in front of me, tears running down his face.

'Don't be angry, Prince,' he says. 'I'm sorry about Narnia. You went away, and I didn't know what to do. You said I could help Mieli, too, but you are doing it all on your own.'

I conjure a silk handkerchief from my sleeve and wipe his face. 'I know, Matjek. I should not have gotten angry. It's not your fault. Something … something bad happened and I have been thinking about it too much.'

'What was it?'

'It doesn't matter.' I smile. 'But that was a nice trick you did, just now, with time. Can you tell me how it's done?'

He shrugs. 'I used to play time games a lot, on the beach, when I got bored. You always need to have a trigger like that that speeds you up if you get too slow by accident, so you don't blink and miss the end of the world.'

Uh oh.

My plan was to sandbox the *Wardrobe*'s vir and slow Matjek's clockspeed down while I was off doing the Iapetos job so that he would not even notice my absence. Clearly, that is not going to work. I could try to design a more secure vir, but I don't have enough time, and I am starting to doubt that any construct I could come up with would even hold him.

I look at Matjek, at the thin dark hair that will go grey too early, at his snub of a nose and serious mouth, and there is an odd, warm tingle in my chest.

I need a babysitter. It would be so much easier if I could just leave a copy of myself here. Unfortunately, Joséphine made sure I'm a singleton white male now, unable to spawn off gogols of myself, and I can't trust a partial to keep up with Matjek. The people of Sirr are compressed data, and until I complete my mission, I can't bring them back. I don't dare to bring in anybody from outside, either: Matjek is hot property, an early gogol of a Sobornost Founder.

That leaves—

I sigh. There are no two ways about it. I need to talk to the Aun.

Carefully, I gather the shards of the thought-mirror and put them onto the table. 'I'll tell you what. Here is a puzzle for you. If you manage to put the mirror back together, you get to keep it. I need to go and take care of something, but I won't be gone long, and after I come back, I'm going to make some hot chocolate. How does that sound?'

Feigning obedience, Matjek sits back down and starts moving the glass fragments around with one forefinger.

'Be careful, they are sharp,' I tell him.

I can almost hear the wheels turning in his head as I walk towards the back of the shop and the many volumes of Sirr.

It is dark there, and the only light comes from the faint silver lettering on the spines of the night-blue books. Everything feels soft, dreamlike: around the edges, the vir forgoes a detailed physics simulation and exploits the brain's ability to lie to itself. In the narrow passage between the looming shelves, I feel like an insect inside a book, pressed between porous, heavy pages.

I swallow. I don't really understand the Aun. They were let loose in the Collapse – or long before that, by Matjek, if you believe what they say. They are pure self-loops, living memes that inhabit minds as parasites. They claim that I am one of them, their lost brother. I'm not sure I believe them. I never claimed to be a god. But the simple fact is they make my skin crawl. And the way you talk to them is by letting them become you.

I run my fingers along the books until I find the right one. I open it, and they rise from the pages, the never-human gods of Earth, serpents of light, coiling and uncoiling, illuminating the stacks around me with a fluttering will-o'-the-wisp glow.

I close my eyes and let them in.

The one that comes to me is called the Chimney Princess. She speaks to me in a voice that sounds like my own inside my head.

Hello, brother.

I am not your brother.

Have you come to join us?

No.

Have you come to deliver our children to our new home?

No. Not yet. I massage my temples. *Sirr.* The last city on Earth, snatched from the jaws of Dragons. A child is one thing, an entire civilisation another. I promised Tawaddud that I would save them. *Only promises left.* I grit my teeth.

Spinning lies is what you do, brother. We hope you have not forgotten your promise.

I haven't. You will have your new home, and so will the people of Sirr. But there is something I need to do first.

Something you need to steal.

Yes. I have to leave the vir. So I need you to look after the boy. Distract him. Tell him stories. Keep him occupied.

What are you stealing, this time? Memories? Stories? Souls? Dreams?

That's none of your business.

How can we be sure you will come back? You left us before.

Because I keep my promises.

They rise in my mind, all of them, the Kraken and the Green Soldier and the Princess, thunderstorms made of thought that wrap tendrils of lightning around my brain.

PROMISES ARE GOOD, they roar. *FEAR IS BETTER. WE ARE ALWAYS HERE. WE ARE ALWAYS LISTENING. DO NOT BETRAY US.*

I fall to my knees. The Aun leave my mind, and the dusty darkness surrounds me. The sudden silence is deafening. Even in my dreamlike mindshell, I shake all over.

'You know,' I say aloud, 'you are starting to convince me about the whole Flower Prince thing. Family really is the worst.'

The Princess speaks again, softly this time, like rain.

We will weave dreams for our father, as we did once before, long ago. But the time will come when he, too, has to wake up.

'Yes. But not yet.'

'His name is not Raoul d'Andrezy,' Chekhova says, looking at me pointedly. 'Isn't that right … Colonel?'

I smile sheepishly.

'Elder, this is Colonel Sparmiento. From the Teddy Bears' Picnic Company. A Sirr-employed mercenary group. On Earth. When your volition push came, I was tasked to check his background. It turned out to be fabricated.'

Barbicane says nothing but his eyes widen.

'So, Colonel,' Chekhova continues. 'How about you tell us your story.' She crosses her arms and looks at me down her nose like a very cross, hot schoolteacher.

I spread my hands.

'What can I say? You caught me. I was with the Teddy Bears. We were not all ursomorphs, although it helped if you liked honey. My apologies for the charade, but I would prefer if my former employers were kept in the dark regarding my whereabouts. The Bears are many things, but they are *not* forgiving. And we … parted ways rather suddenly.'

Conning the zoku is a fine art. But if there is one weakness they have, it's that they always think everything is solvable, that problems are obvious and neat, like in games – and if you make them think they have succeeded, they tend to give up. My identity had another identity concealed within it, a rather more solid one, backed up with the data Mieli collected when she joined the ranks of the Teddy Bears. You can still break Colonel Sparmiento if you poke at him hard enough, but I'm betting that Chekhova won't. Especially now that she is trying to make an impression on an Elder.

'So, you are a deserter,' she says. 'And how exactly did you come by a Verne cannon bullet that is more than two hundred years old?'

'As you are no doubt aware, things are a little bit … restless on Earth at the moment.'

'If by *restless*, you mean *eaten by recursively self-improving non-eudaimonistic agents*, then, yes, I am aware. Professional interest.' There is a hungry look in Chekhova's eyes.

'Well, my unit and I started to smell trouble a few weeks ago, before the chens came. We made it out with the bullet and some other goods from the wildcode desert. We may have taken some liberties with following the chain of command, if you take my meaning. But at least we got out. Most of the Teddy Bears were not so fortunate.'

I look at Barbicane. 'Were you planning on offering us a drink? I'd like to toast to my comrades. Poor bastards: but I was proud to serve with them. And some of them left family behind, family who could do with a new start in Supra City.' The last part is true as well: one of Mieli's fallen squadmates had cubs in the Belt. 'Especially now that the Sobornost has decided to eat everything inside the orbit of Mars. That's why we came here. But I guess it's all for nothing now.'

Barbicane lets out a bellows-like sigh. 'Well, Colonel! That's quite a story! But you are being a good sport! Perhaps we can still work something out.'

Barbicane hovers from his chair to a copper globe showing an engraved old-fashioned map of Earth, but with a strangely tilted axis – the Antarctic is near the equator. He opens it deftly with his manipulator hand, takes out a bottle of a dark amber liquor and three glasses, and pours. He looks at me seriously.

'Names are not important! For us, only entanglement matters. The spime you gave us was impressive. I'm still interested!'

'On the contrary,' Chekhova says. 'If the Colonel's item *is* genuine and came from Earth recently, we should stay as far away from it as possible.'

Barbicane raises his eyebrows.

'You know how closely we are being watched by the Great Game Zoku these days,' Chekhova says. 'What do you think they will do if we acquire something that might be infested with *Dragons*?'

Barbicane purses his lips.

'True,' he says. 'Damn their eyes!'

'The Great Game? What does she mean?'

'A guardian zoku! Protects us from existential threats, or so they claim! Rose to power after the Spike.' Barbicane's face grows dark. 'They converted some junior Club members, to report on more ambitious experiments! Said they endangered spacetime. Phsaw!' He looks at his drink mournfully. 'But I confess, Colonel, Chekhova has a point! It's a delicate time.'

I look at Chekhova. What game is she playing? Does *she* have something to do with the Great Game Zoku? I don't want to risk a direct confrontation with them, not yet.

Perhaps I should pull back and try again via a different route. But it has taken a lot of effort and time to set the current job up. Time that Mieli may not have.

'I have comrades to think about, Elder,' I say. 'As it happens, I've also had interest from a Narrativist zoku in Supra City: I believe they would like to transport it into a Realm and use it for a setting in a confined-space drama of some sort – not that I really understand these things.'

Barbicane sneers. 'Give it to Narrativists! Ridiculous! A piece of matter shaped by nuclear fire, made for a purpose!'

'But we must consider—' Chekhova tries to speak, but Barbicane waves his gun-hand to stop her.

'A great shame, to turn it into a – metaphor!' he roars.

I decide to throw more fuel into the fire.

'I mean, really. I have heard a lot about the Gun Club. Wasn't it your Hawking holeships that stopped the Protocol War from being an even bigger disaster? The only things that can take out a *guberniya*, from what I hear. And you are telling me that you are afraid of another zoku who thinks you are playing with fire?' I shake my head slowly. 'I think I would be better off with the Narrativists. It sounds to me like your children out there have more courage than you.'

I am not just talking to them. I'm talking to the whole zoku: they are acting as its avatars in the Circle of the train.

'I bring you a historical object, a shell from the biggest gun ever built before the post-Collapse era, and you don't want it because it might be *dirty*? Please.' I get up. 'I will take my business elsewhere.'

Barbicane lifts into the air and spins around slowly, thruster legs burning holes in his chair's upholstery. His eyes are squeezed shut, and he is thinking hard. Then he spins around and thrusts his gun arm straight at my face.

'Ah ha! I have an idea, Colonel! A compromise! Will satisfy the zoku volition! Chekhova is a Dragon expert! She will inspect the item in the Arsenal, at molecular level! That way it will be safe. Everybody happy? Hmm?'

Everybody except me, who has hidden a spare miniature body with qupt-ready EPR states inside it. And I was going to use it to steal back my ship from the Arsenal.

But I just smile and nod, and start thinking about a plan B.

5

MIELI AND THE ABYSS

Mieli is standing on a balcony. The sky above is impossibly vast, faded blue, with a white cut across it. The sunlight is bright and warm on her face, but it is diffuse, soletta-light, collected by some giant mirror in space and distilled into this gentle radiance. Strangely, it reminds her of Oort, of home.

Nothing else does.

The building she is in is high and white, made of organic rounded shapes like seashells, bristling with terraces and balconies. Tanned people sit or lie in the sun, surrounded by haloes of jewels.

Below her, there is a canal. It goes on forever, a thread that vanishes into a haze somewhere impossibly far. A golden gondola suspended from two purple balloons floats leisurely above it. On both shores of the waterway, the landscape is a quilt of mismatched buildings and vistas, separated from each other by silver lines. There is a temple of onion-shaped pagodas and spires, rising from a stark field of dark circuitry; a row of coral castles; a mist-shrouded grey city in the distance. Further away lies a white-peaked mountain range, surrounded by red-winged flying specks too large to be birds.

At the very edge of her vision, there is a structure almost as big as the sky, a looming broad arc with a metallic glint, held up by thin white pillars. To right and left, the world is abruptly bound by two cloud-walls, amber-hued.

Mieli feels a touch of vertigo. She has never liked planets: they are too big for her, and the horizons and the skies here dwarf anything she has ever seen. She focuses her eyes on the blue thread of the canal. Hundreds of zoku trueforms dart along it, whirlpools and parachutes of jewels and fog, moving in flocks like birds. They suddenly remind her of the dream that brought her here.

To Supra City.

'Would you like some tea?'

Mieli turns around. Her systems wake up, but detect no threat. It is the usagi-ronin. She is barefoot, dressed in torn blue trousers and a simple green shirt. Here, she is shorter than Mieli. Her skin is the colour of milk chocolate. Her mouth is a bit too wide to fit in the shape of her face, but her eyes are bright. She is carrying a tray with small bowls and a jade green teapot. She motions Mieli to follow her inside.

Warily, Mieli obeys. They are in a small apartment. Its white walls are covered in brightly coloured sheets showing ancient-looking two-dimensional pictures of young people, prominently featuring the words *Manaya High*. There is no smartmatter: the sparse furniture is made of wood and hand-woven, colourful fabrics. The simplicity of it is a pleasant contrast to the madness outside. *Deliberate, of course.*

The usagi-ronin gracefully sets the tray down onto a small table. Then she sits down on the pillows, cross-legged. 'Have some. It's sencha. Unless you would like something to eat?'

Mieli sits down carefully in a kneeling position: the gravity here is heavy for her, nearly the same as on Earth. In spite of that, she feels light and strong, and her limbs no longer ache from days of climbing. She is dressed as she was on *Perhonen*, a black toga, and Sydän's jewelled chain around her ankle. She notices that she is holding the zoku jewel that saved her: a blue oval, smaller than her hand, pulsating with faint light, surrounded by a very faint smell of flowers. She puts it on the table in front of her.

The usagi-ronin girl looks at the jewel and smiles. She places a cup in front of Mieli and fills it with steaming, fresh-smelling liquid.

'Look, I'm sorry about the Realm,' she says. 'The mountain and all that. I can see now that it would have been disorienting for you. We usually try to bring orphans in through Realms, to let them work through their issues: they get the narrative rights to shape their surroundings in the framework we give them. You did *very* well, by the way. I did not see that ending coming at all. Chilling.' She cradles her own cup in her small hands, and sips it carefully. 'But, I didn't realise just how many enhancements your trueform there has. One of its subsystems started fighting back, so I thought it would be best if we started again here. What do you think?'

Mieli looks at the girl sharply. Her Sobornost-made enhancements *are* functioning normally, and she tasks a few intel gogols to scan the environment. In an instant, they confirm what she already knew: she is on a strip of dense smartmatter, tens of thousands of kilometres long and a few hundred wide, somewhere near the equator of Saturn. However, they can't access the local spimescape – either because she is inside a firewall, or because she lacks the right protocols.

'What am I doing here?' Mieli asks.

'Whatever you want. Maybe start by drinking tea? You

haven't touched it. My name in this Circle is Zinda, by the way.'

Mieli frowns. Her experience of the zoku is limited to fighting them. During the Protocol War, she went through a few virs set on Supra City, in case of capture, but they were nothing like this. As far as her sensors can tell, the apartment is what it looks like, down to the molecular level. Zinda, however, is a zoku alter – a mixture of foglets and zoku jewels – although she is running a passable emulation of a human body, down to sketches of internal organs and a digestive system.

'I would like to find out what happened to my ship.'

'Hmm. We'll get to that in a moment,' Zinda says. 'But to answer your first question: you are here because the Rainbow Table Zoku – which you belong to, by the way – found you. They didn't know what to do with your volition. They mostly deal with routers, Realmgates, that sort of thing: they are really more into picotech than people, if you see what I mean. So the volition got passed to *our* zoku, the Manaya High. We take care of … lost lambs, you could say. Those who want to return.' Zinda smiles gently. 'Like you.'

'I don't understand what you are talking about.' Gingerly, Mieli tries the tea. It, too, is exactly what it appears to be, slightly bitter and not completely warm anymore, but in spite of herself, she likes the taste. 'I can't stay. I need to get back to my ship.'

'Oh dear.' Zinda looks serious. 'You are free to leave at any time, of course. But that's not what your volition said to the jewel. You wanted to come home, and here you are.'

Mieli gets up slowly.

'My name is Mieli, the daughter of Karhu, of Hiljainen

Koto, of Oort. I have nothing to do with you.' But deep in her gut, there is a sudden chill. *A tithe child. A child of the sunsmiths, given together with a Little Sun, for the* koto *to protect and cherish.*

'Volition is a funny thing,' Zinda says. 'The jewels don't just respond to what we want, but what we *would* want if we were wiser or smarter or knew more. The zoku as a whole tries to extrapolate what you *really* need, rather than just what you are asking for, and in line with everybody's volition. I'll give you an example. Tell me something you really like. A food, or something.'

Mieli hesitates. 'This is pointless.'

'Come on. Don't take it so seriously!'

Mieli sighs. 'Liquorice. I like liquorice.'

'Great! So, let's say I have two boxes, A and B' – she places two empty cups on the table, upside down – 'and A has liquorice in it. I know that you really like liquorice and are looking for some. You ask me to open box B. Which box should I open?'

Mieli blinks.

'See?' Zinda says.

'But it's not the same thing.'

'Well, it's harder to compute, for sure. The *real* extrapolated volition thing is absurdly difficult, PSPACE-hard or something, so usually we take shortcuts, make approximations. Maybe *you* don't want to be here, but a future self of yours does.'

'I don't think so,' Mieli says.

Zinda smiles reassuringly. 'Look, I've been through this many times. It's completely normal to feel confused at this point. Why don't you try it out for a while? We are not Sobornost – who you obviously have spent some time with.

We don't take away your freedom. We just give you a quantum self, to make you larger than you are now. I think you will find it very easy.' She pours herself and Mieli some more tea. 'I mean, we did study you at some length while you were in the Realm. Your body and mind both have pretty clear signatures of zoku design. A Jovian aegon-family zoku if I had to guess. They used to trade with Oortians – you know, before the Spike. I don't mean to pry, but is it *really* such a surprise for you?'

Mieli sits back down, slowly.

'Why would they do that?' she whispers.

'Many reasons. We *do* weave everybody into the zoku's volition. Children always have a purpose. Making them is kind of a game, too. Perhaps your parents wanted to give you a different life, outside their zoku's volition cone. We could try to find them, if you want. Although if they were based on Jupiter, that could be … difficult.'

Sydän used to joke about it, how Mieli was like the character from a book some ancestor gave her, a queen of presapient monkeys. Mieli only ever knew that she was a tithe child, given to Oortians to raise, a part of a bargain that gave her *koto* their Little Sun. That's why she had spent her early years in Grandmother Brihane's house, until she was big enough to live with the rest of the *koto*. No one except Sydän ever talked about it, and Karhu could not care less. But it was why she had always tried harder than anybody else. It was why she had practised the väki songs until her voice was hoarse, why she did a Great Work younger than anyone else, why she brought an ancestor spirit back from *alinen*.

I need to find Perhonen. Mieli shakes her head. She ramps up the readiness level of her combat systems. Her senses become painfully sharp: it is a good distraction from Zinda's words. It could be a trap. The thief taught her what it is like to be manipulated. Everything this zoku creature is saying could be designed to extract information from her. She remembers the climb with the ronin-Zinda, how easy it was to trust her with her life. Even now, it is hard *not* to trust her. But of course, that is exactly what they want.

She looks at Zinda. 'I have killed your kind, you know,' she says. 'In the Protocol War. Hundreds, maybe more. I took out Metis with a strangelet bomb. Are you sure you want me here, living among you?'

'Oh, we are not that easy to kill. I've died a few times. It's a pain: after you respawn, you have to go back to your jewels and artefacts as a ghost. Most people keep some of them in the zoku bank, just in case. You do get to see things you don't normally see. It's kind of like a sub-game: the Reaper Zoku want to redesign it, but they are not getting much traction. Personally, I think you could introduce a narrative element to it, played across a space of centuries. Every time you die you advance the storyline a little bit. Would that not be cool? But the aegon and alea family zokus don't listen to Narrativists like me—' She shakes her head. 'I'm sorry, I'm babbling. What I meant to say is that it's not a big deal, some people might carry a grudge but any zoku you join never will. And if you were such a big fish in the Protocol War, you probably have a fan zoku somewhere, you know!'

Zinda taps at the table. 'Listen. We need to get you more entangled. You can't do much here if you don't even have a Supra City jewel, even before you think about a primary zoku. The Rainbow Table one you have won't get you very far. Here.' She holds out a small turquoise jewel in a golden leaflike casing. 'You'll find it easier to get around if you have this.'

Mieli accepts the jewel gingerly. It feels warm to the touch, like the other jewel.

Mieli, you fool, the pellegrini's voice in her mind. *What did I tell you?*

And then her systems flood her with alerts and infiltration warnings. Her metacortex show her the tendrils that are pushing into her neurons from the jewel, attaching themselves into her decision-making centres, tapping into the roots of her hopes and dreams.

She lets go of the jewel, stands up and starts powering up her weapons.

'Oh dear,' Zinda says.

'This was another game,' Mieli says. 'All this. You are from the Great Game. You don't take care of orphans. You are here to handle an asset. To extract information.' The q-dot gun embedded in her right hand warms up. 'Well, here is some information for you. You should have kept me in a more secure environment. You are about to find out if they have improved the ghost game after death.'

'No, wait! You don't understand! Why did you have to break the Circle? I mean, all right, I *am* Great Game, but I'm Manaya, too. Everything I said was true! We belong to many zokus, and we can be in them at the same time, in superpositions. I just want to help you!'

There are tears in Zinda's eyes.

'Look, I got activated when you arrived, okay? I'm a bit out of my depth here, to be honest. Could you just sit back down and we'll talk about it? I'd really rather not fight you, Mieli. I have volition to follow, too. I have a combat monster alter, if you insist, but I *hate* the way he smells.'

'I am leaving now. You can either be an asset or a liability.

It's your choice.' Mieli makes her voice as hard and cold as she can.

Zinda takes a deep breath. 'Just give me a minute, okay? You have to understand that it's not just *me*. We created a little zoku dedicated to analysing you. We know a lot about you. If we wanted to break you, we could!' She sniffs. 'I know it doesn't sound nice, but it's true! We could design Realms that would make you into our willing slave, give up all your secrets. But we don't want to break you. We *need* you.'

'Need me for what?'

'Duh huh! There is a war on! The Founders are at each other's throats! As far as we can tell, the chens are winning. And they are going to be looking at *us* next. They were always a threat. The Elders had a gambit after the Protocol War to … neutralise them, but—' She bites her lip. 'Never mind. But anything you know about what happened on Earth, what you know about the pellegrinis and the chens, all their tech, all that stuff – we can use that. Don't worry about any booby traps or defence systems – we can deal with those, given your volition and some time.

'And then – you could be one of us. Do you have *any* idea how hard it is to join the Great Game? You have to *find* them. I looked for them for years. I entangled notches and ithaqui and a whole bunch of others so I could analyse hints they had hidden in our narratives! And I'm just a sleeper. But you – you could be a field agent, fight existential threats, the big stuff. You could save the world. Like a James Bond with wings.'

Mieli blinks. 'Who?'

'What do you say? Come on. It will be fun.'

Mieli lets a q-dot form at her fingertip. 'No,' she says. 'You

73

have ten seconds to tell me where my ship is, and how I get off this planet.'

'Ah, about that—'

'Nine.'

'Are you sure you want to—'

'Eight.'

'I can call for help, you know.'

'Seven.'

'All right, all right! Calm down.' Zinda sighs. 'I didn't want to tell you. Not until you had had a chance to settle in. We traced your trajectory to its origin, of course. This is what we saw.' She gestures, and a small q-dot screen appears above the table. It shows Earth, and a shape that she instantly recognises as *Perhonen*. It is caught in a storm of Hunters, daggerlike Sobornost weapons. Her mouth goes dry. *You stupid, stupid girl. You didn't have to.*

The ship is a spiderweb of threads and modules in the centre of a pair of solar sail wings. It unravels as the Hunters come, swift like beams of light, each impact and scan beam flash taking a piece away.

And then the ship slowly swings around and dives towards the blue and white globe. In a moment, it is a burning scar, drawn across the face of the Earth. It vanishes beyond the horizon, and is gone.

'We couldn't find any traces of it afterwards,' Zinda says. 'That was just before the Dragons came. I'm sorry.'

Mieli closes her eyes but the world does not go away. Her enhancements paint a cold ghost landscape around her. The walls of the apartment are like her skull, squeezing her brain.

She lets out a wordless cry, runs to the balcony, opens her wings and takes to the air.

*

Mieli flies without destination, pushing the microfans in her wings until the air is thin and the strip below is like a road, disappearing into the horizon, crisscrossed by other strip habitats. There are hundreds of them, passing beneath each other, binding the giant planet tight. Playful zoku trueforms try to join her in flight, but she pushes herself harder until the fusion reactor in her thigh complains, outdistances them, flies on until the blue of the sky starts to fade into black and she feels the faint, familiar touch of the Dark Man of the void. She yearns for it, for the hard vacuum and radiation and pressure drop, for the stinging black slap after the heat of an Oortian sauna. But Saturn won't let go of her that easily

Perhonen is gone. *I always loved you better than she did,* the ship said, before it shot her out with the zoku jewel, when the Hunters came.

She lets the planet's gravity pull her into a long, rushing glide, follows it until she reaches the edge of the world.

It is a wall that looks like a mass of sunset-tinted clouds, reaching from the ground to the top of the sky, twenty kilometres high. Up close, it is a mass of cells filled with a gas, held up by thin smartmatter threads, erected on the rim of the habitat strip to keep the atmosphere in.

Then she is above it, wings whining in the almost absent air, and sees the abyss beyond. The mass streams that support the strip are spiderweb pillars that vanish into the yellow-ochre haze of Saturn, far, far below. A storm boils down there, winter blue cream swirling in a giant cup.

Perhaps it will be better to fall like she did.

What happened was her fault. But it was the right thing to do. On Earth, she died a thousand times to find the courage to face down the pellegrini. She drew a line that she would not cross, refused to allow a child's self to be stolen. She did not expect to live, afterwards.

She should let Saturn take her, dive into the ammonium crystal clouds and water vapour and deeper down, until the crushing metallic hydrogen in the planet's depths give her the end that belongs to her. So easy: her momentum will carry her over the edge, down towards the storm and its eyewall, a chain of maelstroms the size of Oortian comets, threaded together like beads on a string, like jewels.

And then something stronger than gravity stops her, a memory rising from the depths. *Sydän.*

She fights the momentum and brakes, folds her wings and dives straight down, at the top of the wall. The wing microfans overheat and moan. She comes down near the edge, hard, rolls like a broken bird. The cloud-wall is soft and slippery and absorbs the impact like water. Her landing sends slow ripples through the gas sacks: the surface is soap-bubble thin, but it stabilises to support her weight. She lies on top of it for a moment, hurting and breathing hard. The air is like watered milk, thin and tasteless.

After a while, she gets up and walks to the edge, slowly, with comical, bouncy steps, treading against the movement of the gas sack beneath her feet. When she sits down and hugs her knees, looking at the endless pale yellow expanse of Saturn below, it keeps rocking her gently up and down, like a mother on her knee.

With a voice that is almost inaudible in the sparse air, she prays to Kuutar and Ilmatar for guidance, and hopes they have power in this dark place where everything changes and nothing is real.

*

As Mieli quiets her mind, she becomes aware of a murmur in her head: the Rainbow Table jewel is whispering to her. Somehow, it has ended up in the folds of her robe. She frowns: she does not remember picking it up. She takes it out and looks at it. The jewel tells her that there are routers and Realmgates nearby, pinpoints them amongst the network of mass streams and q-tubes below, gives her a compulsion to go and make adjustments to a stream buffer controller.

She kills the thought with a quick command to her metacortex. She feels the jewel's disapproval, an unravelling of the entanglement it contains. She ignores it and throws the bauble over the edge. She watches it fall for a long, long time, until it finally disappears from sight.

'It amazes me,' says a warm voice, 'that you have the tenacity to keep praying to your gods, when I'm the only one who ever answers.'

The pellegrini rises slowly from the abyss, a tall auburn-haired figure in a white dress, hands open at her sides, as if ready to embrace Mieli.

Mieli stares at the Sobornost goddess. 'Go away. I told you: I don't work for you anymore.' She feels cold and empty. Even her rage at the woman who has lived in her head for so long is a fading ember.

The pellegrini rolls her eyes. 'And I can't *believe* it took you so long to get rid of that ridiculous jewel. I could not risk being detected. I tried to speak to you, in the Realm. Clearly, you did not listen.' She opens her purse and takes out one of her foul white stick-things, lights it with an elaborately carved lighter, and takes a drag. Then she holds it delicately to one side, sprinkling hot ash onto the eye of Saturn below.

'As for our current relationship – fine. But I can't leave

that easily, Mieli. I am in your mind. You let me in, remember?' She takes another drag from the stick. 'Now that I have calmed down a bit, I must admit that I was impressed by the backbone you showed on Earth. Too bad you had to choose such a misguided moment to do so.

'Well. Here we are. I should have self-destructed when you were captured. But I was made a gogol when I was quite old, and I have always found such extreme measures … difficult.' She smiles. 'So do you, it seems, in spite of all you have lost. We are stuck with each other, like it or not.'

'I could tell them about you,' Mieli says.

'Of course you could. But it would not be wise. You may find them friendly and polite now, Mieli, but if they knew you had a Sobornost Founder gogol inside you? They would have me at any cost, and I am hiding so deep that they would have to tear you apart to get me.'

'Perhaps I'm not afraid of that.'

'No: you do not fear death, you have shown that many times. But this would not be death. You know what I'm talking about: you have interrogated gogols yourself. And *they* don't believe in copies. They would transfer you into one of their Realms, turn the process of cutting me out into a game. You would be changed, utterly. Trust me, you don't want that.'

Mieli shivers. The pellegrini will say anything to get what she wants. But she has a feeling that the goddess is not lying, this time.

The pellegrini gestures with the glowing end of her white stick.

'At the same time, I need you. I always did. I never lied to you. Like my Jean, I keep my promises. I would have given you your little Sydän, in the end.'

Mieli bites her teeth together, hard. '*Perhonen* always tried to tell me. Sydän never wanted me in the first place. She was just trying to escape Oort. I am better off without her.'

'So, why didn't you go over the edge? Why do you still wear that trinket?' She points at the jewelled chain around Mieli's ankle, modelled after the Great Work Mieli and Sydän made together, a dancing formation of comets bound into a chain with q-dot fibres. It feels cold against Mieli's skin, suddenly.

'Let me tell you something, Mieli. When you become immortal and get the things you want, you start wondering why you wanted them in the first place. Sydän regrets letting you go. She misses you.'

She is lying. Mieli squeezes her eyes shut, wraps her wings around her. She will *not* serve the pellegrini again. What would *Perhonen* tell her? To be herself. The ship wanted her to abandon the endless quest for Sydän, to find a new life.

What does that even mean anymore? How could I go back to Oort now? The thief was right. I don't belong there either, after what the goddess made me into.

Mieli opens the chain around her ankle. She wonders how the thief did it so easily: the Oortian gems need a little song to release the thread that binds them. She is close to the edge. If she lets go of the chain, it will fall, into the waiting mouth of Saturn, always hungry for children. She runs her fingers along the chain. Each jewel is a different colour. Choices, moments, in a string, one after another. She remembers their first kiss, in the ice cave, when Sydän's suit opened, warm and wet with life support liquids. The day when they left Oort in *Perhonen*. Venus, where the singularity took her. The last thing she saw was her face, a sad pixie smile, erased by the Amtor black hole's information wind, fading like cream poured into coffee, still looking at her.

Looking back.

Sydän looked back.

Mieli squeezes the chain in her hand. Then, slowly and carefully, she replaces it around her ankle, humming the brief song that makes the smartcoral bind the loop into an unbroken whole.

'What do you need me to do?' she asks the pellegrini.

The pellegrini smiles a half-smile, the rouge line of her mouth twisting. 'That is an interesting question. We are trapped here, hiding, with no means of contacting my sisters. They have begun the endgame, no doubt. The contingency plan we had in case you and Jean failed to steal the Kaminari jewel from Chen.'

'And what is that?'

The pellegrini sighs. 'How do you unite Founders? You give them a common enemy. It wasn't just my Jean you let loose from the Dilemma Prison, Mieli. There is a creature called the All-Defector: Sasha's Archons stumbled upon it. A game-theoretic anomaly of sorts. I don't really understand it, but my gogols tell me it is the most dangerous thing since Dragons. The chaos in the Inner System indicates that my sister inside Jean has deployed him, and that means the *guberniyas* are going to burn.' She frowns. 'I only wish I knew why my sister could not get to the jewel first. If she had, we would know. The entire Universe would know.'

Mieli breathes deeply, lets her metacortex pour cool water on her emotions, makes herself hard and professional. There will be time for proper grief later, and for crafting songs.

'Zinda mentioned something,' she says. 'The Great Game zoku saw Chen as a threat. They were running an operation to get rid of him, but something went wrong. The thief found out how Chen got hold of the Kaminari jewel: from a zoku fleet near the remnants of Jupiter.' She takes a deep breath. 'What if Chen was *meant* to find it?'

The pellegrini starts laughing, a pearly tinkling sound. She sits down next to Mieli and covers her eyes with one hand, overcome with mirth.

'Of *course*,' the goddess says, wiping tears from her eyes. 'Oh, my Jean, how you tricked me.'

Mieli finds herself thinking about the thief. Whatever she feels about his demise is lost in the well of grief she has for *Perhonen*; but in spite of their differences, they worked together well, and there were times when she understood him. Almost. The thought that he might have perished with *Perhonen* or be tortured by Chen stings a little.

'What do you mean?' she asks.

'Never mind now, my dear. What is important is that you are absolutely right. Somehow, the Great Game played poor, overconfident Matjek. They made him *think* he had the Kaminari jewel. And that means *they* must have it.'

The pellegrini touches Mieli's cheek. Her ring is cold against Mieli's scar. 'My dear, beautiful Mieli, we can still both get everything what we want, and more. But first, you have to embrace your heritage. You must join the Great Game Zoku.'

6

THE THIEF AND THE ARSENAL

'So, Colonel? What do you think? Capital idea, eh?' Barbicane beams at me, while I swirl my port around in my glass, in rhythm with my thoughts.

I blink at a fusion flash that creates a new crater in Iapetus's battered hulk below. *Children and matches.* I tug at the thread of the thought, and all of a sudden, my dilemma starts to unravel.

I smile at Barbicane.

'Agreed! My comrades and I appreciate your candour and fairness. If you would allow me to step outside the Circle for a moment to advise them of the developments?'

The zoku Elder inclines his head, making his hat bop back and forth. 'Naturally!' He gestures at the silver boundary of the Circle.

I finish my drink, nod at Chekhova and step over it.

The sudden release from the Circle's Schroeder locks gives me a head rush. The spimescape interfaces to my equipment flash into being in my field of vision. At the same time, the illusion of the drawing room shatters. I am in a featureless white smartmatter tube full of utility fog that floats in the air in powdery, inert form, pollen-like.

I immediately ramp my internal clockspeed up to the maximum that my cheap synthbio body will allow. Behind me, Chekhova and Barbicane become statues in their small green-and-gold patch of Victorian wood, brass and furniture. Another small mercy: the Gun Clubbers are too well-mannered to break the Circle just because I stepped out for a moment.

I take the computronium egg from my shoulder bag. It is heavy and cold in my hand, a beautiful, intricate brass thing, as if laid by some Fabérge bird. The art nouveau tracery on the surface makes it easy to forget the complex waste heat management machinery and the tiny pinpoint of pure atom-scale computational power inside. The egg alone swallowed a large chunk of my pyramid scheme profits, but I needed something to run the bookshop vir and to store the Sirr data in. I carefully erased all traces of them from the restored Wang bullet before handing it over to the Gun Club.

With a thought, I open a quptlink into the egg.

Matjek?

It takes a few moments before the answer comes.

Yes?

Remember when you asked if you could help Mieli, too?

A pause. **It was a long time ago. But yes, I remember.**

His voice sounds … older. The Aun have some strange ideas about time. How much time has passed inside the vir?

Well, maybe you still can, I say.

Tell me what to do! The qupt is so full of enthusiasm that it hurts my teeth.

I hesitate for a moment. Would it be better to just cut my

losses, leave now and find another way in? I don't have to involve Matjek in this. Do I have the right?

I shake my head. There is no time, and I have no alternatives.

All right, Matjek. Listen to me very carefully. Remember to do exactly as I tell you. I form a complex thought, mapping it out in the spimescape, and send it to him. He devours it eagerly.

Then I check the status of the nuclear warheads I sold to the zoku youths as detailed replicas of the Tsar Bomba. While a cursory inspector would mistake them for the biggest hydrogen bombs ever built on Earth, they are in fact disguised qupt transmitters. Their cores hide ion traps entangled with their twins inside the Wang bullet, and their complex layers of deuterium and tritium are designed to send out a carefully modulated neutrino signal, capable of penetrating several light years of solid lead – or the walls of the Gun Club's Arsenal.

To my relief, several of the Tsars are still unused, even though the thermonuclear war game is heating up by the minute. I watch Matjek flash down the quptlink into one of the bombs like a genie into a bottle. I swear to myself I will make it up to the boy, and pray to all the gods of thieves that I will have the strength to carry the weight of all my promises.

Otherwise, the fail will be epic, as the zoku like to say.

'We are happy with the approach you propose,' I tell Barbicane when I return to the Circle. 'However—'

'Yes?'

I look at the zoku Elder hesitantly.

'Would you grant me one favour in return? I would like

to accompany you to see the famous Arsenal. I may be a deserter, but I am still a soldier, and I am still fond of the tools of my trade.'

'But of course!' Barbicane says. 'It's the least we can do!'

Chekhova looks disappointed. I'm sure she would prefer to flash back into her trueform and get on with it. But that would be rude as well: Barbicane has created this Circle, and she would lose face – and entanglement – if she was to leave. I smile at her warmly. She scowls at me.

An exceptionally large nuclear blast goes off in the Turgis Crater, somewhere above the British Isles.

'Was that a Tsar Bomba?' I ask. *Matjek, converted into entanglement and neutrinos, delivered into a body waiting inside the Wang bullet in the Arsenal.*

'By Jove, you are right!' Barbicane says. 'How very astute! We do have a true connoisseur of ancient weapons here, Chekhova dear! You *must* see the Arsenal'

Then he frowns. 'The spectrum was a tad off, though. Only means the young ones still have a few tricks to learn, eh!' He elbows me rather brutally with his massive gun arm. 'But no matter. There's several real ones and more besides where we're going!'

Ahead, the orbital ring sprouts a golden tendril that bends towards the surface of Iapetus, down towards the massive equatorial bulge that makes the whole moon look like a walnut. The ring is a continuous stream of magnetic particles, encased in a tube and accelerated to furious speeds with electromagnetic fields – a giant circular gun, in other words. Diverting a part of the flow to a receiver station on the surface creates a railway track in the sky. We finish our port as the train rides along it downwards, suspended between the looming yellow eye-lobe of Saturn and the fading nuclear fires of the children's war.

The Arsenal of the Gun Club Zoku.

It is a series of chambers beneath Iapetus's formidable equatorial ridge, buried beneath some of the highest mountains in the Solar System. Some of the spaces are tens of kilometres long and several in diameter, although it is hard to determine the strange blue-green illumination. The walls are not stone: they look like a blue sky, stretched and folded into itself. Looking at the smooth surface disturbs the eye. Nothing casts shadows on whatever the material is, probably pseudomatter of some kind, a picotech construct more solid than anything made of atoms.

The weapons themselves are suspended in the air in deadly constellations, rows upon rows of rifles, pistols and cannons. Their colours stand out starkly: black gunmetal, dabs of olive and camouflage and silver. It makes me feel like I'm floating across an ocean floor, surrounded by shoals of deadly multi-coloured fish.

Barbicane, Chekhova and I are carried by a small q-dot bubble, still within our Circle, sitting in the armchairs. The bubble compensates for the low gravity of Iapetus by exerting a gentle foglet pressure on our limbs. I don't like it: it makes me feel confined, and my anxiety levels are already high enough. Chekhova sits in an impatient hunch, barely looking at me, but Barbicane is enjoying his role as a tour guide.

'It has taken a while to collect all these!' he says. 'And we keep at least one copy of everything our members create in here. Everything is perfectly preserved, in full operational condition.'

Zoku trueforms move between the guns like medusae.

There is an occasional flash and a report as a weapon is tested. The shots echo hollowly in the vast space.

'Ha!' Barbicane says, when he sees me flinch. 'Don't worry! Safety first! But guns need to be used! Not like collecting comic books, to be kept inside plastic foil! All hooked up to our gunscape, to be used by all our zoku, everywhere!'

I smile and count seconds in my head. I need to keep Barbicane and Chekhova occupied until Matjek finishes his part of the job. What is taking him so long? Unfortunately, I don't dare to leave the Circle to check.

'This is all very impressive,' I say. 'Antiques are nice. But I thought your zoku's own creations were a bit more ... ambitious. Tell, me, what is the biggest gun you have? *That* is something I'd like to see. I hear the Sobornost have solar lasers, and I always wondered if you could match them.'

Chekhova doesn't even bother acknowledging my question. But Barbicane winks at me.

'Oh, the *biggest* would not fit in here,' he says. 'We make the mass drivers for Supra City's dynamic support members, for example. But I can show you the most *interesting*!' He nudges Chekhova. 'No need for false modesty here, my dear. Show him!'

She sighs and directs the q-dot bubble downwards with a gesture.

The next chamber is *big*.

It contains several holeships – gigantic wingless dragonflies, dull grey spheres with linear accelerator tails, several kilometres long. The insides of the spheres are perfect reflectors: they are used to store black holes, keeping them stable with their own Hawking radiation – until it's time to fire them.

But it is the thing in the centre of the chamber that gives

me pause. It looks vaguely like the head of a vast insect. There are two compound eyes, bulbous, globular arrays of transparent hexagons, joined at the waist. At the point where they meet, *something* rotates slowly, multiple silver spheres joined with spokes, like the model of a molecule – except that as it revolves, parts of it disappear and reappear in a disorienting fashion.

'What is *that*?'

'My ekpyrotic gun,' Chekhova says wearily.

'It does not look *that* big.'

'This is just the main aperture. You need to drop it into a gas-giant-sized mass to fire it. After the Spike, those are in short supply.'

'And what does it do?'

'It generates a gravitational disturbance that makes our spacetime emit a brane into the higher dimensions of the bulk. It bounces off the Planck brane and collides with ours again. It creates a miniature Big Bang.'

Suddenly, it is easier to see things from the Great Game Zoku's point of view.

'Sounds like it would be quite difficult to aim.'

I check my internal clock. What is Matjek *doing*? My instructions were very precise. He should be in the *Leblanc* already. My original plan was to seal the deal and use the Bomba's neutrino signal to qupt myself into the body I have hidden in the Wang bullet – just a loose collection of smart dust, almost undetectable – merely intended to get me aboard my ship, stored somewhere in the Arsenal. Once there, there is little that could stop us from getting out.

But perhaps the boy has gotten distracted.

'Elder, is this really necessary?' Chekhova says. 'I have better things to do than to act as a tour guide—'

I start considering options to break the Circle for a second, but with the internal security systems of the Arsenal, I don't dare risk it. To get here, we had to pass through a Realmgate that took us apart, scanned us at the atomic level for anything potentially dangerous. Of course, they would not do that to valuable antique items, risk damaging their precious quantum information contents: and that's precisely what my plan relied upon.

I interrupt her. 'It's interesting to see so many ships here. I thought you were called the *Gun* Club?'

'It's not so different! Like your own Wang bullet! Ships are just guns pointed away from the enemy! The Robur and Nemo Societies find inspiration there.' Barbicane strokes his whiskers. 'We are often misunderstood! We don't build things to destroy, but to test ourselves! Cannon shell against armour, vessel versus space – same thing!'

There is thunder in the distance.

Both Barbicane and Chekhova look up. I need to buy a few more seconds. I decide to go for the philosophical option.

'So, you don't have any problems with others using them for the purposes of war—' I begin.

And then things start blowing up.

A rapid cascade of booming explosions makes the Arsenal feel like the inside of a drum. Missiles whoosh past us. Shells and bullets ricochet from the pseudomatter walls below. In the chamber behind us, rifles and cannons go off one after another like exploding domino pieces. The q-dot shell around us is like a night sky with blinking stars as it becomes adamantine under the constant fire from conventional weapons. The noise becomes so loud the bubble has to start filtering it out.

Then one of the holeships starts moving, slowly. Its linear accelerator stem swings around, back and forth, like the weapon of a drunkard.

The bubble zips us out of the way. Not that it will make much of a difference if the holeship's weapon goes off. A single shot from one could take out the whole moon.

Barbicane and Chekhova break the Circle. She explodes into a bright constellation of foglets and jewels; he becomes a disembodied head with a stovepipe hat in the eye of a storm of diamond orbs. *To hell with it*. I speed up and hurl a qupt at Matjek.

What the hell are you doing?

There is an apologetic microsecond pause.

I got access to *all* of them, comes a response. **I just wanted to play.**

Well, stop that right now and come and get me! The thought has more anger than I intended. The response is hot with tears.

Okay, he says in a small voice. **I'm sorry.**

Never mind. Just come and—

Invisible limbs seize me. I find myself suspended in the air between them by foglet tendrils, spread-eagled. Somewhere, far away, the Colonel Sparmiento identity pops like a soap bubble. White fire of the explosions in the distance makes the two trueformed zoku members look literally incandescent.

Wait, I qupt at Matjek. **Don't stop. Keep them popping. But stay away from the holeships!**

Barbicane's eyes are bulging with rage.

'*You*,' he says.

'Hello, Barbicane,' I gasp. 'It's been a long time.' I try to incline my head towards Chekhova, but I can't move. 'Jean le Flambeur, at your service.'

'You are causing irreparable damage,' Barbicane thunders. 'Get out of our gunscape now!'

Another cascade goes off in another chamber further down. I'm pretty sure there is a nuke or two this time. Debris bounces off the skin of the nearest holeship. I squeeze my eyes shut, but it doesn't help much: a red sun shines through my eyelids, and a metal brush of second-degree burns caresses my skin.

'I'm afraid I can't do that. Not until I have what I came for. But open the Arsenal exit and I'll see what I can do.'

'It's the *Leblanc* you want, isn't it? Why didn't you just *ask*?'

'This is way more fun. Besides, I never trusted you. What's it going to be?' Something black and sleek is moving in the distance. *Come on, boy. I don't have all day.*

'No deal.'

'Suit yourself.' The holeship turret is still moving, slowly but inexorably. It collides with a silvery seashell – a Protocol War metacloak generator, I now pick up from the Arsenal's chaotic spimescape – and shatters it. 'Oh my. That *did* look rather valuable.'

It's not enough. They will detect Matjek any second. I need something else, something that will sting even outside the Circle.

Barbicane has been subtly different from the man I remember, but zoku Elders do not change. Not unless their q-self changes, unless they join a new zoku. *Could it be?*

It's worth a try.

'Something you may wish to consider, Miss Chekhova,' I say. 'Your Elder is working for the Great Game Zoku.'

Chekhova stares at Barbicane. A torrent of communication passes between them, blurring the spimescape. Her trueform features are a mask of shock and rage.

My low-rent metacortex picks up only a few fragments of the quptstorm between them, and fails to translate it. But I can imagine what they are saying.

'I would never have believed it, but it makes perfect sense.'

'He is bluffing! Can't you see? He will say anything!'

'*This* is why you blocked the ekpyrotic test, you bastard, it's why—'

There is a blinding flash. My synthbio body is jarred to the core. *Matjek fired a Hawking shell, it's all over now,* I have time to think. But my continuing consciousness implies that our lives have not been ended by a dying black hole.

My vision clears, and I see Barbicane coalesce back into his steampunk form, except that this time there is a silver egg-like q-gun floating next to his head. I fall onto the bubble bottom gently. The air is thick with inert utility foglets and scattered zoku jewels. Chekhova is gone.

'Now look at what you made me do,' Barbicane says. 'Or rather, what I made *you do*! That's the official version!'

'Not getting softer in your old age, Barbicane? You used to have a spark of anarchy. Remember the sunlifter job? You were quite happy to break the rules then. That's why I asked your zoku to make my ships.'

'Just playing a different game now, Jean! As should you.'

'Oh, I'm not *playing*. Not this time.'

'Jean, don't be a fool! Work with us! We know you were on Earth. We need intel. The Sobornost is going mad! This is the best offer you're going to get!'

I shake my head.

'I don't work for cops, even ones that wear stovepipe hats,' I say. 'And by the way, *my* best offer is this: I leave now – with my ship – or we'll get to see what Iapetus looks like with a black hole in the middle. Quite a lot like Mars, I would imagine. But then, you wouldn't know anything about that, would you?'

Barbicane hesitates. I can feel the invisible scan beam of the q-gun probing my forehead. I grit my teeth and try not to blink. It's hard when a light show of lasers, particle beams and kinetic warheads turns the chamber above into a red-and-white spiderweb.

'Get the hell out of here!' he growls, finally.

In the spimescape, I see the great gateway of the Arsenal irising open.

You can stop now, I tell Matjek.

Do I have to?

Yes. We are going to talk about this later, young man.

The *Leblanc* rises beneath us. I can feel its cool non-mind touch my own through my quptlink with Matjek. It is a sleek, midnight blue thing, not large, barely ten metres long, a cross between a Rolls Royce Silver Phantom and a spaceship. The glare of its Hawking drive pierces the chaos of the Arsenal.

'You are making a mistake, Jean,' Barbicane says. 'The Oortian *joined* us. She is a member of the Great Game now, in the embrace of our volition cone. She told us everything.'

Shit.

'We know you are not what you used to be. A challenge for a small zoku, nothing more. We *will* catch you!'

'You are welcome to try,' I say. 'As for the Oortian, you can keep her.' I stare at him. 'Next time we meet, I will take more than just toys.'

Then I jump through the q-dot bubble and drift slowly downwards, towards the ship.

We'll be ready, Barbicane mouths silently.

Another gun cascade goes off around us as a fiery goodbye, and then the blue cold skin of the *Leblanc* swallows me.

Interlude

THE GODDESS AND THE FLOWER

Joséphine Pellegrini takes a step, then another. Her legs ache. The sand is wet and clings to her feet.

The beach is dark. The spiderweb of the System map in the sky has faded into a ghostly glow. Even the sea is silent. The demiurges are busy, listening to her, making the partial. The gogol construct is taking shape next to her as she walks, a hollow ghost, a sand-woman, made of fine grains swirling in the air. It matches its steps to hers, waiting to be filled with thought and purpose.

Joséphine gives it memories. They do not belong to her: they are the Prime's, perfect like diamonds, preserved across centuries. They were given to her by her copymother, to make her into what she is. She holds each one tight as they pass through her and into the partial's eager brain.

The time of her branching, in her labyrinth temple in the shadow of Kunapipi Mons, when her Jean came to her, for the last time.

She remembers being the Prime, but only in fragments. *Walking through the gardens of the Engineer-of-Souls, helping him shepherd thought-swarms. Fighting a war against herself in the Deep Time, against a branch who wanted to take the entire guberniya into deep Dyson sleep, to leave behind these troubles and wake up to see Andromeda Galaxy fill the sky.* Like her labyrinth, the thoughts are mere shadows of something greater and high-dimensional that she cannot understand with a mind confined to the dream-vir.

On the other hand, she remembers very well how she felt when the thief made his entrance.

One moment he is not there, and then he is, warming his hands in the blaze of her singularity, in the cylindrical room at the heart of the labyrinth. A cheap trick, as one of her gogols quickly determines: a carefully placed series of space-time cloaks, hiding his approach through the labyrinth even from her eyes.

He wears flesh and heavy blue armour of the zoku, not quite matter, not quite light, and a halo of quantum jewels to go with it. She hopes that they are not for her. He has given her jewels aplenty already, all of them equally disappointing.

He is so much smaller than she is. She is in the rock and the atmosphere and in the computronium beneath the crust of the planet and in the thread-modes of the event horizon of the black hole. He is a mess of carbon atoms and entanglements and q-dots and water, barely larger than the least of her gogols.

And yet—

She creates an image of herself out of modulated Hawking radiation and steps out of the glow of the black hole to meet him. Her gogols show her his point of view: a towering figure of blue fire, wearing a necklace of stars. He flinches, and she smiles. She keeps the intensity of her form just below what his q-stone suit can handle, but not by much.

'Back already?' she asks, in a voice made of gamma rays. Her words incinerate his armour's surface layer. 'It has only been a century or two. Did you grow tired of Mars so quickly?'

He shields his face with a raised hand. 'Mars was ... educational,' he says. 'Could you stop glowing, please? It hurts my eyes.'

'As you wish.'

It only takes a thought to vaporise him and to pour him into a mindshell in her vir. Her gogols do not know what to do with the zoku jewels, so she just leaves them scattered on the floor of the singularity chamber like discarded toys.

They stand together in her heart-vir, next to a murmuring fountain, beneath a starry sky. She, too, is embodied now, in her favourite dress, in the most regal mindshell from her Library she can find. He is simply a translation of the flesh he came in, a little older than she remembers, in form-fitting dark blue. He massages the bridge of his nose.

'That's better,' he says.

'Is it? Were you not happy with that particular self? Your Raymonde seemed to like it. Poor girl. She must miss you so.' She adjusts her ring. 'Perhaps I should bring her here, too, along with the rest of Mars.'

'Joséphine—'

'Do you think you can play with the little people, and then crawl back to me, with no consequences? Other yous have done the same. What do you think I did to *them*?'

'Something involving poetic justice, I expect.' He spreads his hands. 'I was told that this is where you come to pray to the goddess. So I did.'

'What do you want?'

'As unlikely as it may seem to you, I am here on business.'

'I see. And why should I not have my gogols consume you, here and now, and finally find out if there is anything of use in that mind of yours?'

'Don't offend me by thinking I haven't taken precautions,' he says, tapping one temple. 'Touch me, and whatever I have to trade will all burn. Touch me *wrong*, that is.' He grins.

'Do not test my patience, Jean.'

'I don't have to test it.'

'Then you know you should make it quick.'

'Here, where we have all the time in the world? Where each minute takes less than a baseline picosecond? When we haven't seen each other – well, I haven't seen *you* – for nearly two hundred years? You have gotten even more impatient in your old age.'

She sighs and sits down on the fountain stairs.

'Perhaps I have,' she says. 'It tends to happen when you walk a tightrope between Founder sisters and brothers who want to stab you in the back and a fanatic who wants to conquer death, all the while making sure that they don't tear the System apart in another ridiculous war. It's not like designing buildings and having affairs on Mars, Jean.'

He sits down next to her, carefully choosing a step below her. He crosses his hands over one knee and leans back. 'I know. That's why I'm here. Things are about to get worse.'

'What do you mean?'

'Matjek Chen has the Kaminari jewel.'

She takes a deep breath.

'And why are you telling me that?'

'Why do you think? Because I'm going to steal it.'

She laughs. 'I would like to see *that*,' she says. 'And I suppose you are asking for my help?'

'Not exactly.' He takes her left hand in his own. His grip

is tight and warm. 'Joséphine, if I fail, you know where I'll end up.' He gestures with his free hand. There is a flower between his thumb and forefinger, suddenly, with colourful, tapering petals.

'This will help you find me if that happens. If you ever want to, that is.'

She holds it up. *Clever little thief.* It is information encoded in matter, translated by her gogols into vir form. At a molecular level the petals are spiky cathedrals, rows upon rows of them, containing data. It defines a set of modal logic constraints, provable properties for a neural network, like a gogol. The flower is an empty shape of a person, a shadow, waiting to be filled.

'That's very romantic, Jean,' she says. 'Asking me to be your get out of jail for free card. Are you sure you'd not rather receive a file in a cake?'

'You were never much of a cook, even less so a baker. And I didn't imagine for a moment getting out of jail would be *free.*'

She freezes him in the vir's slowtime for a moment and summons a warmind gogol family to scour the flower for traps. They find nothing. It is only then that she lets time resume and inhales the flower's scent. It is delicate and sweet, the memory of a summer, with a hint of honey.

'Jean,' she says, a sudden tenderness in her chest. 'This is *Matjek.* You are going to fail, and it sounds like you know it. Why are you doing this? You were happy on Mars, with the little people.'

'I didn't realise you cared.'

'I don't. I just thought I'd do the System a favour by keeping an eye on you.'

He looks down.

'I talked to a woman of the Kaminari once,' he says, 'before the Spike. Don't give me such a look, it wasn't like that, we were just friends. But one night on Ganymede, we got philosophical. The Universe is a game, she said. It makes us into players. We can't see the moves that are not allowed. Like in chess. There is perfect freedom in the black and white, except that the rules make invisible walls. Two squares forward, one left. One left, whole row forward and backward, one right. That's all you see.

'There is a reason for it, she said. Algorithmic complexity. The Universe is a quantum computer, and over time, it is simply more likely that structure comes out of it than noise. That means rules, patterns. That means a game. But spend long enough poking at it, and you start to see the game engine, the labyrinth of the quantum circuit, wires looping around each other, forwards and backwards.'

'It sounds like the kind of thing the zoku like to say,' Joséphine says disdainfully.

The thief sighs. 'Perhaps. After that, she started talking about this ancient legend they have, about a creature called the Sleeper with a billion hit points, and after it was finally killed by a coalition of a thousand guilds, it dropped a small rusty dagger.

'But there is something to it. I'm tired of games. Mars was not enough. And you were right, I made a mess of it. I need something new, something different.'

'And you think the jewel will give you that?'

'I don't know, but I'm going to try.'

'I know you, Jean, better than anyone. You will never stop. There will always be something else for you to steal.'

He gives her that fake-weary look. 'Oh, I don't know,' he says. 'I think one more thing would be enough. Maybe it always was.' He stands up. 'Goodbye, Joséphine. If we meet again, it will be your choice.'

'Did I give you my permission to leave?' she says, hardening her voice.

'Oh, I'm not leaving. I would never have come here if I expected to *leave*. This is a new branch of me that I created just for you. That self-destruct loop of yours? I stole it a long time ago.'

'Jean—' She reaches for the firmament, for his mindshell, but it is already too late.

'You know, it's good practice for what is to come. Even if you are branching before jumping into the nothing, you have to have the resolve to do it yourself. Take this as a compliment, Joséphine: if I had come here first, it would have been hard to find the courage. Take care of yourself. It's been fun.'

He closes his eyes. He twitches once. The mindshell stands still, chest rising and falling, but Joséphine knows that the gogol inside is gone.

She sits on the stairs for a long time, watching the still form of the thief, standing there with a peaceful expression on his face. She turns the flower in her hands. Finally she stands up and touches her Jean's face gently with her ring hand.

Then she starts thinking about how to best betray him to Matjek Chen.

7

MIELI AND THE LIQUORICE-ZOKU

Mieli is singing to her new garden when the quantum spam rain starts.

She sits in the shade of a young pumptree and hums a wordless hum, softly varying in pitch and frequency. It tells the smartcoral in the garden's soil to grow thin tendrils to hold the soft soil in place, packing it firmer than the gentle gravity of the Farreach Plate can. The humid air is warm and full of the wet rhubarb smell of pumptree breath. The shrill screams of young anansi spiders mingle with Mieli's song. They dart amongst the tree branches, weaving diamond threads between them. The horizon curves up like the fingers of a cupped hand. Far above is the sky of ice, faintly transparent, and beyond it, the sisterspheres.

Only some of it is real, for certain values of *real*. Like almost all inhabitants of Supra City, she is a member of the Huizinga-zoku now, the zoku of Circles. Inside her own Circle, she is free to define her own realities and their laws as she wishes. She cringes at the memory of fumbling with Circle-crafting, turning her hex first into a cartoon world without a third dimension, then into a grey fog where only sounds had physical form.

Reluctantly, at Zinda's suggestion, she turned her longing for Oort into a wish and wove it into the volition of the zoku through her Huizinga jewel. In an instant, several thousand Huizinga members qupted her complete Oortian Circle and Realm spimes, ranging from megaproject construction game Realms to a very detailed Narrativist Circle exploring gender dynamics in an Oortian *koto*. Mieli found the last one promising, until she realised it only allowed communication through song and wing movements, and completely excluded all sexual activity. But there was enough to help her create a patchwork reality that matched her memories.

Now, she could believe she is in Oort. Almost.

The song comes out of her easily, and she can feel the movement in the earth beneath her. She has already planted some cloudberries. Vecbushes and maybe even a small phoenixwood grove will follow. She breathes in the scent of the garden. It almost fills the hollow space in her chest.

A part of her dreads finishing the song. After singing to living things, it will be time to sing to the dead. She has been working on a song for *Perhonen* for weeks. But she can only do it in bits and pieces, when the grief is hiding beneath a blanket of sunlight and comfort. In her dealings with her zokus, she uses her metacortex heavily, to filter her thoughts and emotions. It always leaves her feeling like a butterfly pressed between two glass plates, thin and lifeless. But she refuses to touch her sorrow, and so it remains a wild thorny plant in the ordered garden of her mind.

She mistakes the first falling jewel for a waterdrop from the anansi webs. But more follow: slowly at first, little more than flashes of sunlight that vanish into the grass, then as a relentless glass hail downpour that beats down on the pumptree leaves with a sound like a whispering machine gun. A tiny jewel stings her cheek. An offer to join a zoku dedicated to constructing a perfect life-sized replica of an ancient imaginary starship from notchcubes on the surface of Rhea flashes through her brain, full of shrill enthusiasm. She brushes it aside and presses herself against the pulsating trunk of the pumptree.

Bigger jewels follow, bouncing off the anansi webs and tearing the creatures down from their perches. They make small craters in her soil and completely decimate the cloud-berry patch. Mieli fumbles for her link to the Plate zoku that takes care of all the infrastructure needs, and qupts a frantic request for a q-dot umbrella over her garden. **Conflict with your Circle's Schroeder locks,** comes back the reply. Mieli groans. Clearly, some subtle setting in her Circle excludes non-Oortian technology.

She runs into the rain and opens her wings in an attempt to shield even a few of the delicate berries from the destruction. It is like standing beneath a shower of hot stones. Lightning flashes of entanglement requests bombard her mind to the rhythm of the blows. **Time machine megaproject! Solve the Fermi Paradox! Resurrect Saint McGonigal to save us all!**

'*Perkele!*' she screams and pushes a request to the Huizinga-zoku through the mad thunder of the mind spam. In a flash of silver, her Circle goes down. The ice sky disappears. The horizon lurches from the familiar bowl-shape of a *koto* into the endless gentle curve of Saturn, crisscrossed by the immense blue-and-green arcs of the Strips and the wispy mass stream pillars that hold them up. The vertigo-inducing stairway structure of the Farreach Plate reveals itself around her little hex, the immense set of stream-supported ascending steps, each with slightly lower gravity than the one below, reaching up nearly two thousand klicks from the one-G level near the ochre van Gogh brushstrokes of the giant planet below.

And, finally, with a pop and a faint ozone smell, a q-dot dome shimmers into being. A few thin streams of tiny jewels pour down to the ground from the hollows of the pumptrees and cupped leaves with a faint tinkle, and then the garden is silent.

Mieli stares at the devastation. Her wings and head hurt. The jewels crunch beneath her feet. Everything green is covered in a layer of multicoloured glitter. With a sigh, she summons a swarm of utility fog botlets from the Plate zoku to clean things up. This time, they materialise instantly: the air blurs in a heat haze, and the spam jewels start floating away in streams and spirals. She briefly considers telling them to hide the damage and make the garden look the way it was, but decides against it. Karhu always told her to keep reminders of her mistakes visible.

Mieli? comes a qupt. It's Zinda: the message comes with a mixture of sensory impressions, smell of incense, a glimpse of the ring-bisected evening sky from the Great Game girl's balcony, and a palpable sense of concern. **Are you all right?**

I'm fine, Mieli answers, restricting her reply to a curt verbal message and nothing else. **What do you want?**

Just checking up on you! I got a volition flash that you needed help with something. We are entangled now, you know. She pauses. **Oh dear. What a terrible mess. I knew we should not have set you up on Farreach: the spam zoku must think that the newly joined and expats are easy targets, and the Plate zoku is a bit too loose to sort them out. Are you sure you don't want a Realm?**

Mieli swears silently. Clearly, she has to guard her thoughts even more carefully. Something of her volition must have slipped through to the Great Game jewel without her realising it – and she is still clumsy enough with the quptlink to allow Zinda to see what she is seeing.

Yes. I'm sure.

How tacky! But I understand. A lot of aegon-zokus feel that way, that matter is special. Just let me know if there is anything I can do. Oh, and if it's more matter you are after, can I interest you in a dinner?

Mieli sighs. To all appearances, Zinda has been sincere in her attempts to help Mieli settle in. When Mieli accepted the Great Game jewel, she expected to be sent to some strange Realm where she would be rewarded or punished for answering questions about Sobornost. Instead, Zinda arranged her to join the Loom-zoku as a part of her cover identity – a zoku devoted to the intersection of music and matter, translating sound into physical shapes, who count several expatriate Oortians amongst their members. Conveniently, the Loomers devote a lot of time to individual projects, and the volition flashes tend to be requests for brief musings about what sort of Universe would arise from thread-theoretic particle states if you converted a symphony into the Fourier components of creation-annihilation operators. For the last two weeks, she has mostly been left to her own devices.

No thanks.

I'm not a bad cook, I swear!

Maybe another time.

Suit yourself. Remember to eat, though. You'll need your strength soon.

Why is that? Mieli qupts.

Wait and see! A wink comes down the quptlink, the

feeling of Zinda's eyelid moving. It makes Mieli wince, and then the presence of the zoku girl is gone.

Mieli sighs. What is left of the garden has been cleared, revealing mounds of soil, battered pumptrees and a few angry anansi peeking out of the holes in the ground. *At least it will keep me busy for a while.*

She kicks at the loose dirt. She is wasting time. Perhaps she *should* have accepted Zinda's dinner invitation, to get closer to her, to find out more about the Great Game and the Kaminari jewel. Pretending to be someone she is not, infiltration – that was always the thief's domain, not hers.

She feels grimy and dirty from the rain, and finds herself desperately missing a sauna. Perhaps she should ask the Plate-zoku to make one, somewhere in the microgravity levels, higher up.

The volition flash comes suddenly. In an instant, she becomes aware of her Great Game jewel pulsing. Before Mieli can tell her metacortex to buffer the thought, it is as if a sudden insight has occurred to her after wrestling with a problem for a long time. *Of course.* She has to go to the Irem Plate, in twenty subjective minutes.

The Great Game needs her.

The compulsion to obey the call is like a toothache in her mind. Unlike the whispers of the Loom or the Plate-zoku, the demands of the Great Game are not gentle. Mieli fights it long enough to take a quick foglet shower. She immerses herself in a hazy cloud of nanobots that scrub her clean. It leaves her feeling tender and red, but more alert.

Then she fabs herself a new toga and summons her q-self to her. Her jewels alight from the nooks and crannies where she left them lying around like a flock of bright, startled birds, and form a modest diamond solar system around her head. Collectively, they are a quantum extension of her, containers for slow entangled light that encodes her relationships with other zoku members. From the zoku point of view, it is the jewels and their unique quantum states that constitute who she really is, not her replaceable flesh. Mieli finds the Sobornost notion of endless, identical self-copies almost preferable. *I should have allowed the pellegrini to make a gogol of* Perhonen.

But the Great Game does not allow her time for regrets. She shakes her head and tells the Plate to seal up her hex and take care of the anansi and the few remaining plants. Then she looks at her Tube-zoku jewel – a white disc surrounded by a red ring, with a blue bar across it – and wishes to be taken to Irem, with the caveat that she wants to avoid travel through Realmgates and stay in the physical world as much as possible.

In an instant, the air around her comes alive with a tingling feeling, and she floats up, as if carried by a gentle tide. A q-dot transport bubble flashes into being around her. There is a tickle in her stomach, and then she is flying, faster than even her wings could ever carry her.

First, the bubble accelerates at several dozen G, cushioning her every cell against the crushing force in a gentle but unbreakable nanobot grip. Yet she feels safe, her mind cocooned in the comforting presence of the Tube-zoku. For a few seconds, the varied hexes and Circles and Farseer stairway architecture that is like mathematics rendered into matter flash past her, until the paintbrush of speed smears them into a flickering tunnel around her.

Then, suddenly, it all vanishes, and she is *below* the Plate. The bubble follows a brachistochrone mass stream that takes a shortcut through the vacuum gulf between Saturn's upper atmosphere and the main shell of Supra City. It is a phosphorescent cylinder inside which iron oxide particles flow at an incredible speed in a constant loop. The bubble grabs the stream with EM fields and reaches its intra-Plate velocity of twenty thousand kilometres per hour in moments, while Mieli looks at the scenery.

Above is the inverted world of the Farseer Plate underside – the crumpled depressions of artificial mountains and the plateau of the Basement Sea. It crawls with tentacled zoku kaijubodies, worn by zokus who want to play at being ancient alien gods. The mass stream pillars that support the vast structure are a glowing forest of filaments that vanish into the haze of Saturn below. Traffic flows along them, ranging from a myriad transport bubbles to the feral spider-cities of the Underpirate-zoku. Fortunately, the only one of the latter in sight is thousands of kilometres below her route. It is a black, spiky, many-limbed monstrosity that houses hundreds of thousands of zoku alters; it swings from stream to stream and shoots Underpirate jewels at careless travellers, to entice them to join their crew and to look for quantum booty in Saturn's endless depths.

She joins a cloud of bubbles travelling along the same stream. They are full of zoku trueforms and alters, humanoids of every hue, shape and description. A blue-skinned giant with a grinning sapphire skull and streamlined armour carapace qupts her an invite to join a Stormrider-zoku that is on its way to dive into the hexagon of the South Pole. Shiva-limbed lovers entwined in an impossible tangle of flesh ask her to join a zoku that intends to develop a tantric language.

She turns them all down, tells her q-self to block further qupts and keeps going.

At last, Mieli approaches the Irem Plate, and the bubble begins a gentle climb up the curve of the stream. It is a new Plate, and the act of creation is still in progress. The bright glow of continent-scale fabbers shines through seams between the hexes. There are so many mass streams feeding the growing artificial continent that they look like threads hanging from a loom, weaving a new landscape into being.

When the bubble passes a gap in the structure, Mieli catches a glimpse of the complex self-assembly inside the Plate's cross-section: snakelike piping that folds itself into polygons and complex shapes that become the bones of mountains and hills. Briefly, it reminds her of the Great Works of Oort that she crafted in her youth, chains of tethered comets that gravity folded into convoluted shapes like proteins.

But the scale of this work is beyond her. Mieli wants to close her eyes, but forces herself to keep them open. She has to remember where she is. And she has to remember that she *matters*. The Dark Man could swallow this bauble of a world with one gulp, but she does not fear him. Even one note in a song can make a difference. A butterfly can change the course of a storm, even one the size of a planet, like the great eyewalls of Saturn, swirling and boiling in the depths, ready to swallow the Plate of Irem, should it ever fall.

The bubble leaves her in the middle of an empty continent, on a vast grey plain lit by wan soletta-light. The ground beneath her feet is made of notchcubes, uniform, gunmetal-hued bricks slightly larger than her fist. They are almost too warm to stand on, but they sense Mieli's presence and cool down, conducting their waste heat elsewhere. They are the macroscopic equivalent of q-dots, basic building blocks of many Supra City megastructures.

The landscape is featureless, except for a gargantuan statue in the horizon: a blocky, rough-hewn image of a man holding a pickaxe, a signature of some Notch-zoku maker who has left their mark on the newborn Plate. Every now and then, there is a booming echo of giant machinery, a brief earthquake somewhere far below. A soft wind blows, bringing a faint smell of burning metal dust.

The grid of the cube seams makes Mieli feel like she is a piece standing on some vast chessboard, waiting for a hand to descend from the sky and move her. *What am I doing here?*

Her systems send out a brief alert. Another transport bubble arrives in a rush of air. Mieli glimpses the glowing medusa of a zoku trueform. But the newcomer quickly assumes an alter that is something even stranger, a collection of silvery spheres with red-lipped female mouths. The orbs grow and vanish and disappear at irregular intervals. The mouths are speaking, a constant, faint chatter of feminine voices that blur into a cacophony. Yet, the creature feels somehow familiar, an instinctive recognition that they belong to the same zoku.

Identity: Anti-de-Sitter-times-a-Sphere, it qupts, followed by a burst of dizzying geometrical concepts that Mieli has no names for, like the output of mathematics gogols.

'Hello,' Mieli says. 'My name is Mieli.'

The spheres swirl frantically and electricity crackles between them.

One-to-one mapping: Metis. Termination: timelike geodesic. Valence-intensity spectrum: anger. This time, there is an emotion in the qupt: a wave of loathing that makes Mieli reel.

Shit. The Protocol War. It knows me from the Protocol War.

Before she can respond, there is a sound like a giant popping its mouth with a finger, and another transport bubble arrives.

The newcomer is a Quick One – a tiny man on the back of a four-legged, red-eyed, winged creature. His mount is barely the size of an anansi, and he himself could stand on Mieli's palm – if he was not wearing black, spiky metal armour. He takes a bow without dismounting.

'GreetingsMyLady! SirMikAtYourService!' he says in a rapid-fire, tinny voice.

The Anti-de-Sitter creature crackles again, and Mieli senses rapid qupts passing between the strange duo.

'Fiend!ChallengetoaDuel!' pipes Sir Mik, brandishing his sword, a tiny sliver of bright metal. One of Anti-de-Sitter-times-a-Sphere's orbs begins to glow bright.

Mieli activates her combat systems.

There is another *pop*.

'Good,' Zinda says. 'You have met the team already!' The zoku girl stands next to Mieli. She is wearing the samurai gear and carrying the naginata from the mountain Realm where they met, although her rabbit mask is pushed up over her head. 'I am *very* excited about this – our first mission together!'

'Kuutar and Ilmatar! What exactly are we doing here?' Mieli asks, not taking her eyes off the three zoku members.

'The jewel did not tell you? Not enough entanglement levels yet, I suppose, or best for the volition that I explain it. You are going to like this, Mieli.' Zinda smiles. 'We are going to kidnap a Sobornost Founder mind.'

*

I told you they would hate me, Mieli qupts Zinda.

Oh, shush, it's just they don't know you. It will be better after the briefing, I promise.

Briefing? I thought you were just a sleeper agent.

Oh, I was! But I seriously levelled up when I recruited you, she replies with a wistful sigh. **Now I barely have time for my old primary zoku anymore. And you are right: I should have made a new alter for this, but I thought I would be better if I came along looking like when we met. It makes me feel brave!**

'All right, everybody,' Zinda says aloud. 'Settle down. I am going to make a Circle so we can talk more easily. Mieli joined only recently, and is not comfortable with qupting. Let's all try to be considerate, now.'

Sir Mik scowls at Mieli. Anti-de-Sitter-times-a-Sphere's many mouths are hard red lines.

Zinda gestures, and a silver circle appears on the notchcube ground around them: Mieli sees a flash of the rules through her connection to the Huizinga-zoku. *No violence. Baseline bodies only. Verbal conflict resolution. Qupting allowed for data exchange only. Points for successful team bonding.* The Schroeder locks kick in, and Mieli feels a strange phantom ache where her combat systems should be. She wonders briefly how good the locks really are: they must work through the Huizinga-jewel's connection to her brain, and her metacortex should be able to disable them if necessary.

At least her new teammates play by the rules. Anti-de-Sitter-times-a-Sphere becomes a woman with a small pouty mouth and angular, classical features, wearing a loose rust-coloured gown and flowers and ribbons in her ash-blond hair. Sir Mik increases in size to slightly-smaller-than-baseline proportions, retaining his large eyes, spiky hair, pointy ears and mistrustful expression.

Zinda twirls her naginata experimentally.

'That's better! Now, I'm going to qupt you some data in a moment, but let's cover the basics. The zoku volition has brought you here because you have the right combination of skills for this mission: cryptography' – she points at Anti-de-Sitter – 'spatial coordination and navigation, transportation' – with a nod to Mik – 'and finally, and most importantly, in-depth knowledge of Sobornost tactics and communications protocols.' She touches Mieli on the shoulder. 'We all have a reason to be here.'

She takes a deep breath, and there is a brief flash of uncertainty in her eyes. *She is very young,* Mieli thinks. *Or perhaps it's just an act, a part of this alter.*

'Does anyone here have a problem with that?' Zinda says.

There is a deep silence. Mik smiles sarcastically, sits down and folds his hands across his chest. Anti-de-Sitter-times-a-Sphere closes her eyes and rocks back and forth on her feet.

'No? All right. Then I guess it's time to go over the plan.'

'Let me show you what is happening in the Inner System at the moment,' Zinda says. She qupts a spime at them. A complex diagram in the centre of their small circle: a three-dimensional tangle of coloured regions, flows and vectors.

It takes Mieli a moment to realise that it is a full spime of the Great Game's estimate of the current power structure in the System, fine-grained detail updated in real time from the Game's intelligence assets in the zoku router network. Information is easily available in Supra City: like for every imaginable quantifiable resource, there is a zoku devoted to gamifying it. But during the last few weeks, Mieli has deliberately avoided looking into the events in the Inner System, and this is the first time she sees the full extent of the conflict.

The pellegrinis, vasilevs and hsien-kus are at war. Their *guberniyas* are centres of raion flows, all pumping out vast amounts of waste heat and matter. Major battles and exotic weapon events concentrate around sunlifter mines and Highway hubs. The lines of conflict extend all the way to the Belt and beyond, to Jovian trojans and even the chaotic space near the Spike remnants. The other Founders are biding their time, fortifying their territories and laying low. The chen *guberniya* is still in the Lagrange point between the Earth and Moon – but the spime is notably patchy on chen oblasts and raions, relying on sensory observations rather than direct intelligence sources.

'I think you can all see the problem,' Zinda says. 'We used to have assets inside all the Founder copyclans. Well, not anymore. We lost everybody inside the chens. And that is a problem: so far, they have stayed neutral, but they are going to decide this thing one way or the other. We expected them to support the pellegrinis, but that did not happen. We are blind to the biggest internal Sobornost conflict since the Dragon Wars. The Spooky-zoku claim that there is something anomalous about the entire conflict, but they are unsure as to exactly what.

'So we are going to find out. At the moment, our beloved zoku has several thousand intelligence-gathering operations at work, aimed at the chens. But *we*, dear friends, have a chance to win entanglement and glory for our zoku.' She turns to Mieli. 'Mieli, could you tell us what is the power structure on a Sobornost warship?'

Mieli frowns. 'Most gogols will be branched for whatever

mission the ship is fabbed for: warminds and turks. There will be a commanding gogol of an older generation, depending on the importance of a mission. And there will be a—'

'A chen gogol, as an observer, to protect the interests of the Sobornost as a whole even during Founder conflicts, ever since the Dragon Wars.' Zinda smiles. 'If the ship is destroyed, the chen is usually evacuated in a thoughtwisp. So, there we have it: we will monitor a civil war battle – a skirmish between raions, that is all we need – and look for thoughtwisps we can intercept. Mik here will lay out a q-dot net and take care of navigation. Mieli will convince the wisp that we are a Sobornost ship. Anti-de-Sitter-times-a-Sphere will use Mieli's protocols and Box the chen.' She looks at their faces eagerly. 'Any questions?'

Mik gets up slowly. 'My lady Zinda, I deem this course of action most unwise,' he says. At normal speed, his voice is a deep baritone, at odds with his boyish face. 'You yourself are strong in entanglement, and known to us all. But our new companion? I like her not.' He takes a step forward and looks up at Mieli. 'She is a member of our zoku, aye; but in level, barely more than a lowly squire. Her will is not yet bound to the Great Game like ours is. I have fought the Sobornost: there is often another will within their will that can hide true intentions. And is it not true that she was the truedeath of many a friend of our lady Anti-de-Sitter-times-a-Sphere, in the War of Protocols?'

Mik shakes his head. 'Were it not for the zoku's volition, I would take my leave now, and I have a mind to pluck the Great Game jewel from the hilt of my blade rather than go forth on a dangerous quest with such a dark companion.'

*

Zinda looks at each of the trio in turn. 'Mieli is a part of our zoku, like it or not, and the zoku has made up its mind. You are free to disagree. And you always have your freedom to leave. Now, we have heard from Mik. What do you think, Anti-de-Sitter?'

'Filtered Markov chain state: doom,' says Anti-de-Sitter-times-a-Sphere in a gentle, singsong voice.

'Although the law of Hospitality binds me, as all those in my order,' Mik says, 'a Sobornost warrior with bloodstained hands will not enter my faithful ship, the *Zweihänder*. This I swear, by my blade.'

Zinda looks lost. 'Maybe I made the Circle wrong,' she says in a small voice. 'Are you sure you are not just rules-lawyering here, trying to win some verbal points? I always do this with Circles, tend to come up with mechanisms that generate conflict, it's better for the narrative.'

'Implication via modus ponens: negative,' sings Anti-de-Sitter-times-a-Sphere.

She is out of her depth, Mieli thinks. And winning entanglement in the Great Game is her only chance to get closer to the Kaminari jewel.

She takes a step forward.

'My name is Mieli, daughter of Karhu,' she says. 'And you are all right. I do not belong here.'

She looks at them in the eyes, each in turn. 'But Sir Mik does me injustice as well. I may not truly belong to the Great Game yet, but I am not of Sobornost either. I may have served them for a time, but I have no reason to love them. In my heart, I am of Oort, of ice and darkness and song and void. I, too, was taught that strangers from outside my *koto* were evil. But I was also taught to put aside my grievances to work together for the Million Tribes, when we needed to, to drive the Dark Man back.'

She pauses. It is not that different from singing a song, watching *väki* respond to the notes and words.

'When we met warriors and builders from other *kotos*, we would do something together, to forge a bond. We would go to the sauna and throw *löyly* until the Dark Man himself ran away from the heat. We would tattoo a common symbol to our skins, to forge bonds of pain and ink.' She touches the butterfly tattoo on her chest beneath her toga and feels a flash of guilt on its raised contours. 'Or we would drink liquorice vodka until we were ready to tell all our secrets to each other. We did all these things so we could stand as one, when the Tribes needed us.

'We are supposed to be bound together by entanglement, by a compulsion to do what is best for our zoku. I say it is not enough. The thread that binds our destinies together is too weak, lost in the greater weave of the Great Game.'

They are listening to her now. Sir Mik's eyes gleam. *He is the key*, Mieli thinks.

'I am ignorant of the ways of the zoku, but I understand this to be true: a zoku is not a difficult thing to make. I propose this: let us forge a zoku of our own for this mission, to join our thoughts and wills to a common cause. Entanglement among few is stronger than among many. It will show you that my purpose is true.' She narrows her eyes. 'Sir Mik, if we were in Oort, you would have to defend your words with your blade. But in this Circle, for my friend Zinda's sake, I ask you to join me in a new zoku brotherhood. What do you say?' She turns to the others. 'What do you all say?'

Mik draws his sword and holds it high. 'I say thee aye!' he shouts. He grins. 'My apologies, Lady Mieli,' he says. 'Bound by a jewel of our own, I will be glad to fight by your side.'

After a while, Anti-de-Sitter-times-a-Sphere speaks.

'Set operation: inclusion,' she says.

It takes only moments to create the zoku. Zinda takes out a small Notch-zoku jewel and, at her request, the plain extrudes a fabber that spits out four blank jewels, simple transparent pentagons. As she works, Mieli whispers to her metacortex, tells it to hide all thoughts of the Kaminari jewel until the mission is over, and hopes that the pellegrini is as good at hiding as she claims to be.

Betraying koto *brotherhood*, she thinks darkly. *Another piece of me gone. Is that why the thief wore many faces? Because there was nothing left of him?*

And then the thought is gone, erased.

The jewels are warm from the fabber, almost like living things. The four companions hold them up in the air, and Zinda summons an entangled light beam from one of the numerous routers in the sky. It comes down in a bright pillar, lights up their faces and bounces around the new jewels in dazzling patterns. Mieli feels a new presence through her jewel, a newborn zoku, a diamond-hard purpose of capturing a chen and winning entanglement from the Great Game.

'What shall we call ourselves?' Zinda asks. Thank you, she qupts at Mieli.

They all look at Mieli. 'Well, let this be the first test of our zoku's volition,' she says. 'Who shall name it?'

The answer is clear. It is Sir Mik who speaks.

'Lady Mieli named us already, methinks – if our bond is meant to replace that of liquorice vodka, let us be known as the Liquorice-zoku!'

He brandishes his sword again. Above them, a dark long

shape is distilled into being: a hundred-metre-long black cylinder emblazoned with red runes and bristling with jutting dark blades.

'Gentle ladies, this is my *Zweihänder*,' Mik says. 'It is she who will bear us to our destiny.'

8

THE THIEF AND THE HAUNTED SHIP

My ship is haunted.

It's a feeling I can't shake as I steer the *Leblanc* through the lower cloud layers of Saturn, trying to hide us in the winter blue swirls of ammonia hydrosulfide pockets and egg-white water vapour clouds. It is a gnawing anxiety that mingles with the faint tickle of motion in my stomach that the interface Realm translates the ship's slow dive into, a chilly sense of someone looking over my shoulder.

It could be some echo of my past self, preserved in the ship's neural interface. The pilot's Realm is a floating platform in a cavernous chamber with crystalline walls that provide a fish-eye view of the giant planet's churning ochre depths. I sit on a velvet-cushioned chair at a control keyboard that looks like the bastard offspring of three pipe organs and a typewriter – it even has pedals. But it is all a shorthand for mental commands. As I brush the keys, the ship's cool presence enfolds my mind, snug like a well-worn glove. Who knows what fossilised feedback loops were triggered by my touch and now resonate in my brain?

Or it could be the ship's avatar Carabas, a glass-eyed

mechanical cat in a flamboyant hat and boots. When I last encountered it on Mars, in my old memory palace, it tried to gut me and turn me into a wax figure. Now it never leaves my side, waiting for my commands with arrogant, feline resignation.

Or maybe it is the awareness that the Great Game Zoku is now after me. I shake my head at the notion: worrying about capture at this point is not rational. I am keeping us well away from Supra City's support structures. The closest zoku presence is the Notch stormcrafter playground near the South Pole, with its fluid dynamics megastructures. There is a calculator made from Karman vortex trains – a region near the Sayanagi belt where chains of swirling vortices the size of continents collide and compute, logic gates larger than moons. Each arithmetic operation involves a mass of gas greater than old Earth's atmosphere. To find us, the Great Game would have to throw enormous resources into a neutrino scan of the whole planet – and I don't think they are ready to do that just yet. That will come later.

Or perhaps the ghost is Matjek. I know I need to speak to him, sooner or later, but I can't bring myself to do it. Not yet. Besides, I need to make sure we are well hidden, and the Aun are supposed to be looking after him.

In the end, what chills my spine the most are Barbicane's last words. *She is a member of the Great Game now. She told us everything.* I cannot imagine Mieli as a zoku member. The Gun Club Elder must have been lying, trying to get back at me for breaking his toys.

And yet—

After Earth, Mieli must be lost, looking for a direction, looking for guidance. She has served Joséphine nearly her entire adult life. Perhaps the Great Game has exploited that, offered her a new purpose when she needed it the most. And with *Perhonen* gone, there is no one around to tell her what a bad idea that is.

I thought the job would be straightforward. Get to Mieli before they break her, use the *Leblanc*'s tools to break into whatever Realm they have her in, and steal her. Simple, what I do best. Instead, I now have the Great Game after me – and Mieli is already one of them.

Nothing has changed. I still need to get her out.

It all depends on how entangled she is with the zoku already, how much freedom the Great Game volition leaves her. That is the paradox of the zoku: the more you achieve, the more entanglement you have, and thus more power to impose your will upon the zoku's collective reality. But at the same time, as you advance, you are sculpted by the zoku jewel into a perfect member of the collective. If I know Mieli she will rise through the ranks quickly. Soon, she will be like Barbicane, a shell of herself, trapped inside her role in the zoku Circles.

I need a better plan. The problem is, Barbicane was right. *You are not what you used to be.* I almost screwed up the Iapetos job. I didn't anticipate the Great Game's paranoia about Dragons following Earth's destruction. If it hadn't been for Matjek—

I shake my head. I can't think about the boy, not yet.

Infiltrating the Great Game is not an option. They are too well hidden, and screen their members very carefully. I have to draw them out, break Mieli's link to them. And they only deal with epic, existential threats.

I need to become one. To manipulate them, I need to find something that makes them afraid. I need leverage. And I already know what that is: the ghost that has been haunting me since the Highway.

I find us a slow-flowing layer not too far from the eye-storms of the South Pole.

'Keep us in the hot stratosphere beacons,' I tell Carabas. 'If you see any mermaids, let me know.'

'Yes, Master,' it says in a whirring, high-pitched voice, and takes my place at the pilot's seat, short booted feet hanging in the air.

I sigh. Evidently, my former self thought his own witty banter was company enough.

I leave the cat to its work and head for the ship's treasure room, to open the qupt that Mars died for.

The *Leblanc* is bigger from the inside than from the outside. Physically, it is a marvel, a picotech creation: zoku subatomic engineering, dense pseudomatter and bizarre metastable quark configurations and nucleon soup, impossibly dense but programmable, all whirling around a tiny black hole like those of the Gun Club ships, only smaller. The passenger space is virtual, a network of interconnected Realms. The main meta-Realm is a blue-lit corridor with a moving walkway, lined with humming Buck Rogers machines and Realmgates.

I've barely had time to explore them, but this time, I'm only interested in the treasure room. It is a vault in an ancient fantasy castle, full of loot converted into iconic Realm form, potions and weapons and treasure, representing stolen zoku jewels and quantum software. Sobornost tech stored as firmament code on scrolls, exotic gogols as frozen homunculi inside bottles. There is even a green planet, a stolen biosphere, some design from the world-builders of the Belt, with an entire biological history unfolding on its surface. It makes me realise why Joséphine did not allow me to remember the ship: with these resources, I would have been too difficult to control.

But I'm not here to admire the spoils of past crimes. I take out the qupt and look at it. The treasure room – a small Realm to itself – translates it into a scroll, sealed with hard candle wax. I break the seal carefully, and Isidore's message echoes in my mind again.

Jean! You can't believe what I found! It's not just Earth, it's the Spike, and the Collapse, you have to look at this.

There is an aching weight in my chest when I hear his voice, but I grit my teeth and focus on the task at hand.

The quantum state that came with it floats up from the scroll, countless tiny soap bubbles connected by glowing tendrils. I examine it carefully: it is a delicate thing, a tangle of qubits that does not follow any encoding scheme I have come across. Aboard the *Wardrobe*, I would have no hope of deciphering it. But here in the *Leblanc*, I do not lack tools.

The work takes a long time, and I have to uncork some of the mathematics gogols. Eventually, they inform me that it is a small virtual quantum computer, meant to bootstrap itself in a biological brain, perhaps originally transmitted via complex photon states – a node in a vast distributed machine, computing … something.

I imagine what it could have been like for poor Owl Boy: a flash of light in the sky that you look at, and suddenly this thing enters your brain via the optic nerve, infects you, repurposes the microtubules in your neurons to do coherent quantum computations. But what is it for? For making a viral, System-wide zoku?

There is only one way to find out. I sandbox myself and increase the fidelity of my neural network emulation to the maximum. A full molecular-level simulation of even a single human brain swallows a respectable chunk of the ship's computational capacity. The feeling is strange. At the level of my consciousness, there should be no perceptible difference, but I could swear that my thoughts feel messier, softer, more eager to copulate with each other and form new ideas.

I tell the sandbox to instantiate the contents of Isidore's qupt in my virtual brain. There is a flash of light in my optic nerve, and then I hear a voice.

You live on an island called causality, it says.

Like Isidore before me, I listen to the Kaminari speak. When it is over, I seal the scroll again. I feel dizzy. By accident, I lean on the green planet, and almost fall down as my hand slides along its slick, cold atmosphere.

The System history speaks of the Spike as a Singularity-class event created by the Kaminari-zoku's transcendence gone wrong, a destructive echo of a god-birth that the Sobornost tried to contain by starting the Protocol War. Instead, it seems that the event that took out Jupiter was engineered by the Great Game Zoku, an attempt stop the Kaminari's attempt to break the Planck locks. *Spacetime weapons. I bet Barbicane and his cronies had something to do with it.*

Cold anger comes with the thought. *I'm going to keep my promise. I'm going to take more than just your toys for this. For Mars and the Kaminari both.*

I could try to blackmail the Great Game by threatening to expose them. But that can't be what they are afraid of. The Sobornost would not care, especially not now, and with their sleeper agents in nearly every zoku, in all likelihood the Great Game would be able to strangle any Deep Throat attempts easily.

What the Kaminari did is not enough for the Great Game to destroy Mars. It must be *how* they did it that they fear. Creating a system-wide viral zoku? How was that supposed to break the locks?

We found the answer in the Collapse, the Kaminari said. *We need your help.*

The Collapse is another white spot both in my memory and history itself. If the exomemory was still there, I'm sure I could find further evidence for Great Game interference. The consensus version is a sudden, catastrophic collapse of the global quantum markets used to value upload labour and embodied life on old Earth, a world with a population so large that most people could not afford human bodies. A time of chaos and madness, when the ancestors of the zokus and the Oortians and other System civilisations fled a dying world, leaving it to the wildcode and the—

It is as if a white-hot pen wrote the word in my brain. *The Aun. They were there. They were the ones who took over after the Collapse. They must know what happened. They will know what the Great Game fears so much they destroyed two worlds to hide it.*

I close the treasure room behind me and head for the bookshop vir.

I pass the gate to the main leisure Realm of the ship: the transatlantic liner *Provence* on a never-ending journey across a sunlit sea, offering the charms of a swimming pool, tennis on the deck, and the delightful company of a Miss Nellie Underdown. I pause in front of it, and listen to the faint echoes of sea birds and the rushing waves. Suddenly, I feel tired after my efforts. Perhaps that is what I need: a few quiet subjective hours in a deck chair with a good book laid over my eyes. The smell of sun and old paper and sweat, a dip in the pool, an evening with a charming young lady, even an imaginary one.

A sudden sharp thought stops me.

What would Perhonen *say?*

I can hear the Oortian ship's voice in my head, fluttering like a butterfly's wing.

I know what you are doing, Jean. You are avoiding the boy. And time is ticking away. I'm not getting any deader, and Mieli is still not free. Stop whining and do what you have to do.

That's what is missing in the *Leblanc*, with all its treasures. A voice that only speaks things that are true.

The bookshop vir looks the same – almost suspiciously so – but Matjek is different. He is older now – eleven or twelve, perhaps. He looks up from his book when I enter, frowns and continues to read. The Aun are nowhere to be seen.

I pull up a chair and sit down next to him.

'Hello, Matjek.'

He ignores me.

'How are you doing?'

Silence.

I look at him more closely. His hair is longer, and there is just a hint of grey in it. His eyes have acquired a piercing blue hue, like little shards of ice. I wonder if he has been playing with clockspeed again. I have done my best to make sure that the vir is sandboxed, isolated from the ship's systems, but I'm not sure that provides enough protection from the future Father of Dragons if he gets bored. Still, it could just be mindshell customisation.

'What are you reading?' A lot of the books in the vir represent the fractally compressed city of Sirr and its inhabitants, and the minds of the Aun. Actually *reading* them is not a good idea, unless you want to be possessed by a jinn or a body thief. 'Are your friends around?'

'Why do you care?' Matjek says finally.

I clear my throat. 'Well, I thought it was time for us to have a little chat, man to man.'

He slams the book shut, holds it close to his chest with both hands and looks at me.

'About what?'

'About a lot of things. I wanted to thank you for your help and—'

'You mean about about how you *stole* me? About how my mum and dad are *dead*?'

There is a cold rage in his eyes that is far too familiar from the older Matjek I know.

'Why didn't you *tell* me?' He throws the book at the shop window, hard: it doesn't shatter, but rings in its hinges. 'When are you going to let me out of here?'

I squeeze the bridge of my nose. Everything feels solid now, sharper. The *Leblanc* has enough computational power to run a full physics emulation: the dreamlike feel of the previous version is gone. I wonder if it's entirely a good thing.

'Look, Matjek,' I say carefully. 'You know why your parents put you in that vir? That place on the beach? They wanted to keep you *safe*. In case something bad happened to the world, in case they could not protect you themselves anymore. And I'm just trying to—'

I swallow. I'm pretty sure Bojan and Naomi Chen would not approve of me using their son as a viral weapon of mass destruction. But sometimes, I'm just as much of a slave to patterns as my almost-son Isidore was: when things *click*, when I can see a way out, it's hard not to seize whatever tool there is at hand.

I can't bear to look at him, so I stand up and walk to the nearest bookshelf. I lean on it. The blue and silver backs of the thousand books of Sirr stare at me accusingly.

'I just want you to know that I never meant for you to get hurt. You helped a lot on Iapetus, and I'm sure Mieli will be grateful.'

'I don't care. I hate you both.'

'You have to believe me. I would have told you, when you were ready. I did not want to find out like that, I swear. Who told you? Was it the Aun – your friends?' *I may need them, but if they caused this, I swear I'm going to—*

'No, it wasn't them.' He sniffs. 'It was the gun.'

I turn around. He is hunched on the chair, looking at his hands. His eyes are rimmed with tears.

'It was kind of fun, at first, having a body again, even if it was wispy, like a jinn, coming out of a bottle,' he says. 'I found the *Leblanc*. I thought at it, and it let us in, like you said. And then I found the gunscape. I got bored with waiting, so I played with it. My friends helped me to get in.'

I let out an inward groan.

'There was a spime for every gun. Some even had Realms so you could try them out. There was one called a ghostgun, from the First Fedorovist War.'

Oh, hell.

'I didn't know what it was, so I asked. The gun said *I* started the war, in some place called Iridescent Gateway of Heaven. That it was *my* fault all those people died. I got angry. I thought it was lying. I wanted it to go away. So I started firing the guns. All of them.'

'Matjek—'

'Was the gun lying, Jean?'

I flinch. It is the first time he has used my name.

'You know so much about lying. Was it lying?'

I kneel down next to him. I want to touch him, to take his arm, but he is looking at me with a fury so palpable that I can feel it in the air like a static charge.

'No, it wasn't. But it wasn't telling the truth either. The person who did all those things was called Matjek Chen, that's true. But he *wasn't* you. Just somebody like you.'

'He *was* me. The gun told me all about gogols, too.'

'That's not how it works. Not all gogols are the same. Trust me, I know. Something happened to that one, something bad, and he never got over it.'

'What was it?'

I sigh. 'I don't know.'

'So how do I know I won't end up like him?' His eyes are wide and desperate.

'I don't know, Matjek. I don't know. But I believe we can decide who we are. If you don't like that other Matjek, be someone else.'

'Is that why you do it?' he asks. 'Put on faces because you don't like who you are?'

'Sometimes.'

'I saw you do it. You were just the same underneath.'

'I'm sorry, Matjek,' I say. 'I'm not very good at looking after other people. I know you were happy, on the beach. I didn't want to take you away. But I had no choice.'

'You just said we always have a choice.'

'Not always.'

'How do you know which is which?' He gets up. 'You're just trying to say something that'll shut me up! You want to get rid of me so you can save your stupid friend! And you don't even know why!'

He shoves me, as hard as the vir will allow, and I almost fall.

'Matjek, that's not true.'

'Shut up! Everything you say is a lie! That's what the *other* you said! Leave me alone!'

I blink.

'What do you mean, the other—'

Father wants to be alone.

The Aun flash in my vision, jagged serpents of light. The vir snaps shut and throws me out. Then I am standing in the blue humming corridor of the *Leblanc*, and the stinging feeling in my eyes is just a vir-to-Realm translation error, not tears at all.

'All right, you bastards, I screwed up!' I shout at the empty corridor. 'But so did you! Why didn't you stop him?'

There is no reply.

I scour my mind for the presence of the Aun but find nothing.

'Talk to me! Show yourselves!'

Still nothing. A righteous fury erupts in my chest. 'Come out, or I'm going to take my brain apart to find you. What are you waiting for?'

For you to keep your promise, the Chimney Princess says.

She stands before me, a little girl in a wooden mask, wearing a sooty dress, barefoot. She looks completely alien in the *Leblanc*'s blue meta-Realm.

I look at her. Her eyes are faint embers behind the eye slits of the mask, and I can't tell if their glow is anger or pity.

'Why don't you ever show your face?' I ask her.

Because people give me theirs when they meet me.

'I know the feeling.'

Have you found one you like yet?

'Can't say that I have. But I am trying. I need your help for that. I need to know what happened in the Collapse.'

We cannot tell you.

'There is no need for blackmail. I swore to Tawaddud I would—'

You don't understand. Much of us is lost. We are shards and fragments, self-loops and voices. We are Sirr, we are the wildcode desert. That is where your answers are. Bring us and our children back and we will remember for you.

I can't see her face, but it feels like she is smiling behind her mask. *Or you can remember yourself.*

Then she is gone. The corridor smells faintly of smoke.

I return to the pilot's cabin and watch the coffee-and-cream flow of Saturn while Carabas steers the ship.

I start thinking about how to rebuild a city, how to get enough entanglement in the Notch-zoku to claim an Earth-sized plate. Slowly, in the calm of the ship's crystalline heart, a smile returns to my face.

Barbicane was right. It is time to play a different game.

9

MIELI AND THE GREAT GAME

In the shadow of 624 Hektor, the Liquorice-zoku and the *Zweihänder* wait for the Sobornost civil war to come to them.

'I wish it would *start* already!' Zinda says. 'Don't you want to go to a Circle or a Realm, to pass the time?'

Mieli and her Great Game minder are in the central habitat module of the ship. It resembles a miniature fantasy forest wrapped into a cylinder, with gnarly bonsai-sized oaks, and tiny green-hued humanoid creatures lurking among them. Mieli is sitting in a forest clearing, inside a stone circle that barely reaches to her knees, basking under the glow of the ship's tiny sun – which has its own convoluted orbit – and smelling the rich pine-and-dirt smell of the forest. It reminds her of her garden.

'If there is one thing I have learned about war,' says Mieli, 'it's that you spend most of it waiting. It feels … familiar. I prefer it to your Circles or Realms.' She smiles. 'Besides, I don't want to forget about the physical world, especially not before going to battle. Someone … someone I knew once said that the reality is always there, like a razor blade inside an apple. The Sobornost always make that mistake. I don't intend to.'

Zinda smiles wanly. 'I understand. Still, I would have hoped that by now, you would have found *something* about the zoku lifestyle that you like. You turned down all my Realm and dinner invitations. I take that sort of thing personally, you know.'

Mieli feels the zoku girl's eyes on her and looks up, squinting at the sunlight. Zinda is lying down on a riverbank, almost directly above her on the cylinder surface. She is wearing colourful, oversized sunglasses that clash with her samurai outfit.

Mieli gestures at the green miniature landscape around them. 'In Supra City, I feel like this, only ... opposite. Everything is too big. I grew up in an ice sphere only a little bigger than this ship. If there is too much room, too much freedom, I get lost. I need ... constraints. Boundaries.'

Maybe I'm saying too much, she thinks. But the zoku girl is easy to talk to. Perhaps it is their new zoku connection, or some remnant from the Realm of the witch. Or perhaps – although she does not want to admit it – the days in the confines of *Zweihänder* are starting to try even her Oortian composure, and it is good to talk to someone who is three dimensional and her own size.

'But that's exactly what Circles and Realms are!' Zinda says. 'They are all about the ludic attitude, making things harder for yourself, more interesting! On Earth, they had this game called golf, for example. You were supposed to get a ball into a hole by hitting it with a metal stick – I know, really tacky, don't ask. If the goal was the point, you'd just walk it to the hole and drop it in. But it wouldn't be as much fun.'

Apart from the enchanted forest people, they are alone.

Anti-de-Sitter-times-a-Sphere and Sir Mik made use of the Realmgate at the centre of the ship, the cryptographer to prepare her tools for Founder gogol capture, and the miniature knight to study the Great Game intel spime to determine likely locations for pellegrini, hsien-ku and vasilev skirmishes. His models predict a likely confluence of opposing forces in the local Jovian Trojan space – a Lagrange point hub of a number of minor Highway routes – within a day or two in baseline time.

'It's not the same,' Mieli says. 'It sounds like a … a song without a tune. Just making sounds that do not mean anything, that do not shape any *väki*, or tell a story. At least the Sobornost have a plan, a purpose.'

'Be careful! I am from a Narrativist zoku, you know!' Then Zinda's expression grows serious. She sits up and removes her sunglasses.

'I spent a lot of time studying you, Mieli, before we met. But there is so much I don't know! Forgive me for asking, but if you miss your Oort so much, why did you ever leave? Why did you let the Sobornost change you? I can't imagine what that was like. They do it so differently from us: we give you a way to change yourself, make a new self or an alter in a Realm, and then bring it back here. But they …' She shakes her head. 'Why did you feel you *needed* to?'

Mieli swallows. Something brushes her bare feet: a group of furred humanoids with golden eyes is chanting inside the circle, waving sticks and bones in the air. She is not sure if they are worshipping her or trying to banish her.

In spite of their diminutive size, the crew of the *Zweihänder* has physical specs that many Inner System mercenary companies would envy, and the positive aspects of being a giant are mostly negated by the nauseating Coriolis forces caused by the spin of the ship that creates the comfortable onboard 0.1g gravity. She has learned the hard way to take care not to step on any unwary denizens of the forest, or to swat at the dragon-riders that occasionally circle around them.

Some things are best left alone.

'I'd rather not talk about that,' she says, quietly.

Zinda smiles. 'All right. We don't have to talk. Would you like to sing to me?'

Mieli looks at Zinda. Her deep brown eyes are earnest, and their faint entanglement connection through the two zoku jewels they share betrays no malice, only warm curiosity.

'We only sing,' she says slowly, 'to create, or to uncreate; in great sorrow or great joy.' She pauses. 'Or to a lover. But not to pass the time.'

'Well,' Zinda says lightly, 'then we just have to find some other way to pass the time.'

'Ladies!TheDarkheartedFiendApproaches!' Sir Mik rides his winged steed into the module, fully garbed for battle. 'TheBattleIsJoined! GloryAwaits!'

Mieli peers into the *Zweihänder*'s strange, runic spimescape. The passive sensors Sir Mik spent the last day seeding the Trojans with are detecting energy discharges: neutrino bursts from fusion reactors, and scattered pions from antimatter engines. Hundreds of tiny diamond shards move around the cold red masses of the asteroids like shoals of fish.

Raions.

'I suppose that is your cue,' Zinda says.

'Yes.' Mieli brings her systems up. Combat autism waits to embrace her like a vast cool sea where the world moves slowly and silently, with no room for emotions for mistakes. Yet, this time, she is reluctant to enter it.

Zinda reaches out across the treetops of the magical forest and squeezes her hand.

'Good luck. Tell me, what comes after waiting?'

'Terror,' Mieli says.

'Oh, I think we can do better than that!'

The battle does not look like a battle, at first.

Wrapped in zoku q-armour and the arms of the Dark Man, Mieli watches the raion pinpoints move in swarms and streams, dancing in the gravity well of 624 Hektor. They soak up delta-v and come at each other in battle formations like the lances of two knights, firing nanomissiles as they pass, tiny projectiles piloted by kamikaze gogols. Communication lasers flicker between them, invisible in the vacuum but sketched into the spimescape. During each microsecond pass, electronic warfare ghosts do battle in the ether, trying to break through the raions' firewalls, flooding each other with viruses evolved by genetic algorithms. Both fleets are dumping so much bandwidth that their heat sink condensates are overloading and, in infrared, they glow like bright stars against the cool background of the Trojan rocks.

Mieli is perched on Hektor's surface, watching the battle. It unfolds before her, dream-like, through the viscous lenses of quicktime and combat autism. The Liquorice-zoku's passive sensors — barely more than flakes of condensed matter with topological quantum logic — intercept fragments of the pellegrini fleet's signals and tightbeam them to her. She feels strangely vulnerable: even though the Sobornost ships are thousands of kilometres away, through the sensor network, her presence and self-image extend right into the heart of the battle itself.

The combatants are the smallest class of common Sobornost

vessel, diamonoid wedges barely a metre long, housing computronium cores and millions of gogols. Yet their surfaces are carved with intricate detail. Tetrahedral prows decorated by vasilev and hsien-ku images, a smiling handsome man and a studious, serious woman. The chilling beautiful visage of the pellegrini multiplied thousandfold, both as a proud figurehead and repeated all over the ships' pearly skin across all length scales, down to the atomic level.

The fleets pass through each other again, and this time, antimatter novae bloom at the point of contact, staccato notes of searing light. Her armour complains at the sudden gamma ray bombardment. She tells the spimescape to filter out as much noise as it can. Her gogols fill in missing data and plot likely trajectories. They seek matches to the mission constraints and direct her attention to an optimal target.

There: a pellegrini raion, severely damaged, hurtling away from the main spear of the fleet. Diamonoid fragments float around it in a halo, extruding filaments in a desperate attempt to reconnect with the main hull whose perfect symmetry has been ruined by a deep crater on the port side. But the damage is not only physical: the smartmatter surface boils with the waste heat of a software conflict. Ghostgun bullets have embedded themselves in the ship's white flesh, flooding its virs with invader gogols. In seconds, the raion will be enveloped by the next thrust of the joint fleet of hsien-kus and vasilevs.

Mieli takes a deep breath, and sends the raion the message she has checked and re-checked against her Sobornost protocol gogols during the last few days, a coded burst of wartime code.

To Elixir-4711. This is Balsamo-334. Your sacrifice for the Great Common Task will be complete in four point three seconds in your frame. You are requested to transmit us a gogol of your observer chen.

The tenth of a second that sluggish light takes to travel to the raion gives her a moment to reflect while waiting for the response, truly alone for the first time since the beginning of the journey, with the radio silence between her and the *Zweihänder* isolating her from her zoku companions. She casts a quick glance at the elongated shape of Hektor. The zoku ship is hidden behind the bulk of the asteroid, along with its own metacloak, and even at this distance she can't detect any signs of it – except the faint pulsing of her Liquorice jewel.

There is something she has been wondering about the mission ever since Zinda described it. Given the intensity of the Great Game intelligence operations elsewhere, is she really that important?

Or is this a test, designed to probe her loyalty? And if that is the case, does she dare to fail? She has to remain useful to the Great Game, has to win entanglement, to get closer to the Kaminari jewel.

The response from *Elixir* comes, preceded by a rapid burst of protocol. Mieli sighs with relief. At least her Protocol War codes are still approximately up to date. But the message itself makes her grit her teeth.

Founder code authorisation required.

Mieli whispers a fervent prayer, first to Kuutar and Ilmatar, and then to the pellegrini.

'What a waste of gogols this is.'

Mieli blinks. The Sobornost goddess is standing next to her on some invisible surface. She checks her metacortex, to make sure none of her perceptions will filter through to the rest of the zoku.

'Oh, stop fretting, dear,' the pellegrini says. 'Please give me more credit than that. Once we are done, I will edit your memories to make sure it looks like your old Protocol War codes still worked. But first, let me send a confirmation to my sisters.'

With disturbing ease, the pellegrini takes over Mieli's systems and answers the *Elixir*'s message with a quick, coded burst.

'There. All done. Now we just have to enjoy the show. I would dearly like to exchange a few words with my sisters, to get an update on the situation in the Inner System, but you are right, the zoku is testing you. In all honesty, I am surprised that things have not escalated faster. I would have expected the All-Defector to move against my brothers and sisters by now, and that should have made Anton and Hsien give up on petty squabbles such as this. But then they were always too blind to see what was right in front of them.'

The sensor data from the zoku nodes reaches Mieli just before the confirmation that the thoughtwisp containing the ship's political officer chen has been launched. There is a flash on the *Elixir*'s prow as the ship burns a portion of its antimatter to propel a tiny thoughtwisp towards Hektor at an impressive fraction of lightspeed.

'See?' the pellegrini says. 'Nothing to worry about.'

Mieli sends a brief qupt to the *Zweihänder* to alert them to the success of the first part of the mission, and to get ready for pickup. Everything is in the timing: if they perform the grab fast enough, the Sobornost fleets will still be too involved in their battle to do anything about it. Even the will of the Founders must bow to Newton.

We're ready, comes an answer, tinged with the mingled presences of her zoku, the austere calm of Anti-de-Sitter-times-a-Sphere, the fiery enthusiasm of Sir Mik, and a warm touch from Zinda. The pellegrini gives Mieli a faint smile, but says nothing.

Mieli tracks the thoughtwisp with her lasers, ready to fire them to decelerate it for the grab. As soon as she has it, *Zweihänder* will swing past at full blast of her antimatter engines, and grab her with a q-dot field. She is so focused on the tiny reflective disc, its colours warped by blueshift, that the details of the battle are lost to her for a moment. But the pellegrini is still watching it through her eyes.

'Curious,' the goddess says. 'That is not what I would have done. You never know with these high-generation branches, fallen so far from the original. But still—'

The thoughtwisp is within a millisecond of Hektor. Mieli fires the armour's lasers at it in short bursts: it dances from side to side in the coherent light like a feather in the wind, reflections decelerating it rapidly. *That's it: I've given away my position if they are suspicious.*

'Mieli,' the pellegrini says. 'Something is wrong. The *Elixir* just sent a communication burst to the hsien-ku/vasilev fleet. It doesn't make sense. Are they *negotiating*? Why would I do that? No tactical advantage whatsoever!'

Something tickles at the back of Mieli's mind. *Spooky-zoku's quantum oracles found anomalies.* But the razor focus of combat autism washes it away. The wisp is almost within range now, and she starts launching a volley of q-dots to grab it.

Sharp breath hisses between the pellegrini's teeth. 'Mieli! Stop! It's not a civil war! It's theatre! They are faking! Don't—'

The thoughtwisp explodes.

The light rips the spimescape apart. The wisp's ghost warhead burns itself out in a white-hot jolt of bandwidth, aimed straight at Mieli. Attack software comes with it like hard burning rain.

Mieli's suit screams. Her tactical gogols flounder and panic. The suit's outer armour bubbles and fluctuates. It forms a spike that stabs *inwards*, through her subdermal q-dot armour. Pain lances in her side before the combat autism dulls it into a damage report.

Abort, Mieli qupts at the *Zweihänder*, urgency mingled with pain. **Repeat, abort! It's a fake battle, the hsien-kus, the pellegrinis and vasilevs are cooperating!** *And I did not follow the script.*

She is losing control of the q-armour. Its lasers send out flickering comms bursts at the two raion fleets. Mieli focuses on her Liquorice-jewel, pushes through one more volition command at the suit. With a sickening, tearing feeling, the suit ejects her, spits her out to the Dark Man's embrace, into the hard vacuum of Hektor's surface. She rolls in gravity that is too sluggish for quicktime, digs her fingers into the rocky surface, pulls herself down like a rock climber for balance. Her zoku jewels follow under their own power in a faithful, scattered halo.

Dark blood bubbles out from her pierced side, boiling in the vacuum. She regards it dispassionately: another parameter in the problem she has to solve, in the ten minutes she can survive in hard vacuum without external life support. In the thirty seconds it will take *Zweihänder* to reach her. In the seconds it will take for raions' first kinetic missile volley to fall on Hektor.

She stands up, in full combat mode. Time slows down.

Dust particles swirling in the air become static brushstrokes. Her wings bloom from her back, radiating waste heat. The fusion reactor in her right thigh pumps energy into coherent payloads of the q-gun in her right hand. She is already firing the ghostgun in her left: war gogols in nanomissiles, hurling themselves at what used to be a Great Game warsuit.

Even in quicktime, the suit moves like a raindrop in a powerful wind, shivering into a new shape on the moon's surface. It rises up on thin silver limbs. It extrudes a face that is not a face, a hollow oval atop a sketched neck. Lasers fan out from its shoulders. Mieli's ghostgun bullets and their gogol pilots evaporate in tiny, brief flashes.

She follows with a pattern of a dozen charged q-dots that become extensions of herself as soon as they are launched, plunges them at the suit's weapon systems like gouging fingers into eyes. They detonate in blasts of coherent light. The suit-thing's skin becomes a dazzling mirror.

Then the raion kinetic needles hit, soundless and invisible in the vacuum. They shake the ground beneath Mieli's feet. New craters appear around them like the holes of a god's shotgun blast, and slow pillars of dust rise from them. Without flinching, Mieli keeps firing. A high-explosive dot gets through, splattering the suit's material into the vacuum in tiny droplets – until the suit catches them in a q-dot web and absorbs them back into itself.

Mieli risks a glance at the tattered spimescape. Both raion fleets are converging towards their position. The space around Hektor is full of roaring electromagnetic noise across the spectrum. *They are trying to make sure no information leaves this moon.* She detonates her passive sensor network with a thought. Not much a distraction, but she is going to take everything she can get.

Mieli, we are coming, Zinda qupts. **Hold on. Ten seconds.**

The suit-thing is whole again, in a more humanoid shape this time. Mieli reviews its specs. New weapons are forming beneath its skin. It contains nuggets of zoku picotech, able to translate quantum information into matter, and an antimatter power source. And without a fragile human inside, even controlled by a warmind with no experience of flesh-combat, it is orders of magnitude faster than her.

Jumalauta, Mieli swears. *My only hope is to pierce the antimatter containment.* She extrudes a q-blade from her hand. She is almost disappointed that in the combat autism, a moon-shattering explosive death feels just like another tactical option. *At least that would take my zoku jewels as well.*

But the suit's electronic warfare barrage has died down, and the thing stands still, as if its empty face had eyes, looking at something standing next to Mieli.

The pellegrini.

The Sobornost goddess is still there, pale, staring at the faceless silver thing.

'Do something!' Mieli shouts at her.

But the pellegrini only shakes her head.

'Mieli, she says, fear in her voice. 'Meet the All-Defector.'

The suit-thing tilts its head to one side, as if listening. Then the void in its un-face seals itself into a perfect mirror oval. The pellegrini's features appear on its surface, sculpted from silver by invisible fingers.

'It is an unexpected pleasure to meet you here,' it says, in an EM whisper that sounds like the pellegrini's echo, targeted at Mieli's communication systems using a Sobornost military protocol. 'I have to thank you for offering me the chens. They are now me, as you can see. So are younger generations of you. And your Prime has chosen to serve. Perhaps you will, also.'

'No,' the pellegrini whispers. 'Never. You are *our* creature. *We* released you. What are you doing, playing games with the hsien-kus and vasilevs? You are supposed to *eat* them!"

The All-Defector smiles the pellegrini's own serpent smile.

'My appetite is greater than that,' it says. 'But, as your other self thought, I *have* given them a common enemy.' It takes a step forward. It even moves like the pellegrini now, swaying lightly.

'But what's this? Your pet project. The Oortian. Interesting. Now that she is here, I think I will take her, too.'

Mieli is frozen. The thief did not like to talk about the All-Defector – All-D – but from what she knows, the thing somehow models its opponents and finds an optimal strategy against them, without ever cooperating. Her game theory gogols compute payoff matrices, and they all look bleak. *The* Zweihänder *won't make it here in time.*

That's why All-D is not attacking. It has already won.

To hell with it.

Another volley of raion needles falls. This time, they divert their course away from direct impact, and blast up a curtain of rock shards and dust in a circle around them. *Of course. Can't break the new toy it wants.*

'You want me?' she whispers through gritted teeth. 'Come and get me!' She raises her q-dot blade. *It is still moving like the pellegrini. Need to use that.*

She lunges forward. Her toes dig into the rock, propelling her forward like a *väki* spear. She aims a lightning blow at the dense hot spot of the antimatter container in the suit.

Silver hands seize her right arm and twist. Her dermal armour bursts. The thing swings her around and slams her down against the moon's surface so hard that the quickstone-enforced bones in her arm and ribcage snap. The back of her skull digs deep into the crushed rock. Her wings tear and fray beneath her. The control system of the fusion reactor in her thighbone goes mad.

All-D looms above her. She drops out of combat autism to stop from blacking out and screams a silent scream. Her right arm is on fire, but she forces it to obey, stabs upwards with the q-dot blade, but the thing is not there. It stretches a willowy arm towards her. The fingers become spikes that impale her forehead.

There is no pain. She always thought there would be pain in a forced black box upload, living all possible lives in one white-hot moment.

'No. You are not taking her,' the pellegrini says. 'She is mine.'

Like so many times before, the pellegrini becomes Mieli, wears her body like a glove. Mieli is looking down at herself, from above, a broken pale angel lying on dark rock, a silver monster looming over her, its fingers growing into her head. *The jewels*, she thinks. *The jewels are caching my mind.*

The other Mieli's eyes below snap open. For an instant, she looks up at Mieli, smiles the pellegrini's smile. *Remember*, she mouths. Then she squeezes her eyes shut.

I could self-destruct, the goddess said.

Mieli's body twitches rhythmically. Her eyes flutter madly beneath her eyelids. All-D jerks to the same rhythm and pulls away: its tendrils come out of Mieli's head, bloodlessly, easily.

A discontinuity.

Mieli is back in the blood-red madness of her body. Its

systems are dying. Her brain is on fire. The fusion reactor is overheating. The only thing that does not burn is the awareness of her zoku, getting close.

But All-D is still moving, shaking off whatever recursive self-annihilation algorithm the pellegrini tried to use to destroy them both.

An itinerant fact from combat autism floats into her mind. *Hektor. Escape velocity: 0.13 km/second.*

She sends a command that shapes her power source's tiny dense magnetic bottle into a funnel.

It does not take much strength to move in the low gravity, but it is almost more than Mieli has left. She slides forward so that her right leg is right beneath All-D.

Then she overloads her fusion reactor.

The damage reports become a white noise. Her eyes pop. Through the few sensors that still function, as if in a dream, she feels a pillar of plasma below her, taking her up from the surface of Hektor. Milliseconds later, the zoku suit's antimatter containment collapses. She sees a god's incandescent gaze for one quick eyeblink, and then there is nothing, nothing at all.

10

TAWADDUD AND THE BOTTLED CITY

Tawaddud, Dunyazad and the thief Jean le Flambeur stand on Saturn, on the newborn Plate of Irem, ready to plant the seed of Sirr.

It is Tawaddud who carries it: an intricate snowflake shape inside a transparent bubble. It is heavy, and she has to hold it with both hands against her chest. She wonders if this is how the women of the Banu Sasan feel, holding their infant children, shielding something unutterably precious from the world. Then she remembers that by carrying the seed, she is carrying all of the Banu Sasan as well. It is difficult to let go.

'Come now, sister,' Dunyazad says impatiently. 'The hour grows late.'

Le Flambeur smiles, and the strange, diffuse sunlight of the vast gleaming plain glints in his blue sunglasses. It is still difficult to see the small, slim man in a white jacket and trousers as the Sumanguru she knew – a towering, dark-skinned giant, a warlord of Sobornost – but every now and then, he makes a small gesture that feels familiar.

'You should take your time,' he says, smiling a little sadly. 'You want to do it properly. In the future, in the Palace of

Stories, perhaps they will tell the tale of two sisters who saved the city of Sirr.'

'And what about you, master thief?' Dunyazad asks. 'Will they tell stories about you?'

'There are enough stories about me already,' he says. 'I don't think I'll be needing any new ones. Besides, I like the one about the sisters better.'

It was only hours ago that le Flambeur brought Tawaddud and Dunyazad back, from the pages of a book, he said. One moment Tawaddud stood in the razor whirlwind of a wildcode desert storm, drowning in the voices of the Aun, and then she opened her eyes in a dusty bookshop that felt real, but wasn't. Then they stepped through a silver gate that Duny claimed *made* them real, turned quantum information into matter, wrote the Names of their atoms into reality, like the bright beams of the Sobornost Station in Sirr.

They are on Saturn, a thought that makes Tawaddud dizzy, on an artificial continent larger than the entire Earth. A part of her wonders if le Flambeur can be trusted as a guide in this place. But she is Tawaddud, daughter of Cassar Gomelez, trained in many arts in the House of Kafur, and if there is one thing she can do, it is reading men. Besides, Duny claims a connection to the zoku who rule here, and now wears a ring like a jinn ring, but with a bright purple jewel that glows with an inner light of its own. While Tawaddud has had her differences with her sister in the past, she knows that Duny will always think what is best for Sirr, and deal swift death to those she deems its enemies. Now, she is starting to look impatient, running the jewel of her ring back and forth along her lips.

Tawaddud kneels on the strange, hard ground that is made of interlocking geometric shapes, like the floor tiles of

Sirr palaces or jinni skin. She puts the seed down carefully, reluctant to let go.

'Wait,' le Flambeur says. He removes his glasses, and looks at the sisters.

'I have an apology to make,' he says, 'and this is as good a time as any. I came to Sirr to find the place you call the Lost Jannah of the Cannon, and to learn the secrets of the body thieves. I did not care what I had to do to get what I wanted. If not for me, Sirr might still be on Earth.' He kneels next to Tawaddud. 'I could spend forever apologising for the things I have done, but it is you, Lady Tawaddud, I have wronged the most. I threatened you, blackmailed the jinn Zaybak by holding a gun to your head. I want you to know I would never have pulled the trigger. Will you forgive me?'

Tawaddud looks at him. She remembers kneeling on the floor of the Sobornost upload temple, the black eye of the barakah gun, how helpless she felt, how the Sumanguru she had trusted betrayed her. The anger is still hot in her, and if le Flambeur did not look so different from Lord Sumanguru, she would recoil from his presence.

But she also remembers the moment in the desert, when all hope was lost, when black Dragons were falling from the sky, when the man in the blue glasses came to take Sirr away.

She sighs. Hate and gratitude are entwined in her like a muhtasib and a qarin, and she can't tell where one ends and the other begins. So she remembers old, mad Kafur's advice: *tell them lies they want to hear.*

'You are forgiven, Lord le Flambeur,' she says, '*if* my city is the way I remember it.' In all honesty, she is not sure if the whole thing is a dream: a city in a bottle is a tale like the mutalibun tell, visions born from the madness that the wildcode desert brings.

He smiles a crooked smile. 'I suppose I will have to take what I can get.' He replaces his glasses and stands up. 'Whenever you are ready, my lady.'

Tawaddud kisses the seed's smooth smartmatter surface and mutters the Secret Name of Al-Mubdi the Initiator, for good fortune. She does not know if the Names have power here, but it is as if the seed senses her thoughts. The shell of the seed vanishes with a hiss and a whiff of ozone. The fractal snowflake crumbles into a dust that flows into the cracks of between the ground tiles with a swift purposefulness, quickly like water spilled in the desert.

Le Flambeur touches her arm. 'We had better step back,' he says. 'This is something we will want to see from above.'

He gestures, and a bubble forms around them – this place's version of magic carpets, as she has already learned – and takes them up with dizzying speed.

Below, the city of Sirr begins to rise.

At first, it is gleaming cubes and spheres and polygons the size of mountains, slowly growing from the metal skin of Irem. Squinting, Tawaddud can make out the great ribs of the Shards, curving up, built by invisible hands. Then, a white mist swirls at the base of the structures, glittering like the snowflake in the seed, and where it passes, colour and detail emerge, suddenly, like a mirage in the desert. It sketches the hive cities of Qush and Misr, where the Fast Ones live; the dark grid of the City of the Dead, the mazes of gogol markets. Only the great diamond needle of the Sobornost Station is absent. Tawaddud does not miss it: it was always a false axis of the city, and in time, they will build a new one.

And it is not just the buildings that Irem is making. Already, Tawaddud sees the first glimmerings of athar, the shadow of the Other City where jinni live, where the Secret Names are written.

It takes hours. Heat rises from the birth-pains of the city, and Irem grows pillars that glow white-hot. Their bubble keeps them cool, taking them higher up in the sky. From a greater height, they can see the circle of the whole city. Tawaddud gasps: it is not just the city that is taking shape, but the strange contours of the wildcode desert, the mountains of the rukh and the distant Fast Cities.

'The Aun insisted,' le Flambeur says. 'It is where they live. It is their flesh, their body. It's all going to be there, when it's ready. Every distant corner of the Earth, every forgotten buried city, every bone in every desert, every grain of sand.' He looks sad, and angry. 'With them, it was always like the story of the scorpion: it stings, since it is in its nature to sting. I can relate, I suppose.' He squeezes the bridge of his nose. 'Well, no matter. It is almost time for goodbyes, but I have two gifts before I go.'

He turns to Tawaddud and presses a heavy book bound between blue covers in her hands. It has the same kind of strange feel as the seed: smartmatter, somewhere halfway between imaginary and real.

'These are the people of Sirr,' he says. 'I leave them to you. They are all there, good and bad. Your father. Your friend the Axolotl. Even that scoundrel Abu Nuwas, somewhere. Every story needs a villain. The Aun will show you how to bring them back. I thought it would be better if you two did it.'

'A better story?' Tawaddud says.

'Much better.' He takes something from his jacket pocket: a necklace with several large, multicoloured jewels that shine like the one in Dunyazad's ring.

'There is much you have to learn about this place, and

you may wonder how it is that the people of Saturn allow an entire city and a planet's worth of wild nanotech to just appear at their doorstep. The answer is simple: I stole this Plate. Don't worry, the zoku are not going to ask for it back, they have plenty to go around. But you will be needing this.' He holds the necklace up between two hands. The jewels shimmer like dewdrops in a spiderweb.

Dunyazad looks at it a bit too eagerly for Tawaddud's liking.

'Lady Dunyazad,' the thief continues, 'to you, I suggest a trade. Your zoku jewel and whatever mental code you seal it with, for these. It's a bargain, I assure you. They took some effort to obtain. They have enough entanglement to make you a goddess in this place.'

Dunyazad frowns. 'Lord le Flambeur, my apologies, but it sounds a little too much like a jinn's bargain. If I give you my jewel, what will you do with it?'

'I know it binds you to the Great Game Zoku. I have some unfinished business with them.'

Tawaddud's sister hesitates. 'I dealt with the zoku as a diplomat,' she says. 'What you ask was given to me as a sign of trust, in confidence. I will give it to you only if it is the price for restoring our city. But I thought you were beyond holding people for ransom.'

'Touché,' le Flambeur says. 'Not as a trade, then, but as a gift, for me to remember the city of Sirr and its people by.'

Tawaddud lays a hand on his arm. 'Lord le Flambeur,' she says. 'Would you accompany me on a short walk to some suitable quarter of our city? I feel I require exercise, after all those weeks squashed inside your dusty blue book.'

Le Flambeur looks at her, surprised, then offers her his arm. 'It will be my pleasure,' he says.

I'll handle this, Tawaddud tells Dunyazad with her eyes. And she can't help but feel a twinge of satisfaction when her sister slowly nods.

They walk along the top of the Gomelez Shard. Le Flambeur keeps casting nervous glances at the narrow walkway ahead of them and the sheer drop on both sides. Tawaddud smiles to herself: one has to use a man's weaknesses when necessary, and Sumanguru was always afraid of heights.

She takes her time to enjoy the view. The city is almost ready, and if not for the lack of echoing, moaning jinn music, smells of food and other faint noises of the city's breathing, she could almost imagine she is home. The empty city should feel eerie, like the Fast Cities of thinking buildings that the mutalibun speak of, but somehow it doesn't. Instead, there is a pregnant silence, as if the city is merely sleeping, waiting to wake up.

It is le Flambeur who breaks it.

'I apologise, again,' he says. 'I will find another way to my enemies. It's not for me to ask your sister to betray her trust.'

'Leave my sister to me,' Tawaddud says. 'You make many apologies. What you have not told us is why you are here, or what you seek.' She pulls her arm away from his. *There is a time for lies and a time for truth.*

'You hurt me, and the one I once loved, and these things I do not forgive, in spite of my words. But I can pity. When I look at you, I see a lonely man, a divided man; one, perhaps like our qarin and muhtasib, a man wrapped inside another creature, be it the Flower Prince of the Aun as you say, or a thing you have made yourself. Men and jinni have told me many false names, and I recognise their sound. I do not think you are called le Flambeur any more than Sumanguru.'

She pauses.

'In Sirr, a story is told of a mutalibun who journeyed to the wildcode desert many times, and saw many miracles. His skin grew rough with sapphire growths, but he kept going back. One day, his wife told him to choose her or the desert. That day, the man put his affairs in order, sold his house, saw that his wife and children were provided for, and said goodbye to his friends. Then he walked through the gate of Bab, the gate of the treasure hunters, never to return.

'That is the man I see when I look at you, Lord le Flambeur, who was Sumanguru when I knew him.' She points at the city below. 'I cannot forgive, but I can extend a hand. Whatever promise it is that you go to keep, I ask: don't. Do not walk through the gates of Bab. We need guidance in this world you have brought us to. You helped to save this city, and by the name of Gomelez, I swear you will have a place in it, if you wish. The gate is open.'

Le Flambeur stands still and looks at the city, lost in the haze below. In the strange light of Irem, the purples, golds and blues have a different hue. But it is still Sirr the blessed, Sirr the hidden, more beautiful than ever.

'I thank you for the offer, but I cannot. I owe someone a debt, an even bigger than is due to Sirr. I need your sister's jewel to find her, as well as the help of the Aun.'

'Her?' Tawaddud says pointedly.

'It's not like that. A … friend.'

'I see.' She looks into his eyes. 'And are you sure this is not a story you tell yourself? I know what mine was: *Tawaddud the lover of monsters, the black sheep of the Gomelez.* These are just chains, my lord of many names, chains made of words.

'And whenever I hear a man talk about moving mountains and great quests, there is always someone he is doing it *for*, and that someone is not just a friend. It would be better for you to go to her, and make things right.'

'The … other woman and I have danced that dance many times,' le Flambeur says. 'We have hurt each other too much.' There is a wistful look in his eyes.

She takes his hand. 'Then what do you have left to prove to her? Sirr can be a place of healing, too. We know much about the Aun. My father and the muhtasib council know many Secret Names. Perhaps we could free you from your … other side. Perhaps then you could find peace.'

He smiles a bitter smile. 'I'm afraid it is far too late for that. And I need my other side, where I'm going. And the story will be better for that.'

He kisses her forehead, gently, and pulls away. 'Still, I thank you. I shall not forget Sirr, or gentle Tawaddud. But there are monsters even she can't heal.' He looks past Tawaddud's shoulder. 'Speaking of which – you'll have to excuse me for a moment.'

Tawaddud turns around. The Aun stand there, near the edge of the Shard, on the side of the wildcode desert. The little girl in a mask, the old man in green, and the thing that shifts and glows. Le Flambeur squeezes her hand and goes to join them.

I look at the Aun in the eternal soletta twilight of Irem, standing on the edge of the Shard, the wildcode desert and its arabesque patterns of light behind them. They look much more real now, not just echoes inside my mind, but thought-forms made from the matter of the reborn desert. I can see the grains in the Princess's mask, the creases in the Soldier's uniform, the play of light in the glassy innards of the Kraken. But even now, it is hard to look at their faces: they always remind you of someone you once knew, but have forgotten.

'Happy now?' I ask. 'Not a story for a boon, this time, but a city.'

'They are one and the same,' says the Princess.

'The lords of this place will be coming for you soon, brother,' the Soldier says, in a voice like gravel. 'Are you ready?'

'We shall see,' I say, and glance at the sky. He is right, the Great Game or their pawns will be here soon. The use of Notch-zoku entanglement on this scale is not something that will go unnoticed, no matter how carefully I tried to be to hide my tracks.

It wasn't easy: creating a Notch identity, endless concept mining in the design Realms to build up enough entanglement to make the transition to matter. Then there was notch-cube grinding, improving the impact tolerances of Plates and Strips, sculpting a trollface on a fresh mountain range. My mind still echoes with the countless hammer blows. And then, finding the Ender Egg in the Sayanagi Belt, the entrance to the hidden Realm of Vipunen the Notch-zoku Elder whose jormungandr body is a thunder-and-lightning storm that circumscribed the entire planet. I broke into the zoku jewel bank inside his hurricane gut and got away with a few Plate-level jewels.

I shrug. Does that make me ready for the Great Game Zoku? Not a chance. The moment I give up the Notch-zoku membership, they will come.

'We are whole,' the Kraken says, in a voice like a glass flute. 'We remember now.'

'So, what was it?' I ask. 'What caused the Collapse?'

'You did,' the Princess says.

*

I stare at them.

'Why would have I done that?' I whisper. 'You are lying.'

'You are the only one of us who lies,' the Soldier says.

'We do not judge,' the Kraken says. 'It was Father who set us free from flesh. But it was you who broke all old things, so we could grow.'

The Collapse. Sirr falling from the sky. Cities waking up, full of gogols, breeding uncontrollably. The machine nervous system of the world, flooding with mad minds. Fleshbodies repossessed by the millions by automated corporate entities, black box uploading their inhabitants who could no longer afford to live—

It's too big. It's too much to bear. I belong with Chen and Joséphine and the Great Game. I deserve them. I would leap from the Shard and let the wildcode desert take me, except that it already did, once, and spat me back out.

'It was you,' I hiss at them, the desert devils. 'You planned it. Your Flower Prince came into my mind in the prison, to have an agent in the flesh-world. He *made* me do it. He broke the world so you could be free. I have been his puppet for centuries. Saving you was a mistake. Chen was right to try to wipe you out. You are nothing but a disease.'

The Princess steps forward. I raise my hand to strike her. Then I see her eyes, embers full of truth, see my face reflected in them, contorted with hate.

She reaches up and removes my sunglasses, touches my cheek. Her small hand is hot. I breathe in the smell of smoke. It reminds me of a tent in a desert, of a brazier burning in the night, of waking up and a hard-faced woman watching me.

'We never made you do anything,' she says. 'We do not choose. We simply are. We call you brother because we miss him. But you are not him. No one is ever just one thing, except us.

'He touched you, through the crystal stopper. But all your choices were your own.'

There are tears in my eyes.

'But why? Why the Collapse?' I whisper.

'For the same reason you did everything,' the Princess says. 'To please the goddess.'

Joséphine. I served her, on Earth, I know that much. She opened a door for me. I gathered the Founders for her. There was a time I would have done anything to make her smile. *No. I freed myself from her. That's why I went to Mars. It was the best thing I ever did.*

And this was the worst.

I lock the feeling away. I let the metaself calm the storm between my temples, make it smooth and cool and empty like the wildcode desert.

'That's not the answer I need,' I say slowly. 'I need to know *how*, not *what*. I need you to show me.'

'We told you already,' the Princess says. 'You need to remember yourself.'

'But I don't. It is one of the secrets I burned when I was caught—'

The Princess smiles a wooden smile.

'The other me,' I breathe. 'Matjek said something about the other me who spoke to him. *That's* why the *Leblanc* felt haunted. There is a partial of the old me there, or a gogol even. It was watching me.'

The Princess hands my glasses back.

'See?' she says. 'Which one is it who loves secrets so much? The boy from the desert, or the Flower Prince?'

She steps back, to stand with the others. They fade away into the light, become sand and wind.

Farewell, brother. We will be here when you return.

When le Flambeur comes back, he is uncharacteristically quiet. There is a strange fire in his eyes, and Tawaddud leaves him to his thoughts during the descent along the curve of the empty Shard, in one of his magic bubbles.

In the end, Dunyazad gives him the jewel, and he offers her the necklace. Tawaddud has to admit it suits Duny: the brightness of the jewels against her dark skin makes her look like a queen.

'I trust you will not misuse them,' le Flambeur says. 'People of Sirr will need jewels of their own, too. And jinni may want bodies. This place has the power to give it to them. It may become a very different city from the Sirr on Earth.'

Tawaddud thinks of the Axolotl. *Perhaps there are other monsters I can heal.* She gives the thief a smile for that, a small one.

Dunyazad's smile vanishes, suddenly. 'Look.' She points at the sky.

Fear opens a sharp-nailed hand inside Tawaddud's chest. 'No. Not here, too.'

The new pinpoints in the sky are deceptively beautiful. They are beyond counting and their numbers grow as she watches, like glittering sand poured onto a mosaic floor. They arrange themselves into patterns, polygons and wedges, with a clear purpose.

'Don't worry,' le Flambeur says. 'They are not here for you, but for me. And I shall not tarry long. Why is it that there is never enough time for proper goodbyes? Nothing ever changes.'

He kisses both of their hands and bows deep.

'I am from a desert, too,' he says. 'Yours is harsher, and less forgiving. But as long as you two are in it, it will always be a garden.'

A glowing bubble takes him up to the sky. He blows them kisses as he goes. A moment later, there is a distant boom, and a white line is drawn across Sirr's new sky. The dancing stars follow it, a flock of bright birds, and then they are gone.

During the hatching of Sirr, the sky has grown dark, and it is as if Tawaddud sees it for the first time. She looks up at the wide sky road of the rings, the discs of the moons, and the glowing threads in the distance that hold up other skies. She takes her sister's hand, and for a while, they breathe it in. Finally, they turn back to the blue and gold mandala of Sirr.

'Do you think it's time yet?' Dunyazad asks.

'Yes,' Tawaddud says. 'Let's go wake them up.'

Interlude

THE GODDESS AND THE BIRTHDAY PRESENT

There are two Joséphines, walking by the night-grey sea, one with bare feet on sand, the other stepping in the water, making small leaps every now and then. One of them is old, and the other is young, her auburn hair a dark curly banner in the wind.

Every now and then Joséphine loses herself in the partial, in its firm flesh and bright eyes. But the work is not finished. She still has memories to give, and so she has to look inward, to cut and keep and choose. As she walks, a constant stream of words for the demiurges pours from her lips, mingling with the deep, slow breath of the waves.

The last day she truly loved him was her birthday.

It was after they lost the first war. Even centuries later, Matjek never wanted admit defeat, and so that early stain in the shining history of the Sobornost was wiped from gogol memories. But Joséphine remembers it.

After all, it was she who brought them together, from different parts of the world, sent her Jean to gather them and gave them a common cause. She made them into something more than just scattered fanatics.

She made sacrifices. She made mistakes. She always regretted the way she brought Anton Vasilev into the fold, for example. He was perfect for what they needed: a virtual pop star, a media cyborg, worshipped by millions, the demagogue, the ideologue, the stealer of souls and hearts. But she left him with a wound that never healed.

In the end, she made them into an army.

They fought to liberate uploads, those bound to insurance heavens, those slaving away in black box upload camps and in the cloud. Shenzen was a mistake. The liberated gogols went wild, took over the infrastructure of the city, a swarm of sentient computer viruses. It created a backlash against the Fedorovism movement. The struggling nation states, corporations and liquid democracies organised a response. They fought back, and won. The Founders – except for her, still bound to flesh – fled to space, minds distributed in swarms of nanosatellites, sent to orbit by loyal followers using microwave launchers, vowing to return.

Matjek, Sumanguru and the others swore that they would expand, build resources, unbound by a little planet, and return to conquer. They did not understand. She knew it would be much better if the gogols would come to them, out of their own free will.

And the problem was that the world that rose from the ashes of the war *worked*.

A world of gogol labour markets, vast virtual economies based on the potential future labour of uploaded minds and their copies. An endless variety of complex financial instruments, traded across quantum markets – the first killer app for quantum computers. Entangled instruments, determining if dead souls had the right to live. The most efficient resource allocation system in history: superpositions of portfolios, entangled derivatives, applied to everything: gogol labour, the right to wear a fleshbody, energy, space and time.

Cancerous growths, standing in the way of true immortality. She wanted to cut them out, and she so made a hand to wield the knife.

Joséphine is dying, in her bedroom on the island. The sun is shining. Most of the time, the smartbed's beemee feeds her lifestreams from the young, slim, trim employees she uses as proxy selves, but today, she watches the sunlight and the blue sky with her own eyes. The artificial retinas make everything clear and sharp. She wants to see the view better, and the bed shapes itself to her movements, supports her as she sits up. The window shows the white masts of the sailboats in the harbour. The ropes and the rigging make a distant, tinkling sound in the wind, like improvised music.

She has resisted a full brain transplant into a cloned body. After all, there are already other hers beyond the sky, young and beautiful, perfect like her pearls, and just as identical. The DNA nanomachines repairing her chromosomes can only do so much for someone who was already old when immortality arrived.

And there is always the black box upload, the sharp-edged crown waiting inside the softness of her bed.

For a long time, it made her angry to admit the hopelessness of the fight. It was Jean who told her to think of the last vestiges of her flesh as a cocoon, something that she would hatch from, even more beautiful than before.

It was the kind of thing he liked to say after making love.

She thinks about the last time and falls asleep for a

moment. When the bed wakes her gently, he is there, sitting by her side, hands folded.

'Happy birthday, Joséphine,' he says, and makes a blue flower appear from thin air. He holds it out to her to smell. Again, the bed brings her up, and the scent takes her back, to her childhood, running up the vineyard hill in the morning, when the towers of the old village were purple in the distance and it didn't matter that the sun shone right into her eyes and the dew got her trainers wet.

She must have fallen asleep again: the bed shakes her gently awake. Jean holds her hand in a firm, warm grip. She frowns at him.

'Flowers,' she says. Her voice is dry, and she does not want to ask the bed to make it stronger. If her Jean has earned anything, it is right to see and hear her as she is. 'Why does it always have to be flowers?'

'Well, I like flowers. But it's not just flowers today,' he says.

'Jewels? Paintings? Poems? You really are a terrible poet, you know.'

'Touché,' he says, smiling. 'It is a very expensive gift, Joséphine. I have made you very poor. I hope it's worth it.' He holds out his hands to her, cupped, as if cradling a tiny bird. Then he spreads his fingers wide. Between them is the blue globe of Earth. He gestures, and it expands to fill the space between them. Around it is a cloud of data, a visualisation of quantum markets, pillars and curves and geometries, like aurora borealis.

'I made a machine out of money,' he says. 'Mostly yours. Although a few of the other wealthy ancients made ... involuntary donations. They were very generous.'

'What is this? It hurts my eyes.'

'Look closely.'

The bed forms a cool helmet around her head, and then she does not just see the data, but *understands*, senses the tension in the flow of it like a drawn bowstring, feels the uncountable trading bots across the world connected by neutrino links, ready to be fired by a thought.

'It's very pretty, Jean,' she says, 'but what is it *for*?'

He leans back and looks up, the way he does when is feeling guilty.

'I had a hunch about something. I always thought there was a flaw in what the exchanges have been doing. I talked to the zoku. They gave me some hints. I … found the insurance gogol of a physicist they quoted. I'm afraid I have made him work very hard. He provided the details.'

'Jean dear, I am sure you know I have little time or patience for *details*.'

'I remembered that meeting with the others, where you said it would be better if people would follow us of their own free will. That the world worked too well.'

'You are delightfully cryptic today, Jean. What is my birthday present? It's the last one, so it had better be good.'

'Well, I thought the world would make a pretty musical sound if we broke it,' Jean says.

She takes a deep, rattling breath.

'What do I have to do?'

'Just think of something beautiful. Think of a secret. Something no one else knows.'

She sees on his face that he wants her to choose a shared, beautiful moment, the first night on the seastead, or the first time they met, in that awful stinky cell. He refused to come with her, saying that he liked her pearls and would come for them three days later. When the guard closed the door behind her, she could see in his eyes that he was free. And for the first time in a long, long time, so was she.

But she can't help it: it is a different secret that rises up to swallow her and the world. It is the worst night of her life, long ago, that comes to her. Lying in bed, on rough, sticky sheets, holding the dead little red thing, being eaten by the emptiness that comes after enduring the world-filling pain. Looking into its tiny closed eyes, vowing to survive its death. Vowing never to die.

He sees it, sees the pain on her face, and flinches. But then it is too late: his machine is set in motion, and the world starts to unravel. He squeezes her hand gently, and they watch it together.

She cannot be sure what comes afterwards, how much of what she sees through the beemee and Jean's little spime is a real memory. More likely it is a combination of fragments of Prime thought and data absorbed throughout the centuries, re-interpreted to fit the context of that birthday.

The markets that control life and death collapse.

Swarms of repo bots, come to reclaim bodies, descend upon a seastead off the shore of California.

Upload cities in China shut down, unable to purchase energy.

The great exodus begins. The infant zoku escape on desperately crowdfunded ships. Improvised transmitters beam gogols to the loving arms of the Sobornost in the sky.

She watches it all, exhilarated. The slate of the world is wiped clean, and it will be her writing that appears on it next.

She turns to Jean to thank him for a beautiful gift, to kiss him like she once did, to tell him how much she loves him.

*

That is the last moment she gives the partial. The rest, she keeps to herself: seeing the horror on his face, the sad eyes wide, all innocence and joy and freedom gone. She does not understand why, it is all like clockwork.

Something else is loose, engulfing gogol minds, burning, consuming.

The weather ghosts who control the climate of a warmed Earth go mad and make winds dance like whips.

There is a fiery arrow in the sky outside. She looks at it, and the faithful bed provides annotations in her field of vision. Sirr, the great city in the sky, is falling.

There are rains of miniature bodies above London, suddenly vacated and deactivated.

Wildcode, they would later call it, serpents that sting minds, madness that consumes a hsien-ku fleet in a great Cry of Wrath, beings born from the machine that Jean made.

'No, no, no,' he whispers. 'That can't be, I didn't plan for this, I don't understand.'

It is not a breaking, it is a burning, a cleansing. Joséphine closes her eyes. *It is time to go,* she tells the bed. The upload crown descends upon her head. The blades start whirring. The bed pumps optogenetic viruses into her brain. She grabs Jean's hand as hard as she can.

'Stay with me,' she whispers. 'I'm scared.'

He wrenches his hand away.

'I can't. I have to go, Joséphine,' he whispers. 'I'm sorry.'

And then he is gone, running footsteps echoing down the hall. How could she not see before that he was weak?

She has no voice left when the upload begins, so she just thinks so that the words will be preserved to all her selves that come after.

You can't run away forever. You can't help what you are.
You will come back to me.

11

MIELI AND THE REBIRTH PARTY

There is sunlight filtered through ice. The air is warm and moving in the slow flow of pumptree breath. The horizon is a pair of cupped hands.

A *koto* in bloom, in the Little Summer of passing close to a sun.

Mieli is floating high up, close to the Weightless Eye in the centre of the ice sphere, where the air medusas live. Her wings are open, catching the mellow thermals from below. She is whole again, unhurt, and the sudden absence of the pain is almost like a loss. Something else is different: she can't feel her systems anymore. Or the pellegrini.

Did she sacrifice herself for me? What would make her do that? It doesn't make any sense. But it is difficult to think. Flashes of the battle on Hektor's surface are stuck in her brain like slivers of glass.

'How are you feeling?'

Zinda is wearing Oortian garb, a black toga, floating in the middle of a medusa swarm. It does not suit her: she is shorter than native Oortians, and the large fabric is loose, billowing around her, making her look a little medusa-like herself.

Mieli finds herself smiling. It is good to see the zoku girl. Then she shakes her head. *Don't forget what you are, what you are here for.*

'Confused,' she says aloud.

'I hope you don't mind that I made this Realm! I heard from the Huizinga-zoku that you had asked for a design like this. I was tempted to include some narrative element, but I tried to make it as Simulationist as possible, almost like a vir. What do you think?'

Mieli says nothing.

'I mean, it's a local one, only until we get into router network range, then we can just 'port you straight home and get you a new body. Trust me, you would *not* want to be seen dead in the one you had! We barely got you through the Realmgate in time.'

'What happened?'

'Well, Mik did some *amazing* flying. The raions chased us, but the *Zweihänder* has a really big antimatter drive: it's not easy to stay on the tail of something that is shooting a plume of gamma rays at you, if you know what I mean.' She pauses. 'But I could ask you the same thing! What was that thing on Hektor?'

Mieli shudders. *I can't tell her. Not yet. I need to think.*

'A warmind, a new type. It took over my suit, wanted to upload me.' She shrugs. 'I dealt with it.'

'I'll say you did!' Zinda grows serious. 'When you blew the suit's antimatter, I thought ... I thought we lost you, Mieli. I've never known anyone who has been near truedeath before.' She takes Mieli's hand. 'You don't need to lie to me, Mieli. You look at me like I was your jailer. That's okay. I don't mind. But I want you to know that I'm glad you made it.' Her smile is a mixture of sadness and joy. 'We all are. The others are here, too, if you want to see them.'

Mieli notices her zoku jewels for the first time: they are here with her, only invisible, hidden beneath the blanket of Realm reality. The Liquorice jewel is sending a steady stream of subliminal qupts filled with concern.

Mieli sighs. 'All right. There are things we need to talk about.'

They wait for Mieli and Zinda on the surface of the *koto*, near a roofless smartcoral house that marks the entrance to the honeycomb beneath the ice.

'My lady,' says Mik, in his baseline form. 'I doubted you. I grieve for the wounds you suffered. Should anyone question your honour ever again, my blade will have a ready answer for them.' He kneels in front of her, head bowed.

'Functor: isomorphism,' says Anti-de-Sitter-times-a-Sphere.

Mieli's connection to them feels stronger, and there is something new between her and Zinda as well. *Entanglement? Is that what it feels like?* At the thought, her jewels whisper to her: she is now a Level Twelve Badass of the-Liquorice-Zoku, and a Level Seven Existential Risk Manager of the Great Game.

'But I *failed*,' she says.

'No. No, you didn't,' Zinda says. 'You discovered that the Sobornost civil war is a great sham, a cover for something. Anti-de-Sitter worked it out. We have already sent the results to the rest of the zoku. You can't believe how much entanglement that got us.'

'Show me,' Mieli says.

Anti-de-Sitter-times-a-Sphere opens the Great Game

intel spime. It looks strange in the Oort-realm, a multi-coloured ball of twine floating in the air.

'Bayesian inference: different prior. Operation: process tomography.'

The spime expands until they stand in the middle of it, threaded orbits and colourful potential fields.

'If you work from the assumption that the civil war is a distraction, *this* is what the zoku thinks they are really doing,' Zinda says.

The raion and asset flows shift. Subtle anomalies that can be attributed to metacloaked ships are highlighted and interpolated. Even without her tactical gogols, Mieli can spot the pattern. A new hub forms in the network, a blue knot of activity near the Broken Places of Jupiter-that-was.

'They are assembling a fleet,' Mieli says. 'You could hide it in the topological defect webs in the Broken Places. Even *guberniyas*. Better than a metacloak. Can you tell how many assets they are moving?'

'As far as we can tell … possibly all of them,' Zinda says.

I have given them a common enemy, the All-Defector said.

'Our ancient enemy is moving!' says Sir Mik, grinning. 'My blade Soulswallower thirsts for Sobornost blood!'

'We still don't know what's up with the Founders, who or what has managed to get them to cooperate. But it does look like they are getting ready to invade Supra City!'

That's it, Mieli thinks. *All-D is also after the Kaminari jewel. But why did it want me?*

She stares at Zinda. The zoku girl's eyes are gleaming. A strange enthusiasm filters through her zoku jewel.

'I don't understand. This is war we are talking about! Why are you all smiling?'

Zinda laughs.

'Oh, Mieli. Because it's going to be so much fun!'

Mieli's rebirth party is just getting started when she arrives.

Her transport bubble leaves her at the opening of a cavern of leaves that leads into the depths of a forest. Ahead, there are warm, coloured lights, shouts and faint music. The party zoku jewel – a small robin's egg blue thing glittering in her complex hairdo – pulls her forward insistently. She straightens her back, unused to walking with open wings and uncomfortable in her elaborate black dress – another detail Zinda insisted on – and clutches the small handbag she brought for her zoku jewels. Then she takes a deep breath and walks in. The warm heady smell of a summer night greets her.

She had a perfect view of the party Circle from the bubble. The Strip has transformed into a vast woodland garden. The hex where Zinda's house used to be is overgrown with wild forests, meadows and steep ravines. The river is the only familiar feature, and small boats with colourful sails drift along it. Zinda is expecting a lot of guests: a mass stream has been diverted and hangs in the sky like a silver rainbow. Transport bubbles drift drown from it, mixing with the Chinese paper lanterns that float everywhere above the trees. The solettas have been turned away from the Strip, and the sky is almost as vast as outside a *koto* in Oort, full of faint stars and the bright discs of Rhea and the other inner moons.

Mieli sighs. Cypress leaves rustle and tickle her bare feet as she walks. There is a clearing somewhere ahead, and the voices grow louder. She is not looking forward to meeting more zoku strangers, more faces that are just masks for something else, that shift and change between every Realm and Circle faster than she can keep track of.

'Of course you have to come!' Zinda said and gave her a shocked look, when she hinted that she was tired. 'It was my first field mission, and it would not have happened without you! We *have* to celebrate!'

Mieli just wants to pray and meditate in her garden, but it is difficult to sit still when her new body is a chorus of noise. She was remade after the battle on Hektor. The Great Game offered her a trueform – a completely artificial shell of foglets and diamond – but she refused, insisting on a synthbio replica of her biological body, preserving whatever original components survived. It is not baseline, of course: she kept her metacortex, tactical gogols and reflexes, and added a few choice zoku q-tech enhancements. Having a high level of entanglement in the Great Game Zoku turned out to have some advantages, after all. If she ever meets the All-Defector again, she will be ready. But it is taking a while to adjust. Her gogols constantly complain about the unfamiliar interfaces, a subliminal neural chatter that leaves her edgy, and there are phantom tingles in her right leg, in spite of her attempts to filter them out with the metacortex.

Yet it is nothing compared to the thoughts racing through her mind, in circles like horses in the brass-and-neon carousel she glimpsed in the party clearing from above. *The invasion. The pellegrini. The Kaminari jewel. Sydän.* Round and round.

She reaches the edge of the clearing. The carousel is ahead, and a few scattered guests are standing around it. There are small tents and tables, long-legged golden robots in tuxedos serving drinks. The party jewel is urging her on. Others are floating down from the sky, trueforms shimmering into well-dressed baseline party guests. Zinda is clearly trying to make her comfortable: the Circle rules specify human forms only.

She blinks when the ground shakes and an angular, robotic kaijuform from the Big Game Zoku that towers above the treetops steps into the party Circle, and instantly evaporates into a shimmer of foglets, leaving behind a small party in evening wear: two girls in twin yellow dresses, laughing, and an elf-man in a tuxedo who reminds her a little of Sir Mik.

Mieli frowns. *How can they be so carefree?* There is an invasion coming, perhaps within days, certainly not much longer – now that the Sobornost ruse has been discovered, the obvious tactical move is to strike immediately. The fleet and the *guberniyas* with their Hawking drives may already be on their way. The zoku must know that with the vast energies of the Inner System under Sobornost control, Supra City is at an enormous disadvantage – yet the Liquorice-zoku talks about the coming battle like it was a difficult level in a game. If the Great Game is doing something about it, she is not included in the effort: that jewel has been silent ever since their return from the Jovian Trojan belt. And in spite of her enormously increased entanglement within the secretive zoku, she has not dared to request any more information.

One problem is that she does not know what questions to ask.

She reaches the carousel and watches the whirling horses, most of them riderless. There are people on the other side of the structure and the party jewel is pulling her there, but she does not want to go just yet. She would rather hide in the tinkling music, the light and the motion: in the small sphere of carousel glow, she can imagine the vastness of Supra City does not exist.

Sydän would love this place. They could have come here, when they left Oort. But no, she wanted true immortality, the kind that only the Sobornost offers.

The thought pinches her with sharp claws. The cold touch of the jewelled chain around her ankle mingles with the phantom pains of her leg. *I am losing her.* The pellegrini's constant presence in her mind was a reminder of her mission, a sharp rock she could squeeze in her hand when in doubt; a peach-stone in her mouth.

The pellegrini. Mieli first met the goddess – or the Prime – in her temple on Venus, jealously guarding the singularity she had made out of Amtor City and the matter of Lakshmi Planum and sacrificed minds. A tiny captive star whose event horizon still holds the soul of Sydän and countless others. *What will you give me, little girl?* She was always a vengeful, hot-tempered taskmaster, *a cold bitch*, as *Perhonen* often put it. Never one for self-sacrifice, as the goddess herself told Mieli. *Why did she save me?* The pellegrini-gogol in her head was one of uncountable billions, but Mieli knows well that it does not make death any less real, sacrifice any easier. She remembers her own copies who died fighting in the wildcode desert of Earth, the pain and sudden nothingness she felt through her metaself.

Remember, the pellegrini said.

And she does. Invasion or not, Sydän is still trapped in a black hole, and the Kaminari jewel is the only way to get her out. She must stay inside the Great Game, find out what they know about the jewel, and think of a way to get to it – all before the Sobornost invasion comes. Again, she wishes the thief was here: he would know what to do. Or *Perhonen.* Mieli's song for her is still unfinished. She does not want to think about the ship: she knows too well what it would say.

Mieli is alone, and there is no more time for the past.

She takes a deep breath and walks around the carousel, to the sea of light and conversation.

And that's when the zombies attack.

They come at her from behind the carousel, four rotting bodies in tuxedos and evening dresses, lurching forward slowly, arms outstretched. She recognises the two women in yellow from before, except that one has a broken neck now, head hanging at an odd angle, and their skin has a deathly pallor. A sickly sweet smell of formaldehyde and rot surrounds them.

The undead elf-man in a dinner jacket reaches for her and brushes her cheek with clammy fingers. Without thinking, Mieli swings her handbag at his head as hard as she can. The force of the blow lifts him off his feet and tosses him into the spinning carousel. The riders of the white wooden horses scream – with delight or terror, Mieli is not sure. She takes a step back and stares at the dead women in yellow, wondering if the party Circle would allow her to try out her new weapon systems.

'What did I tell you? No zombie games!' It's Zinda, in a beautiful green dress that creates an impression of large green leaves made of lace, silk and pearls, but leaves her olive-skinned shoulders and neck bare. She is holding a champagne flute in her hand, and looks furious.

There is a howl somewhere in the distance.

'Or werewolves!'

The girls in yellow shimmer into more warm-blooded forms and scowl at Mieli. 'The Circle rules specify a rebirth theme,' one of them protests, a chestnut-haired girl with an imperious expression on her cherry lips. 'And it's appropriate for the period!' Her honey-blonde companion nods vigorously.

Zinda rolls her eyes. 'Duh huh. But you don't have to take it so *literally*. Look at me: plants. Green. New life. Spring.'

'Or envy?' the other girl says. 'I can understand, with *that* alter.'

'I'm sorry, Mieli, this will only take a moment.'

Mieli can't suppress a smile. Zinda puts her hands on her hips.

'Zombies get their own sub-Circle, starting now. All right?' The chestnut girl's eyes harden, and she brings her hand forward in a challenge. Zinda scoffs. They wave their hands rapidly in the air in the same rhythm, three times. In the end Zinda's hand is open and flat, and the other girl's hand is curled in a fist.

'Damn!' the chestnut-haired girl swears, stamping her foot. 'I spent *so* much time on this alter!' She takes the hand of the other yellow-dressed girl and they walk towards the busier areas of the party.

Zinda sighs. 'Can you believe her? I wanted to do something simple and old-fashioned, but once the party zoku got bigger, it got out of hand. I'm afraid the whole thing is a bit inconsistent in terms of style and theme. And it seems some people can't tell their Fitzgerald from their Lovecraft. So don't be surprised if you see a few flapper Deep Ones tonight.'

'Am I supposed to know what those are?'

'Frankly, it's better that you don't. The only ones who are worse than the Mythos Zoku are Manaya High fans, like me. But what am I thinking! It's your party, and here you are, without a glass in your hand, and being attacked by the undead!' She hooks her arm through Mieli's and pulls her towards the music. She smells of a soft perfume, fruit, peach perhaps. 'Come on. Let's go meet some people!'

*

The party proper is a dazzling, whirling clockwork of talk, dance, music and drink. A white-clad band plays jazz. Most guests are elegantly dressed baselines, but there are a few odd ones out, pushing the boundaries of what the Circle allows. One of them is a cyborg with bushy sideburns and a tall black hat that Mieli reckons is even more ancient than most of the party wear, a brass barrel of a man with an elaborate moravec arm that is clutching several champagne glasses at once. He is the centre of a small group of anthropomorphic animal alters, a fox, a badger and a white creature that looks like a pointy-eared hippo; it keeps adjusting its bow tie awkwardly with small paws.

'And *boom!*' the man in the hat says, gesturing. 'They all started going off! To be honest, we should have thought of it ourselves, to arrange something like that! Perhaps for the centennial of the zoku! But it was so *rude!*' He shakes his head. 'And to cause truedeath – but I won't tarnish this happy occasion with sad memories. Although Chekhova would surely have liked to be here. Ah, Zinda! And this can surely only be the lady of the hour!'

'Mieli, this is Barbicane, from the Gun Club Zoku,' Zinda says. The name is familiar to Mieli from the Protocol War: the Gun Club creates many of the zoku warships and weapons, eccentric and elaborate, but effective designs. **He is Great Game**, one of us, Zinda qupts. **An Elder. A good person to know.**

Barbicane kisses Mieli's hand. His sideburns brush her skin, rough like steel wool. He smells of gun oil and a heavy, stinging aftershave. *An Elder*, she thinks. *He must know more about the jewel. But what should I ask?*

'Charmed! Please join us.' **Congratulations**, he qupts. **In a very short time, you have achieved great things.**

I only want to serve.

The fox and the badger greet her politely. They appear to be a couple and are from a zoku called Dancing Cat. The white creature is too shy to say anything, just shakes her hand quickly.

My goodness, what has Zinda been telling you? Barbicane qupts back, with an amused tone. **The Great Game is not just about serving. It's about having fun!** He offers Mieli a champagne flute. She accepts it and takes a sip. The golden liquid is sweet and tickles her throat as it goes down. It makes her feel bolder.

'The honour is mine. I am … familiar with your work,' Mieli says. It is not a lie: *Perhonen* was once caught in a Gun Club holeship blast when an oblast destroyed it, and they had to surf the Hawking radiation front to safety.

I keep hearing that word, she qupts. **It's not one I would use myself to describe a Sobornost invasion. What is Great Game going to do about it?**

'Capital! Then you will be interested to hear my news! I was just telling these gentlemen about a spot of bother we had on Iapetus recently,' Barbicane says. 'A most audacious break-in! An artefact stolen, irreparable damage caused to our collection. A blatant Circle violation.' **This is hardly the time and the place to discuss such matters, and it could be considered rude towards our lovely hostess, to boot. I suggest you direct your enquiries directly to the zoku itself: I note your volition cone has increased considerably, and we will listen.** This qupt has a firm undertone that suggests that the conversation is over, even if the link is still there.

Mieli smiles at him. 'How interesting,' she says. Zinda gives her a puzzled look. 'Do tell us more.'

We Oortians are not known for our courtesy, she qupts at

Barbicane. **So, is inaction simply a sign of a tired civilisation whose time has run out? Or do we just feel safe because we have the Kaminari jewel?**

The quptlink wavers. Briefly, Mieli sees a flash of something unutterably alien, a twisting sheet of light, like a skin beneath the skin of the Universe, impossibly far and right next door at the same time. Then the link is gone.

Barbicane is just lifting a glass to his lips but is stopped by a sputtering cough that turns into a giant belch. A jet of vaporised champagne shoots into the air from his mouth. The Dancing Cat members duck, and Zinda stares at the zoku Elder in stark horror.

Barbicane gives Mieli a fatherly smile and wipes champagne from his sideburns with a napkin held delicately between a few of his smaller manipulator limbs. 'My sincere apologies! I'm afraid I was in such a rush to answer the young lady's question that I poured some of this lovely stuff right into my boiler! If you will excuse me, I shall go and perform certain urgent mechanical engineering operations to prevent an explosion that no doubt would spoil the mood entirely! It is not time for fireworks yet, hmm?'

He vanishes into the crowd, weaving back and forth a little unsteadily on his leg-jets.

'What was that all about?' Zinda asks. 'Don't tell me you were *flirting* with him?' She covers her mouth with a tiny hand. 'Disaster!'

'Of course I wasn't!' Mieli protests. 'What makes you say that?'

Zinda sighs. 'Well, to be honest, that was the most likely explanation for all your strange expressions! Especially given that you have been living like a nun ever since you got here.'

She punches Mieli in the shoulder gently. 'We are going to have to fix that!' Then her eyes narrow.

'Okay, I believe you. Unless looking angry is the way Oortians flirt. Whatever it was, it's making you far too serious. That won't do, not at all. Whatever you are worrying about, it can wait.' She takes Mieli's hand and starts leading her through the party, towards the forest.

'Where are we going?' Mieli asks.

'Hunting,' says Zinda, picking up a champagne bottle and two glasses from a passing botlet waiter.

'Hunting for what?'

'Treasure eggs, of course!'

There are eggs hidden all over the forest, small blue things that look like the party zoku jewel, with glowing golden numbers written on them.

'Do you like it?' Zinda asks, sipping her drink. 'It's an egg hunt lottery – every number has a prize attached to it! I figured you wouldn't like the more mainstream games like jeepform or fastaval – they tend to be all grimdark anyway – so I thought I'd go for something simple. The more difficult the hiding place, the better the prize.' She smiles. 'Besides, I figured you would like to have an excuse to get away from all the people. It's just difficult to throw a *small* party in Supra City, you know.'

The zoku girl's eyes are clear and kind. *She is trying to help. I don't understand what she is doing, but she is trying.*

Mieli empties her fourth glass and listens to the soft sounds of the forest, and the faraway clamour of the main party. The floating lanterns above give the forest and its leaf labyrinths and the river a fairy-tale tinge. The gold and blue twinkles of the hidden eggs in the undergrowth and in the trees tickle something deep in her belly, like the aftertaste of the champagne. *The end of the world is coming, and we are going to play children's games. Well, why the hell not?*

She wonders if it is just the drink, or perhaps the strange intoxication emanating from the party zoku jewel in her hair that is making her giddy. In any case, she is, for the first time in a long, long time, pleasantly gloriously drunk.

'All right,' she says. 'I'm going to play. And win. Unless you are planning on cheating. Wasn't it you who designed this whole thing?'

'Oh no, it was the party zoku! The idea came from my volition, but I have no idea where they are, or what is in them. But let's make it a little more interesting. If I find more eggs than you do, I get to make a wish. Not a zoku wish, just a wish, an old-fashioned one, like the ones you make when you see a star fall. What do you say?'

'Fine,' Mieli says. 'I want a wish too, if I win. Let's meet by the river in one hour. But you are forgetting one thing.'

Zinda grins. 'And what is that?'

'I can fly.'

Mieli spreads her wings and lets the microfans lift her soundlessly to the level of the paper lanterns. Below, the forest is full of tiny blue stars.

12

THE THIEF AND THE CRYSTAL STOPPER

There are zoku ships everywhere above the Irem Plate. I glimpse them through my q-dot bubble's magnifying skin as pinpoints as I rise towards my ship's geostationary orbit. Then the entanglement beams between them become visible in the thin ammonium and water vapour, turning the sky into a silver net, woven to catch me.

Transitioning into the *Leblanc*'s Realm through its gateskin is perfectly smooth now, like slipping beneath the surface of cool water. The pilot's chamber flows into place around me. Carabas stands to attention and takes its hat off with a mechanical flourish.

The ship's sensors show over two hundred ships in Plate space, ranging from the Notch-zoku's Replicators – tiny, blocky insects – to green dense Dyson trees, sleek, spiky, purple pseudomatter vessels of the Evangelion-zoku, and even individual baseline quicksuits, silver humanoids with large, circular waste heat fins. In spite of the diversity, they are clearly members of one temporary zoku, moving in a seemingly random dance that nevertheless covers all possible escape vectors. What did Barbicane say? *A challenge for a small zoku, nothing more.* It looks like the Great Game has spun off an entirely new quantum collective to catch me.

I suppose I should feel flattered.

I fire up the ship's Hawking drive and uncloak. The distributed information attack starts immediately. Qupt probes and attack software bore into the ship's firewall from all directions. *It seems they want me alive.*

'Two hundred baseline milliseconds until firewall collapse,' Carabas says, '3.07 subjective minutes at maximum clockspeed.'

I wave the cat aside, sit down at the control keyboard and brush the brass keys gently. The ship's non-sentient presence is a calm cool armour around my mind.

I can't help but pause to think for a moment. *What if I let them catch me?* After what the Aun told me, I feel like I deserve it. It would be easy. I feel the possible vectors now, and there is nothing I can choose that will get me past the Plate and into either trans-Saturnian space to flee or into the planet's dense depths to hide. Even tiny course corrections I make provoke an immediate response from the zoku all around. *Is this how Mieli felt when she wanted to fight the Hunter swarm?*

A quptlink request comes, through the tiny Great Game jewel Dunyazad gave me, safely in its own sandbox. I let Carabas and its agents examine it, and then let it through.

That was very sloppy, dear boy! It's Barbicane, of course. The qupt comes with an aftershave smell and the echo of hollow brass. **Did you think we wouldn't notice? What have you done to a brand new Plate?**

Hearing the zoku Elder's voice brings a burst of welcome anger. I tell my metaself to use it to help me focus.

In the trade we call this breaking and redecorating, I

respond. Stay out of Irem. You will find that it is under the control of a Notch-zoku member called Dunyazad. It's all perfectly legitimate. Unless you want to take it up with Vipunen the Elder in the South Pole? I believe he ate the last expedition that tried to find his Realm.

Capital! Barbicane says. Perhaps he would like to join our brand new Ganimard-zoku! Detectives and manhunters extraordinaire. They get entanglement based on how close they get to you, of course.

He's trying to distract me. Think, Jean. What would Mieli do?

Unless, of course, you want to surrender and we can settle this like gentlemen! They would be terribly disappointed! I am certain young Mieli would be pleased to see you and discuss the matter of her ship *Perhonen* with you as well – I believe that is the civilisation that destroyed it that you have helped to recreate down there, yes?

But of course, that is precisely the wrong question.

Incidentally, Mieli is such a bright young lady! I have a mission in mind just for her, and I expect her to succeed admirably – and be rewarded accordingly, of course. It is amazing how the volition system shapes you, how your zoku comes to mean everything to you. Why deny yourself that experience, Jean? You always lacked a purpose. We can offer you one. Pipe tobacco and the clink of fine china with the qupt. He is enjoying this, the bastard. No matter. I know what to do.

This is the last time I ask you to join us. If the Ganimards catch you, they will give you to our information retrieval specialists, and the games they design are much less enjoyable than the Great Game.

'Twenty subjective seconds until firewall collapse,' Carabas says.

I plot a tight arc just along the skin of Irem and pass it to the cat. 'Come on, boy,' I tell it. 'Time to earn your keep, for a change.'

Don't get the wrong idea, Jean: reshaping Plates or not, you are nothing more than a nuisance. You are out of your depth. What do you think you have that you can fight an entire zoku with?

Carabas gives me an offended look. I hold my hand up.

Family, I qupt at Barbicane, and cut the link. Then I bring my hand down. 'Now.'

The *Leblanc*'s Hawking drive fires, a great white torch, and we dive straight at Irem and the wildcode desert.

We only see ourselves, the Aun told me once.

The photon tail of the *Leblanc* cuts a scorched letter in the skin of Irem. My stomach tickles as the ship spins around, turns the mad dive into a parabolic arc following the Plate's curve.

The Aun get the message. The wildcode desert rises behind us. Walls of dust and sand, jinni the size of mountains who grasp at zoku ships with sapphire fingers. Aerovore protuberances shoot up. For a moment, the wildcode data storm gets through the *Leblanc*'s firewalls, and I glimpse vast serpents of light, striking at the sky. They brush my mind like the hot fingers of the Chimney Princess, recognise me and release the ship.

The Ganimard-zoku ships are not so lucky. The wildcode enters their technology. A Dyson tree makes a green, fragmented impact on the shifting dunes. A Replicator fires signals at the notchcubes beneath the sand, but only twisted, dysfunctional copies of the von Neumann craft rise up, drawing short arcs before crashing and exploding. The Evangelion ships turn their weapons at the desert and white antimatter flowers blossom behind us like a string of blazing pearls. For a moment, I fear for the integrity of the Plate itself.

Then the body thieves come. They enter zoku minds through code fragments, through stories told as geometric patterns in the sand, and manipulate the Ganimard-zoku's collective volition. The converging wedges of ships intercepting us turn away, scattering in all directions. It is a temporary reprieve – the zoku are not nearly as vulnerable to mind-hacking as sobortech, and will no doubt develop countermeasures rapidly – but it buys the *Leblanc* enough time to get past the edge of the Plate and follow the glowing flows of the dynamic support beams down to the depths of Saturn, away from pursuit.

As soon as we are in the relative safety of the sub-troposphere layers, I turn to Carabas again. The Ganimard-zoku won't give up, so there is no time to waste.

'Is there another Jean le Flambeur on board?' I ask it. 'Another copy?'

On Mars, my past self left me a series of clues, partial ghosts of myself, to guide me to the memories hidden in the Oubliette. Could I have done the same here?

The cat's metallic whiskers shiver. 'Prime authorisation needed,' it purrs.

I frown. After all the iterations I went through in the Dilemma Prison, the probability that I am sufficiently identical to the Jean the *Leblanc* would recognise as Prime is vanishingly small.

'All right, never mind. Carry on.'

There is another possibility. The *Leblanc*'s technology is a hodgepodge mixture of Sobornost and zoku. The Sobornost have a concept called a Library: a repository of gogol snapshots, of people you once were and want to retain. Is it possible that the ship has one? I haven't found it yet, but perhaps it is hidden. Could Matjek have accessed it somehow? Old virs like the bookshop are based on demiurge gogols, custom minds that maintain the illusion. Sometimes it's possible to trick them into linking things that are not supposed to be linked, a kind of sympathetic magic.

I would have to ask Matjek, and at the moment the conversation would not go very well.

So where would I keep the Library of the ship? Where would I store self-fragments that I was too sentimental to throw away?

Of course.

I return to the Realm corridor and step through the gate leading to the white sunlit deck of the *Provence*.

I find the book on the deck chair by the pool. No one looks at me twice here; it is a timeless Realm where I am a Monsieur d'Andrezy, a first-class passenger across an endless Atlantic, spending my days on the deck and nights in the gambling saloon and dining hall.

Golden flashes of sunlight reflected from the pool water dance on its cover when I pick it up. *Le Bouchon de cristal.* An old favourite, an anachronistic paperback edition with a colourful cover, a dark monocled silhouette of a thief and a crystal bottle. The pages are yellow and well-thumbed. I sit down comfortably, put on my blue-tinted sunglasses and open it.

The pages are blank.

I flip through them rapidly, looking for clues. The book is out of place in the Realm: even as I touch it, it feels unnatural, a kernel of another reality embedded in this one. It is as if the pages are waiting to be filled with something. A key. A memory.

I close my eyes. *Prime authorisation required.* It's the same approach the Sobornost Founders use: an image that is the core of who you are, stable across copies, a neural configuration much more difficult to duplicate than any password, used to unlock secrets.

I search my memories. The Prison. Wearing the face of Sumanguru the Founder, getting caught. *It must be older than that.*

Fragments from Mars, glimpses from the corridors of the memory palace. Getting drunk with Isaac. The first date with Raymonde. The affair with Gilbertine. The Corridor of Birth and Death. No, none of that. Something older.

I reach for the ship. There are tools on the *Leblanc* I can use, metacognition software to dig through my own mind, treat it like a memory lockpick, find the right shape that fits when you wiggle it.

I can't move. My world is made of blank pages that swallow my gaze.

'You have been identified either as a divergent copy of master-Prime or an intruder,' says the voice of the cat, somewhere. 'You have thirty subjective seconds to provide a Prime code. After that, I am authorised to use countermeasures.'

Bastard. I waste a second cursing my past self. *I wish I had never been born.*

That's it. When *was* I born? Does the book want the moment when I first opened it in Santé Prison, when the Flower Prince first started growing in my mind? Too obvious, too easy.

'Twenty seconds.'

Or when Joséphine opened the door to my cell? Her young-old face, a key turning in a lock. *No, not her. She does not define me.*

'Fifteen seconds.'

The pages are a desert, empty and bright with the glare of a harsh sun. I feel lost in them.

'Ten seconds.'

There is a desert inside me, too, the blank paper on which I was first written, the first letter in the shape of a boy lying on a sand dune.

I whisper to him and he steps out of me. The book accepts him, and its pages are filled with the black ink of memory.

13

MIELI AND THE ANTHROPIC PRINCIPLE

In spite of herself, Mieli enjoys the egg hunt.

The search keeps getting harder as she goes. It is not a simple matter of finding peculiar hiding places, although, at first, she finds a few small eggs in streams, tree holes and under leaves, all easily spotted from air. But one particularly large egg, sitting in the crook of a tree branch, grows slender white legs when Mieli approaches it, and flees with amazing speed. She chases it on foot through a thicket, and a burning chasm suddenly appears in front of her. The egg leaps over it effortlessly, and Mieli almost falls in.

She stops and stares at the hot lava at the bottom of the deep fissure, hissing and spitting sparks. The fleeing egg is lost among the shadows of the trees.

'How do you find flying now, Oortian?' rings Zinda's taunting voice from the other side. 'You have to be smarter than that!'

Gritting her teeth, Mieli sits down on a rock and starts listing the craziest possible hiding places she can think of. *Barbicane's hat. Clouds. Inside flowers.* Then she starts going through them, one by one.

Most of them turn out to be dead ends, although she does find swooping down from above to snatch the zoku Elder's hat away quite satisfying. He shouts something at her she can't hear. Fortunately, the Circle prevents his gun arm from working. The hat turns out to be empty, but she wears it for the rest of the night anyway. Eventually, she does notice a suspiciously low cloud over the party – far too white and fluffy to be natural – and inside it she discovers a large floating egg with the number 890 written on one side.

When the time is up, Mieli returns to the riverbank with her loot and gathers them in the stovepipe hat, five eggs in total. Surely, that must be a respectable result, especially the cloud egg. She leans back on the grass and watches the wavering golden and silver reflections of the lanterns on the dark water. She imagines herself drifting along the river with the small zoku boats, sailing somewhere far away.

After a while, a sound wakes Mieli up abruptly. She sits bolt upright and sees Zinda kneeling next to her, angular face lit from below by blue light.

'I'm sorry,' the zoku girl says. 'I didn't want to wake you up. You looked so calm. But I'm afraid I have to tell you that you lost.' At Zinda's feet, there is a glowing pyramid of at least a dozen eggs of different sizes. 'I even found the one that I think is the main prize.' She holds up a tiny egg with the number 999.

'Where was it?' Mieli wipes her eyes. She feels more awake now, but the night and the river still hold her in their grip. Or perhaps she is not ready to let go of them.

'In my purse! The last place I could think of. But I don't think it was actually there before I looked – Great Timbo! Is that Barbicane's hat?'

'It was the last place *I* could think of,' Mieli says.

Zinda laughs a long, pearly laugh. 'Well, I'm glad you have been having a good time, Mieli,' she says.

'Me, too. And thank you. It has been a good party.'

'It's not over yet! Do you want to go back to collect our winnings?'

'No, not really.' Mieli looks at the glowing contents of her hat. 'Maybe I prefer to imagine what I would have won.' She holds up an egg with the number 27. 'An unsung song, perhaps. Or a new beginning.'

Zinda takes her hand. 'That's a nice thought,' she says. 'Maybe we need one, too.'

A warm wave of desire leaps up within Mieli. *No, not like this. She is just wearing a mask. None of this is real. I am doing this for Sydän, maintaining my cover, getting close to her for information.*

Mieli pulls her hand away.

'Speaking of winnings,' she says, 'what is your wish going to be?'

Zinda looks down. 'I'll tell you later.' She puts Barbicane's hat on. It is far too big for her, and she has to tilt it back at a ridiculous angle to wear it.

'I don't know about you, but I feel like doing something forbidden,' she says. 'I think it would do us both a lot of good. What do you think?'

Mieli sits up. 'Listening to people say that is the story of my life,' she says.

'So, what happens next?'

'Usually, we find out why the forbidden things are forbidden.'

'Come on! On nights like this, we need to climb over fences and break into graveyards. Suggest something forbidden.'

'Well,' Mieli says carefully, 'your friend Barbicane said that talking about the Kaminari jewel was forbidden.'

Zinda looks at her, eyes wide. 'I didn't realise you even knew about *that*,' she says in a hushed voice.

Mieli shrugs. 'So you don't know *everything* about me,' she says.

Zinda smiles. 'Are you trying to play me, Mieli? Are you flirting with me to try to get me to talk about things I'm not supposed to?'

Mieli takes Zinda's hand. It is small and warm in her own. *Kuutar help me,* she thinks.

'Don't you *want* to be played?' she says aloud.

'Mieli, daughter of Karhu,' Zinda says, 'are you suggesting that we *twink*? That I help you to level up, tell you zoku secrets you are not supposed to know? That's bad. That's very bad. How do you think we are going to get away with that?' She grins wickedly. 'I like it. Give me your Great Game jewel!'

Mieli opens her purse and passes the trinket to Zinda. The zoku girl holds it up.

'This really is forbidden, you know. We could get bumped back to level one! But you just leave it to Auntie Zinda.' She touches Mieli's jewel with her own, like clinking glasses. Mieli feels a surge of entanglement, like in meditation, a sudden, sharp awareness of everything around her: the Great Game Zoku members, everywhere in Supra City, minds close to her like her own heartbeat. Then the feeling settles down like the surface of a glass of water.

'There you go. At least three extra levels, for free. How do you like that?' Zinda hands Mieli's jewel back. 'Don't worry, everybody does it, sometimes.' She lowers her voice. 'So, what is it that you want to hear? I can't tell you anything that really goes against the zoku volition, you know. Anything you *need* to know, you should just know.'

'I'm just trying to understand,' Mieli says. 'The Kaminari jewel. Why doesn't the zoku *use* it?' She looks up at the stars and the curve of Saturn's rings, dashed across the sky like a brushstroke of light.

'It wasn't that long ago, before I came here, that I wanted to die,' Mieli says quietly. 'A truedeath, not one of your games. I almost got my wish, too. But these last few days, I've been thinking – I want to live. I want to hunt eggs. I want to sing. I want to ...' She pauses.

'I know the Sobornost. If they win, they will erase this place, take your minds, take away the thing you call the q-self, and make you work for their Great Common Task, forever. And I'm not sure you – we – can win without something bigger than we are.'

'Wow. You really are not very good at flirting, are you?'

Mieli gives Zinda a dark look.

'I'm only teasing!' Zinda says. 'But seriously. Using the jewel – can't you feel how *wrong* that is? It would be against everything the zoku stands for. Protecting the Universe. Managing existential risk. Do you know what the jewel *does?*"

Mieli shakes her head. 'Only that is something big. Something that the Founders want. Something that could be used against them.'

'Duh huh! That's putting it mildly!' Zinda purses her lips. 'There are two problems, really. The first is that we can't solve any *hard* problems. Not really. Anything that's NP-complete. The Travelling Salesman. Pac-Man. They are all the same. All too hard. Even if we had a computer the size of the Universe! It drives the Sobornost crazy. *We* don't mind it so much: that's what makes most games fun. And we have quantum shortcuts for some special cases, like coordination. And for throwing parties, of course!

'But if you *could* do it, things would be very different. You could predict the future. Recreate history. Automate creativity. Make minds truly greater than us. Fulfil all those Strong AI nerd dreams from the pre-Collapse times. So you can see why the Sobornost has been trying for centuries now.'

'Yes,' Mieli says, remembering Amtor City, falling, the glowing whirlpool of the singularity, burning in the flesh of Venus.

'The second problem is that no physical machine we know of can do it. It's almost like travelling faster than the speed of light, or making a perpetual motion machine. Quantum computers can't do it, synthbio machines can't do it, doesn't matter how big you make them! Pretty early on, everybody agreed that the only place where NP gods could hide was quantum gravity.

'Use a big enough magnifying glass, and spacetime breaks into tiny pieces. At the Planck scale, causality becomes a variable. You can even have little time machines, closed timelike curves. Nothing like DeLoreans or Grandfather Paradoxes, those don't fit into quantum mechanics. But maybe you could squeeze a computer in there. And if you could, you could turn time into memory. You could solve NP-complete problems, and more. Sounds too good to be true, right? Right.'

Zinda leans closer to Mieli. The night air is still mellow, but Mieli is glad of her warmth.

'Just say if I start to bore you,' the zoku girl whispers in Mieli's ear. Her tickling breath sends a shiver through Mieli's body. Then she pulls away again. 'My usual technique does not involve theoretical computer science, I can assure you.'

Mieli shakes her head. 'I'm not bored. Go on,' she breathes.

'Okay, then,' Zinda says. 'Where was I? Oh yes. So, of course, people tried. Pretty early on, too, before the Collapse, with tiny black holes. And they discovered the Planck locks. Try to build a quantum gravity computer, and you get nonsense out. Some say they are artificial, that the Universe is a construct, and the locks were put there to keep us in our place. The old Simulation Argument. But I'm not sure. It could be that they *have* to be there.'

'What do you mean?'

'Think about it. Imagine that there are many possible universes, with different rules. The Spooky-zoku claim that that's how it works, that there are bubbles of possibility, that they collide and make Big Bangs. So imagine worlds where causal structures are broken, where spacetime can rewrite itself, where there are no stories, no games. Is that a world where *we* could exist? Is that a world where messy, silly humans arise and stumble through life and build cities and make mistakes? I don't think so. That would be too tacky. We could not have evolved in a world where the Planck locks do not exist. They have to be there. If they weren't, we wouldn't be *us*.'

Zinda takes Mieli's hand again.

'So, let's say the Kaminari-zoku did it. Let's say they broke the Planck locks. Let's say they left behind a zoku jewel. You take it, make a wish, and maybe it accepts you. But your wish can rewrite spacetime, make a new world where everything else except what you wish for is different, create a bubble of false vacuum that wipes out the rest of the Universe. Would you destroy what you have now? Is there anything in the world that you want *so* badly?'

Mieli says nothing.

'Don't worry about the Sobornost, Mieli. They are just another level boss. We can beat anything when we have a clear goal. When they come, all of Supra City will join the war zoku. They won't know what hit them. You'll see.'

You haven't met the All-Defector, Mieli thinks.

'Have you ever seen it? The jewel, I mean,' she asks aloud.

'Me? No. It's in a safe place. Only the Elders know where.'

Mieli remembers the flash in Barbicane's qupt. *A twisting sheet of light, close but impossibly far.*

'What would you wish for?' Mieli asks. 'If it didn't destroy the Universe, that is?'

'For the same thing you already owe me,' Zinda says.

'What is it?'

'Something small.'

'Tell me.'

'A kiss,' Zinda says. 'For starters.'

Her fingers caress Mieli's neck. Her lips are soft and warm and slick and taste of champagne and peaches. Mieli touches the curve of Zinda's hip, feels the hot flesh under the flimsy fabric of her dress.

The guilt feels like the q-suit's spike, between her ribs.

She pushes Zinda away.

'I can't,' she whispers.

'Why not?' Zinda says. She looks hurt. 'I know there was someone, Mieli, the girl the witch had on the mountain. But she is not here now. I think she is just a doll the witch has made, in your head.'

'No. It's not that!' Mieli stands up. 'You don't know – you are not even flesh. This is not who you are, it's an alter. Something you created to *handle* me. A mask.'

You idiot. This is not how it's supposed to go. She hugs herself, unable to face the zoku girl.

'Is that it?' Zinda says. 'Mieli, I don't think you understand us at all. That's what I was trying to tell you earlier. We find ourselves here, together, because we are who we are.'

'I—'

Zinda touches her face, cups her chin, turns her head gently. 'Ssh. I want you to watch.'

She presses her hands against her chest. Something glows between them with warm light, emerging from beneath her smooth skin. Zinda cups it between her hands: a zoku jewel, like a pearly tear in a delicate golden frame. She places it on the ground gently, next to the eggs. 'Great Game,' she says. Another jewel follows, a round red eye in a silver disc, and then another, and another. 'Manaya High. Supra. Huizinga. Strip. Liquorice. That's my whole q-self.'

She smiles. 'Remember, we always have the freedom to leave. You can always stop playing the game.' She points at the jewels on the ground. 'They are just pretty rocks to me now. What you see is all you get.'

She pulls her dress down and steps out of it with a rustle. Her body is slim and small, her breasts tiny buds, her bare sex a pink comma in the brackets of her hips. She steps forward lightly and stretches her arms like a dancer, wraps them around Mieli's neck.

'So, who is a big bad Great Game Zoku member now, hmm? Who is out to exploit a poor, innocent girl?'

Mieli answers with her hands and lips and tongue, and pulls Zinda down to the bed of grass, treasure eggs, and scattered quantum jewels.

*

Mieli sings to her, afterwards, a soft, quiet song that lovers sing. In Oort, it makes tinkling *väki* flowers grow in a *koto*'s walls. But here, it fits with the rhythm of Zinda's breathing in her arms, with the warm breeze that the forest makes to dry the cooling sweat on their skin.

She feels free and light, unmoored, for the first time on a world bigger than a *koto*. Zinda is a small and precious and true thing against her.

I can't do this. I can't lie to her with my body. I have to tell her the truth.

The pellegrini may have sacrificed herself for her, but no doubt it was for selfish reasons. After years of service, Mieli owes her nothing.

And Sydän? *She looked back.* But she got what she wanted. An eternity. A life without end. Would she begrudge an end for Mieli, or a new beginning?

Promises and vows, chains made of words and false hope. I am done with them. Perhonen *was right. She would want this. She would want me to be happy.*

I always loved you more than she did, the ship said.

Perhaps this is the best song I can give her.

'Why did you stop?' Zinda asks.

'There is something I have to tell you.' Mieli takes a deep breath. 'I'm not one of you. I'm not sure I ever will be. I only joined because I was looking for the Kaminari jewel. And you were right. There was someone. And there was a witch, too. My friend *Perhonen* once told me the same thing you did. I have been a fool.'

'Mieli, you don't have to say anything.'

'Yes, I do.' Haltingly, she tells Zinda about Sydän, about Venus and the pellegrini; her long journey with the thief and *Perhonen*. And the All-Defector. It gets easier as she speaks, and it takes a long time. When she finally runs out of words, there is faint rosy soletta-light glinting in the infinitely distant horizon of the Strip.

'I understand if you have to share all that with the Great Game,' Mieli says, after a while.

Zinda hugs her bare knees and looks at Mieli. 'I won't, if you don't want me to. I'll leave the zoku, if I have to.'

'I can't ask you to do that.'

'Of course you can.'

Zinda stares at the river water, weighing her pearly Great Game jewel in her hand. Then she squeezes her eyes shut. 'Shit, shit, shit,' she whispers.

'What is it?' Mieli touches her shoulder. 'Tell me.'

'I'm not sure you would understand.'

'After you listened? Of course I will.'

Zinda smiles a sad smile. 'I know you pretty well, Mieli. I knew you even before we met. And I know you won't like it. But after everything you said, I can't keep you in the dark. You don't like lies, Mieli, you really don't. And like you said, you will never be one of us.'

'I don't understand.'

'I was made for you, Mieli.'

'What?'

'I *told* you about zoku children. We are never born without a purpose. You are mine.' She bites her lip. 'It's not artificial. It's not a mask. It's not a jewel putting thoughts into my head. I want to make you happy and to love you. It's who I *am*.'

Mieli looks at the jewels lying on the ground. They sparkle in the morning light, in many colours. *It was a trap, all a trap.* She stands up.

'I'm sorry, Mieli. But you have to understand, it doesn't make it any different.'

'I thought the Sobornost were cruel,' Mieli says in a cold voice. 'But they have nothing to learn from you. They deserve to have this place, and everything in it.'

She turns her back to the zoku girl and starts walking into the woods.

Mieli walks for a long time. She is naked, except for Sydän's chain, and her zoku jewels, which follow her like a flock of birds. She ignores them, ignores the qupts from Zinda, and keeps walking. Rage and guilt and confusion swirl inside her like the eyestorms of Saturn, until finally she can't bear it and uses her metacortex to filter the emotions out. But that is even worse: there is no room for anything else in her mind, and she is left a blank sheet of paper, a mindless point in motion.

The landscape is changing around her. The party is over, the Circle erased. The building blocks of the world are showing through: the surfaces of rocks and trees are melting back into smooth notchcubes, and after a while, she is the only living thing in a roughly sketched, blocky forest of gunmetal.

What finally stops her is an insistent impulse from her Great Game jewel. *Stay where you are.* She regrets not throwing it into the river, but cannot summon the energy to do it.

Impassively, she stops and waits. A Realmgate pops into being, and Barbicane floats through it, a rotund splash of colour against the grey cubetrees.

'I suppose you want your hat back,' Mieli says, folding her arms.

Barbicane raises his eyebrows, and smiles a little awkwardly. 'My dear, young ladies at parties do what young ladies at parties do! My headgear is hardly the issue here. I do apologise for intruding upon your privacy at a difficult time, but the zoku has an urgent need for your services, and your handler, the lovely Zinda, failed to contact you. I thought my presence would carry more … weight!' He clangs on his brass belly with his heavy gun arm.

Mieli turns away. 'Whatever it is, I'm not interested.' She reaches for her Great Game jewel, ready to throw it away.

'Oh, but I think you will be! I believe you are familiar with a rascal by the name of Jean le Flambeur?'

Mieli stops and looks at Barbicane, eyes wide.

'He is *here*?'

'In a manner of speaking.' Barbicane licks his lips. 'We received a communication from him. He claims that in precisely fifty-seven minutes, he is going to steal a ring of Saturn.'

14

THE THIEF AND THE CLUTTERED SELF

The boy is lying in the hot sand with the sun beating down on his back, thinking about stealing.

The robot moves along the edge of the solar panel fields. It looks like a plastic toy, a camouflage-coloured crab. But there is a bioprocessor inside the cheap shell, and One-Eyed Ijja will pay well for it.

His mouth is dry. The sun is hot enough to peel even his parched neck, and bright lights are starting to flash in his eyes.

Tonight, his mother will come home again, bone-weary, and he won't have anything to show her. Last week, he tried to bum cigarettes from the soldiers in the village, spoke French to them and did magic tricks to make them laugh. But when Tafalkayt found out, she beat him, called him a clown, a no-man who would never be *amenokal*. The memory makes his cheeks burn hotter than the sun.

The soldiers are laughing, smoking next to their low vehicle, just visible beyond the wavering glare of the panel field. He calculates: fifteen steps to the robot, a few moments to open it with the multi-tool he took from Ijja's shop at the souk.

It is as if there is a clock ticking in his head, counting down seconds to the moment when he needs to move. Before he even realises, he is sliding down the slope of the dune. His bare feet barely whisper on the hot soft surface.

He pauses to grab a handful of sand, throws it into the robot's sensors, follows with a spray of paint from a can, watches as it scutters around in a circle. He fumbles with his phone, squints at the screen, presses the app with his thumb. The robot jerks and is still. He starts working on the plastic carapace. It takes all his strength to break off a palm-sized piece with the tool's plier head. The sun glints off the plastic tubes inside, the prize, the thinking bugs that are the crab machine's brain. He only has to stretch out his hand and take it and his mother will smile and all will be well.

'What are you doing, boy?'

He grabs the prize. The sharp plastic edge tears at his hand as he pulls it out. Then he runs. But it is harder to go up the dune than to come down: his feet sink into it like in a nightmare. A hand grabs him by the neck, and he rolls down, right into a circle of towering figures, their faces and rifles black shadows against the stinging sun.

One of the soldiers pulls him up, roughly, a thick man whose face is shaded by blue stubble. He smells of black tobacco and sweat. He backhands the boy, hard, harder than Tafalkayt ever hit him. Something metallic on the man's wrist bangs against his teeth. The boy's brain shakes in his head like an egg yolk.

He begs for him to stop, in French, screaming as loud as he can.

The big man laughs. He kneels next to the boy, grabs his face between his big fingers.

'Goddamn. You are Theo's boy, aren't you?'

Shaking in the man's grip, he nods. He is not supposed to know his father's name, but he'll say anything to stop them from hitting him again.

'Well, boy, your daddy isn't here, so I guess it's up to us to teach you a lesson about stealing.'

The rifle butts come down, on his ribs and arms and back, to the rhythm of laughter and curses, each impact a new crater of pain. After a while, they blend together into white agony.

He is not sure when they stop. He comes to when another repair robot scutters past him. The men are gone, bored of their game. He feels like a ragged doll: the sand beneath his face is black with his blood, and his face is numb and sticky, a puffed-up mask. Pain lances through a rib when he tries to move. It takes a while to sit up: his body wants to curl up and stay down.

He opens his right hand. He is holding the big one's watch, a thick band of metal, silver and precious stones.

And that is the moment he remembers forever: not the prize, but becoming more than he is with a single act. It feels like being born.

He will look for it his whole life: on the other side of the sea, in cities and palaces and other worlds, and beyond. He won't always find it. There will be times when he will die the death of getting caught. And one day, in a prison cell, he starts to read a book.

The boy becomes a young man with pencil eyebrows and dimpled temples, and weary Peter Lorre eyes. He is dressed in a dinner jacket and a red-lined cape, as if he was on his way to the opera. There is a white flower on his lapel that smells faintly of summer. He is me.

We are standing side by side in a crystal labyrinth, lit by some unseen sun far above. There is a bone-deep chill here, and our breaths steam in the air. There are glass cells on both sides of the narrow, twisting corridor. The light filters through their walls and makes dazzling rainbow patterns on the smooth mirrored floor. Inside each cell is a wax figure of me, as a young man, as an old man, with zoku jewels around my head. Each cell is framed in cast iron wrought in the shape of flowers and birds, and has a label written in old-fashioned cursive lettering: the design reminds me of the Paris metro entrances. The door to the cell behind me is open, and a rush of heat and desert wind blows out from it. The label above it reads THE BEGINNING.

It reminds me far too much of the Dilemma Prison.

The other me smiles, walks past me and closes the door behind me. Then he gestures at the glass labyrinth with a white-gloved hand.

'Well,' he says. 'Here we are. All of us.'

I follow the other me down the corridors of the crystal gallery of my selves. He hums to himself as he walks.

'Here,' he says, finally, pointing to another cell. The label above it says THE END. He takes out a small golden key, inserts it into the iron lock of the glass door and opens it. 'This is mine. We will be a bit more comfortable here. The Gallery is far too cluttered. But that is really the point of you being here, isn't it? Time for spring cleaning.'

Inside is a small table and two heavy mahogany chairs, facing each other. He points at one of them.

'Please. Sit.'

I sit down carefully, watching him. The environment does not feel like a vir or a Realm, and as far as I can tell, everything is solid and real. I can't feel the interface of the *Leblanc*. There is an uncomfortable pricking in my neck.

'Any traps I should be worried about?' I ask. 'And if you want to play games, I didn't bring my gun.'

'Oh no,' he says. 'No games. No guns. Not anymore. Not here. Just the truth.' He leans back in his chair, smiling. 'First of all, Jean – I take it I may call you Jean – congratulations! You are the first of us to make it here. It's quite an achievement.'

I raise an eyebrow.

'Second, please note that I am not a full gogol like you – just a partial, a sketch, with limited autonomy. I may not be able to answer all your questions. I certainly cannot help you with any pressing problems you might have – which I believe include a rather strong-willed young man whom I spoke to briefly when he first entered this ship. He was very intent on exploiting every single vulnerability he could find in our systems, so I thought it best to have some words with him.'

'Yes, thank you very much for that. Very helpful.'

'Oh, but I had to give you a hint of some kind, didn't I? Is he part of a plan to steal the Kaminari jewel from Matjek Chen? If so, I might as well tell you that you are wasting your time. Chen does not have it.'

'Hm,' I say. 'I was wondering about that.' I review the memories I got from the sumanguru on how Chen got his hands on the Kaminari jewel. With the wisdom of hindsight, there is something decidedly fishy about the whole thing.

'The zoku gave up the jewel far too easily. Almost like the chens were meant to find it. It has the Great Game Zoku written all over it.'

'Precisely.'

'But how do we know he doesn't have it?' I ask myself.

He smiles a familiar smile. 'Well, I tried to steal it from him, of course. It turned out to be a booby trap. A nasty viral thing that would have taken out the whole chen copyclan. The Great Game do not kid around. I was almost surprised it wasn't an exploding cigar, or a poisoned diving suit.' He sighs. 'Nothing ever changes. I kept the fake as a memento, as a reminder of that. It should be lying around here, somewhere. Just to keep things civilised, I left a replacement in its place – with a calling card, of course.'

'Well, that would have been useful to know. You know, before I spent several months and lost friends trying to *steal* your calling card.'

He waves a hand at me. 'Calm down, calm down. I could not tell you anything before you got rid of Joséphine. You are here now, that's all that matters.'

'So, what about the real jewel? I take it that the Great Game has it?'

'*Now* we are getting somewhere,' he says.

'After trying my luck with Chen, I went after the real thing. And yes, the Great Game have it, unless they have done something spectacularly stupid recently. I'll spare you the details. I found it. I just had to stretch out my hand and take it. Except—' His eyes are far away.

'Except what?'

'It didn't *accept* me.' He removes his gloves, closes his eyes and squeezes the bridge of his nose. 'It was frustrating. To hold a piece of thinking spacetime in your hands, and then it—'

He makes a small sound, halfway between a laugh and a sob. Then he shakes his head.

'Anyway. Doesn't matter. But the Kaminari really did it.

They figured out what caused the Collapse. A hidden non-linearity in quantum mechanics itself that manifests when your entangled states get large enough. In the case of the Collapse, it was quite literally a global wavefunction collapse, a sudden decoherence of the whole system into a definite state.'

'A decoherence that *we* caused,' I point out. 'How? And why?'

'Oh yes, you were curious about that,' the other me says eagerly. 'One of my functions is to provide you with information. Here is some recent work by our esteemed collaborator, Professor Zhu Wei.' He pulls a pile of papers from his pocket and places them on the table. The heading on the sheet on top says THE BREAKDOWN OF LINEARITY IN LARGE-SCALE ENTANGLEMENT DISTILLATION FOR MULTI-AGENT SYSTEM COORDINATION. I pick them up carefully. 'You may not want to look too carefully into how we obtained this,' the partial says. 'The same goes for the why.

'In any case, the Kaminari used the same nonlinearity in a different way: to crack the Planck locks. They formed a huge, System-wide temporary zoku to do it, like the old story of all the guilds fighting the Sleeper together. The Great Game tried to intervene, but they only managed to cause some pyrotechnics. The Kaminari went God knows where and left behind one entanglement jewel. It works like the rest of them do: you tell it what you want and it asks the zoku.' He sighs.

'Except it doesn't *give* you what you want. I think the damn thing actually computes the Universe's coherent extrapolated volition. Trust a zoku to take a bizarre concept like that, and make it reality. *I'll give what you would want if you were wiser and stronger and smarter and better? Oh, and by the way, it has to be in the interests of the entire Universe.* In other words, what you would want if you weren't you anymore.'

I close my eyes. Domino pieces are falling into place in my head, tracing a shape in a cascade of clicks, and I don't like the way it looks.

'So you decided to become someone else.'

'Yes. You.'

He gets up. 'You know, I can't do this without a drink. It's like Isaac said: it's not the chemicals, it's the meme. Besides, I'm hoping we'll have a few things to drink to, before we are done. Whisky?' He produces two small glasses and a gentleman's flask from his pocket, puts them on the table and pours. 'There is a zoku called the Society: they get pretty obsessive about these things. They simulated an entire parallel biosphere to produce this.' He smells one of the glasses. 'Fortunately for us, they are better at distilling their whisky than at guarding it. It's unique, of course. Quantum information, no-clone theorem, all that.'

I pick mine up and smell it: smoky, vanilla, and something deceptively candy-flavoured.

'Why?' I ask.

'Well, I do think it's rather interesting to drink a substance that combines flavours that never even existed on Earth, that don't even have names, that you need a billion-year atomic-level quantum simulation to even conceive.'

'That's not what I mean. Why change?'

He spreads his arms and smiles, sadly.

'I was tired. I had been tired for a long time. Worn thin. Too many names, too many crimes. Some of them started to weigh down a bit.'

'It was about Joséphine, wasn't it? It was always about her.'

He ignores me, sips his drink and closes his eyes. 'Vanilla. Tar. A hint of rosemary. Something a bit like a superposition of chocolate and charcoal. Something I don't have a name for, but I imagine it's a bit like liquid love. And, of course, a hint of guilt.' He tosses the contents of the glass back, sighs and pours more. 'You know, I didn't think it would be such an emotional moment, but it is. To see you here, finally. I mean, it has only been an eyeblink for me, but still. To feel hope again. To know one's death meant something.'

'What did you do?'

'What has dying always meant for us? Getting caught. I pretended to go after Chen again, just clumsily enough that he would catch me. And I made sure Joséphine would have reasons to get me out, gave her a template of myself to find from the billion variations in the Prison.'

I bow my head and squeeze my head between my fists.

'You went to the Prison on *purpose*? Are you *insane*? Do you have *any idea* what it was like?'

He shakes his head. 'Only in theory, I'm afraid. That was the point. But I'm hoping it will have been worth it for you.'

I throw my glass against the wall. It shatters, and the amber liquid pours down the crystal surface.

'What do you mean, you bastard? *Nothing* is worth it!'

He looks at the shards and shakes his head. A second later, the tiny fragments rise to the air, a tiny galaxy of crystal, and reassemble themselves back into the glass in my hand. Only the whisky is gone. 'The Gallery tries to keep things the way they are, so your temper tantrums will have little effect, I'm afraid. Except for the waste of a good drink. Oh well. Easy come, easy go.'

I roll my eyes. 'So are you telling me that you went to the Dilemma Prison to become a *better person*?'

'No, just different. But there are things we were never very good at. Altruism, compassion, cooperation. Or regret. I bet you've regretted past mistakes, tried to make up for them.'

'But I *haven't*—'

'It doesn't matter, as long as you tried. The template I gave Joséphine wasn't *me*, precisely. Evolutionary algorithms are still one of the best ways to create new things. If you are here, if the book let you in, you are the best approximation of me – as far as I can tell – that the jewel might actually accept.'

He takes a deep breath. 'There is one more job to do, Jean. A theft to end all thefts. Show them all. Steal the fire of the gods when it's right under their noses. I will tell you how. And then – *change things*. The Sobornost clings to immortality that turns souls into cogs in a machine. The zoku get lost in silly games and Realms that lead nowhere. Chen always had a point. We don't have to accept the way things are. We don't have to do the same things, over and over and over.'

He smiles. 'And don't you just *hate* all those damn locks? Some bastard, a long time ago, made this Universe into a prison. I would imagine that you, of all people, would have a problem with that. What do you say?'

I sit down. I look at him, like looking into a mirror, only not. It burns in him, the sheer *wanting*, the fierce hunger of the boy in the desert. I can feel it on my face, too.

I remember *Perhonen*. *What are you going to do when this is over?* the ship asked me once. I think of Mieli, and Matjek.

Who have I been kidding? It's never going to be over.

'All right,' I say. 'I'm in.'

He clasps his hands together and grins. 'Excellent! Let's seal it with a drink.'

We clink glasses.

'Here's to being Prometheus,' he says.

'That sort of thing,' I say, nodding.

We drink. He is right: there is a warm undercurrent in the whisky that tickles the throat and makes you want to laugh. And an afterglow that settles into a heavy feeling in the bottom of your stomach. But that's not all: something else passes into me with the complex quantum information that encodes the taste, a liquid key. Then the *Leblanc* is back in my head, with Prime authorisation this time. I can see the firmament underlying the Gallery, software cages for past sins.

'That's better, isn't it?' he says.

I nod and place the glass back on the table, stretching.

'Much better. Thank you.'

'Now, do you want to hear what the plan is?' He smiles conspiratorially.

'No.' I wink at him.

Then I punch him in the face as hard as I can.

It's not much of a blow. It glances off the underside of his jaw, and the impact of bone on bone jars my hand painfully. But it is quite satisfying to watch him fall down, eyes rolling in his head. I take the bottle of whisky from the table and walk to the door.

He looks up at me, genuinely astonished, rubbing his jaw. 'What the hell was that for?'

'For a lot of things. We're done here. I just played along to get the *Leblanc* back. I do have one last job to do, but it's not yours. I'm going to save Mieli, pay my debts, and then it is over. No more Jean le Flambeur.'

'You don't know what you are saying. You are not *that* different from me. That's just a story you have told yourself.

The only way to escape the desert is to turn it into a garden. Trust me.'

'Not trusting myself was a lesson I learned pretty well in the Dilemma Prison.'

He gets up, slowly, face dark with anger now. 'Do you really think you can just walk away? I have protocols for scenarios like this. You are not the only le Flambeur out there. There are plenty more in the Prison.' A shudder goes through the *Leblanc*'s systems: a sudden conflict with access rights. The partial me is attempting to regain its control of the ship. *That's not good. The Ganimard-zoku can't be far behind.*

'There is always a way out,' I quote myself.

'Not always,' he says with a sad smile.

I grin and hold up the small golden key I stole from him when I smashed my glass.

'Touché,' I say. 'Goodbye.'

'Wait!'

I slam the glass door in his face and turn the key. It makes a small, final click in the lock. The glass frosts, and the other me becomes a statue, hands pressed against the door, mouth open to say words I no longer want to hear.

I stand in the Gallery, looking at the endless rows of frozen statues. I think about the other me – not the partial, the Prime who died to become me. What could have been so bad that he decided to become somebody else?

Here we are. All of us.

I could find out. All that I ever was that I thought was worth saving, past selves and identities, they are here, put in boxes like old letters that you can't bring yourself to throw away.

217

I close my eyes. *He was right about one thing. It is time for a spring cleaning.*

I reach out my hands and mind to the *Leblanc*, and close the Gallery around me. I hold it in my lap. There is sunlight on my face again. The world is rocking, gently. There are screams of birds, and the soft, endless sound of the sea.

'What is it that you are reading, Monsieur d'Andrezy?' asks a female voice.

I blink, remove my sunglasses and squint at Miss Nellie Underdown, who is looking at me from beneath a white parasol with her great dark eyes, smiling. 'It's just that you seem so terrifically engrossed in it, I should want to read it after you. One does get bored on this long voyage, you know!'

'Oh, it's nothing.' I get up and give her a slight bow. 'Just a collection of rather weak detective stories. I could not finish it, in fact, and cannot in all honesty recommend it to you. But if you wish to be entertained, I am, of course, at your service.' I offer her my arm. 'How about a walk to the upper decks?'

She smiles demurely and hooks her small arm into mine. Later, standing in the bow of the ship, I make her gasp by throwing the book far into the sea. Its pages flutter like wings as it goes, and then it is lost in the foam of the *Provence*'s wake.

15

MIELI AND PROMETHEUS

The thief looks at Mieli. He looks younger than she remembers: his hair is thicker and jet-black, his eyebrows charcoal-dark. But his eyes and his arrogant smile are the same.

'Dear friend,' he says. 'I am Jean le Flambeur. I steal things. Maybe you don't remember me. I have been away a long time.'

'Jean?' she asks, in spite of herself. Her heart pounds. *If he made it, maybe* Perhonen *did, too.* She bites her lip. It is too early to give in to false hopes. The sting of Zinda's betrayal is too fresh in her mind for her to have any confidence in the Universe.

The thief raises his eyebrows. 'I'm afraid you have me at a disadvantage!'

Of course. It's just a partial, not a full gogol, just a conversation tree with a few neural states for colour. Mieli wraps her freshly fabbed toga tighter around her, suddenly self-conscious. Barbicane is looking at her thoughtfully. They are in a featureless grey room in the Invisible Realm of the Great Game, and the Elder looks just as out of place as she does.

It feels like only the thief belongs there, in his minimalistic white suit, leaning back in the metal chair.

'Never mind,' she tells it. 'Go on.'

'I freely admit I have a lot of catching up to do, especially when it comes to making the acquaintance of charming ladies. The fault is all mine.' He leans forward towards Mieli. 'To make it *very* clear to the entire System, I am going to demonstrate what I do. A comeback with a splash, if you will, as I already told your colleagues. Any signal boost would be much appreciated – I don't want anyone to miss it!'

He looks at a large silver watch on his wrist and taps it with a deft forefinger. 'In approximately fifty-six minutes, baseline time, I am going to steal all the quantum information stored in the F-ring of this planet.'

Mieli looks at Barbicane. 'What does he mean?'

'An excellent question!' the thief-partial says. 'You will have to ask your friends at the Gringotts-Zoku if you want a full answer to that one. But to put it briefly, no self-respecting zoku member wants to carry *all* their zoku jewels around all the time – a bit incovenient without Bags of Holding. And in case of wars, accidents and such, you want to keep at least a part of your q-self stashed away somewhere safe, so that if the Reaper visits, you don't have to start again as the quantum equivalent of a level one kobold.' He sighs.

Mieli frowns. *He doesn't seem like himself. There is some hidden purpose behind this.* But the thief she knows is only the latest chapter in his long life, and flamboyant announcements of upcoming crimes are something that the Jean le Flambeur of times past was well known for.

'Apparently, one hot jewel banking trend these days is that sufficiently advanced technology should be indistinguishable from nature. So if you want really long-term storage, you make your quantum memory look like natural objects. The rings are a good candidate. Introduce some rubidium impurities into the icy bodies there, couple them to the magnetosphere of Saturn, and you have a natural setting for quantum information storage. Hard vacuum, cold temperatures – a bit retro, but much more long-lived than the warm wet synthbio components the routers use. The F-ring has a few petaqubits of zoku data, mostly relating to Supra City infrastructure zokus, as I understand.'

The thief looks at Mieli from behind steepled fingers. 'I am going to take it all.' He glances at his watch again. 'In fifty-six minutes! We're in a fast-time Realm, I see. Very clever.' He looks around. 'Is that why the setting is so pedestrian? Or is it just traditional? Is one of you the bad cop?' He leans towards Mieli again. 'Is it you? You are far too beautiful to be the bad cop.'

Mieli narrows her eyes. 'You have no idea,' she says.

'Ooh! Now I'm intrigued! At least it sounds like we have time to get to know each other. And by all means, think as hard as you can. It won't help you.'

'Why are you doing this?' Mieli asks.

'Why does a scorpion sting? It's in my nature!' He purses his lips. 'But yes, I know, *property*! How pedestrian, Jean!' He winks at Mieli. 'Well to be completely honest, this whole thing is a farewell gig. I have decided to retire after this one last job, and this little planet of yours caught my eye – Saturn is the god of old age, after all. And *Jean le Flambeur, King of Saturn* has a nice ring to it, don't you think?'

Mieli turns to Barbicane.

'What are you – we – doing about this?' She glances at the partial. It is smiling impassively, and giving her a lewd look she does not care for at all. 'I take it can't eavesdrop?'

'No, we are in a sandbox here – nothing gets out.' Barbicane plays with the coarse red hairs of his sideburns, braiding them with the tiny golden fingers of his manipulator arm.

'My dear, the problem is not so much the nature of his crime, but certain information we believe he has in his possession. That is the reason we are involved. Please go on, my villainous friend.'

'Thank you,' the thief says. 'You are far more polite than most of the people I have been speaking to. And your sandbox is hardly secure, by the way. Well, if you are a three-year-old child, perhaps—'

'Please,' Barbicane says, exasperated.

'Just pointing out obvious facts! And speaking of obvious, I know what you must be thinking. You are zoku – distributed quantum minds with billions of members! What is to stop you from forming a dedicated detective zoku to apprehend Jean le Flambeur, that mischief-maker, and just throwing enough jewelled sleuths at the problem until you catch me?'

The thief inspects his fingernails. 'How did it work out for you last time, Barbicane?'

Mieli takes a deep breath. In a way, the purpose radiating from the Great Game jewel and a touch of her old irritation at the thief make her feel clear-headed. *Perhaps this is an opportunity*, she thinks. *If I provide useful information to the Great Game, I can get closer to the Kaminari jewel again.*

But it means betraying the thief.

The thought makes her gut wrench. *We had our differences, but we fought side by side. This place deserves every misery he can serve them. Is it really even him, or some other copy from the Dilemma Prison?*

Or – is he still working for the pellegrini? He must be after the Kaminari jewel. He knows they have it. Then this is a distraction. I can reveal anything that does not compromise the true goal. It might even help him.

How do I get a message to him?

She looks at the partial. It is tapping at the surface of the table now with its fingers in an annoying irregular rhythm.

'Young lady, you seem thoughtful,' Barbicane says. 'It goes without saying that anything you can share with the zoku about your experiences with young le Flambeur here would be much appreciated.' The zoku Elder's expression is grim. The jolly gentleman is gone, and only something much harder and older and colder remains.

He lowers his voice. 'Let us be grown-ups here. We are aware of your background, Mieli. We offered you an opportunity to start again. Your quantum self is all that matters to us. If you feel any misplaced loyalty towards le Flambeur, I suggest you discard it quickly. You have formed your own zoku here already. There are people here who care for you. Do you want him to destroy all that?'

Barbicane hovers up from his chair and floats next to the thief-partial. It looks at him curiously, with uncharacteristic, infinite patience.

'Let me tell you something about le Flambeur. You may think you know him, but you don't. He will charm you. He will wear whatever face he needs to get what he wants. I knew him, when I was young and foolish, and he did that to me. But when the time comes, you are just another tool to him, to be used and discarded when you have served your purpose.

'When he disappeared, I thought his sins had caught up with him, or that he had finally abandoned his profession.

He reappeared a few days ago. He came to my old primary zoku, the Gun Club, in disguise, to steal an old ship of his. Making it was one of those youthful follies I regret. Making his escape, he killed one of the younger Gun Club members, a girl called Chekhova, not much older than you. A truedeath: all her jewels were destroyed with her mind. She got in his way.' He leans closer to the partial. 'I don't think you can hear me, le Flambeur,' he says, 'but if you can, you are not going to get away with *that*.'

He presses his gun arm against the partial's head. There is a boom and a white flash, and the dull wet thump of falling simulated flesh.

Barbicane takes a deep breath. 'Excuse me,' he says. 'I feel a little better now.' He extends his manipulator arm to Mieli. 'Shall we go and talk to the rest of the zoku now?'

In the Invisible Realm, fifty-six minutes is a long time. Mieli was expecting something like the battlespace virs of Sobornost, direct sensory awareness of vast and complex systems, a hub of coordination and control. Instead, it resembles nothing as much as a vast board game, played with thoughts; an endless black space, where colourful beads joined by silver string form a labyrinth of threads. She can zoom in to each of them with a thought, receive a qupt of the most recent thought in the chain, contribute her own insights, routed to where they matter the most by quantum coordination algorithms. It feels like being inside a vast song.

She picks a thread at random.

—**Purpose**. Lenormand of the Ganimard-zoku, devoted to the meme of crime in the posthuman context. **What is his purpose, really? I do not believe this is the real le Flambeur** but a work of conceptual art created by an as yet unidentified zoku—

—Conceptual art: our Martian agents have indicated that le Flambeur under the alias of Paul Sernine has a history of conceptual art—

Mieli feels lost in the torrent of thought, tells her gogols and metacortex to condense it as much as possible. The Realm allows her to glimpse the entire history of the zoku's thought-web at will, and the current threads are thin and frayed compared to the vast, shining tapestries of the past.

She turns her attention back to the thread she was following. *I do need to contribute. Barbicane is watching me.* She looks for a connection and casts the first thought that comes into her mind into the mix. Other minds seize it immediately and devour it.

—Paul Sernine – in his case, the conceptual artwork was created to conceal stored quantum information—

She feels a pleasant tingle from her Great Game jewel: the contribution is successful, and she is rewarded with a modicum of entanglement.

—Stored quantum information: it would make perfect sense, he would find the Gringotts F-Ring project fascinating—

—F-Ring: Schroederian tech, with the goal of making a long-lived storage mechanism indistinguishable from nature. Possible connections to the Fermi Paradox spam zokus—

The thread branches into involved speculation about the nature of the Fermi Paradox, and if the absence of any visible alien life has anything to do with the thief is attempting to do. Mieli traverses back along the thought-beads, chooses one that actually provides more information about the ring itself.

—The F-Ring: what are the likely physical mechanisms for actually carrying out the theft? The ring has little distributed hardware. The primary retrieval mechanisms are on Pandora and Prometheus—

—Prometheus, Mieli qupts instinctively. **Stealer of fire. Prometheus means something to him.** *Being Prometheus, that sort of thing.*

—**Prometheus. A thematic connection, a common feature of le Flambeur crimes.** The sharp cool joy of more entanglement, like fruit juice on a hot day.

—**Put an agent there. Someone who knows him. Me.** She attempts to weave her volition to that of the zoku, push at it with all her new-found entanglement. *I need to at least try to get a message to him. And find out about* Perhonen. A flash of anger comes when she thinks about the last moments on the ship, staring down the thief and the pellegrini both. *They are alike. Barbicane was right. They will do whatever is necessary to get what they want. But I need to know what happened.*

A flash of insight comes directly from her zoku jewel. A compulsion to be on Prometheus, as soon as possible.

The jewel is pulling her away, filling her mind with the need to allocate her resources to best serve the zoku. She fights it with her metacortex, tries to reach out to the bead game, to find at least a hint of the Kaminari jewel. Sensing her will, the zoku sends her a thread fragment.

Should we reconsider it?

To expose it to an individual's volition? Never. And the resources required to access it would be prohibitive, especially in the case of invasion.

Resources: a better way required to transfer information between branes. Spooky-zoku has been harvesting dark matter particles entangled with the Planck brane, required

for superdense inter-brane communication. The original jewel storage operation exhausted all the resources so far, but a new collection has been assembled at—

A personal qupt comes directly from Barbicane, and she pulls hastily away. The severed thread scatters random thoughts in her mind, like a rubber band, snapping at her painfully. *A flash of the sheet of light, far away and close.*

Mieli? A word, if you please, the Great Game Elder says.

Barbicane smiles at Mieli, his mouth a waxy line.

'I noticed what you were doing, my dear,' he says. 'I do need to remind you that a decision on the subject of the Kaminari jewel has already been made, and the zoku volition will not allow it to be used. You will see what I mean if you try to pursue that line of thought further.'

'But—' Mieli starts to protest. Barbicane holds up his manipulator hand.

'Bear with me, my dear. I was not finished. Perhaps you do not take me seriously. Perhaps you laugh at the body I wear, at the Circles I choose. I do it because I celebrate what I lost. You of all people should understand.

'I was a soldier, in the Fedorovist War. I believed I was protecting my people, fighting for my comrades. And then the Collapse came. Everything breaking. Chaos. An enemy we could not fight. All because of a tiny quantum effect we could not anticipate. Because we made a thing that was bigger than us.

'Mieli, I think you know what it feels like when the world you love suddenly lurches and turns into something utterly alien, into something you never knew at all. You of all people should want to prevent that from happening to anyone else.

'That is where my love of guns comes from, you see. Guns

are predictable. Guns make sense. In a gun, you channel the destruction. You aim it. You make it do work. Or you use it as a threat, to maintain balance. With things like the Kaminari jewel, you can't. To think otherwise is folly.

'Le Flambeur is the same. When I was younger, I thought he could be aimed and controlled. We used him to attack a Sobornost sunlifter mine. The operation succeeded – but he used the mine for his own purposes. And now his scheme has brought the Sobornost upon us.

'The Great Game's purpose is to remove elements of chaos. Today, le Flambeur is one of them, just like the jewel. Do you understand?'

Slowly, Mieli nods.

Barbicane smiles. 'Capital! In that case, my dear, we both have work to do!'

Prometheus.

The rings are a tilted mirror sea, glinting razor blades with dark gaps between them. Saturn itself is a vast sunrise that fills the sky. A silvery spiral of aurora borealis gleams near its south pole. The interwoven threads of Supra City's Strips and the larger hexagonal blue-and-white shapes of the Plates are like a harlequin mask on the giant planet's face.

She clings to the surface of Prometheus. The moon's twin, Pandora, is a clumpy shape in the distance, nearly motion-less, synchronised to the orbit of its brother, its partner in shepherding Saturn's outermost ring.

Prometheus itself is subtly alive beneath her. On the sur-face, it looks just like a lifeless moon, elongated in shape, with large craters, barely enough gravity to hold her down. But in the spimescape, Mieli can see the hidden interfaces to the picotech embedded in the moon's atoms, designed to last for aeons. When Supra City itself is gone, Saturn will survive – and the zoku legacy will be hidden inside it, there for some unimaginable archaeologist to discover in the distant future.

It is not just the moon that is seething with hidden activity. The space around Prometheus is full of metacloaked Great Game and Ganimard-zoku ships. Even though Mieli does not want to admit it, there is something satisfying about how during an operation, the zoku fulfils even her unconscious wishes. She is heavily armed, with an array of q-guns and a rather satisfying replica of a Sobornost multipurpose cannon.

Five minutes left to the thief's deadline. Even without her enhancements or spimescape, she can see the F-ring itself in greater detail now, a twisting, kinked string of ice and dust.

The wait has been long: she has spent much of it in quick-time, engaged in collaborative planning with Lenormand of the Ganimard-zoku, mapping out the space of possible trajectories that could intersect with the F-ring. The Great Game agrees that to actually retrieve any quantum information from the rubidium atoms scattered around the ring's icy objects, the thief will require access to the hardware on Pandora and Prometheus. The Gringotts-zoku is spinning further layers of cryptography around the data retrieval systems. Watching the entire circumference of the ring is difficult, but not impossible. With the resources the zoku has deployed, any attempted theft seems like madness.

Waiting. Always waiting. She allows herself to wonder what Zinda is doing, and regrets it immediately: even a fleeting thought of the zoku girl makes the wound inside her chest bleed something bitter and black. She almost tells her metacortex to extinguish the feeling, but decides against it. She needs to stay sharp, now more than ever. It will be walking on a razor edge: appearing as if she is acting in the best interests of the zoku, making sure the thief is not captured, sending him a message if possible. *Damn you, Jean. What are you doing?*

Three minutes. Prometheus is swinging closer to the F-ring. Its gravitational field sends a wave through the white weave of ice, makes it twist and dance. After a moment, Pandora follows, right behind its twin, adding its own smooth ripple to the ring's movement.

One minute.

Perhaps it is a trick. Perhaps the real crime is happening somewhere else.

There is a sudden shiver in the F-ring that is not due to Pandora or Prometheus. Mieli's systems, linked to the Great Game, find solutions to the inverse problem, look for gravitational sources that could explain the anomaly. *That can't be right.* Several huge masses, approaching fast. Seven of them.

Guberniyas. *Not now, not yet. He is working with them. This was all just a distraction.*

The spimescape goes white with zoku chatter. The ripple in the rings grows into a tear. Mieli's systems register something impossibly blue-shifted for an instant.

Then a vast knife slices through Saturn's rings.

There is a wedge-shaped disturbance that plows through the silver bands of F, D, C and B, leaving behind a deformed cut, fraying at the edges, pulling icy bodies behind it. Then, a single flash of light on Saturn's surface.

The Sobornost just hit a Plate with a kinetic weapon, she thinks. *No matter. It's just another level boss, like Zinda said. All of Supra City will join the war zoku.* Already, she can feel a new thread in her q-self, pulling at her will, and she gets ready to flow in the cool stream of the zoku volition, anticipates the heat of battle.

A discontinuity. A flash of a scintillating web, overlaid on the face of Saturn. Then, a sudden emptiness.

It takes her a moment to realise all her zoku jewels are dead, devoid of entanglement. The sudden utter freedom in her head is like falling, naked, from a great height, towards the abyss of Saturn. A great terror rises within her. *Is this what Zinda felt like? And she still did it for me?*

The spimescape fills with the white noise of non-qupt chatter. All quptlinks are broken. All entangled states in zoku jewels have decohered. All zoku – the Great Game and the Ganimard and the Notch and the Evangelion alike – are in utter disarray, their perfect quantum order dissolving into chaos, like melting ice.

And the Sobornost is coming.

What have they done?

The nova of her anger surprises her. She pushes herself off Prometheus on her suit's thrusters. The raions and nano-missiles will be coming soon. She launches autonomous q-dots in a sphere around her to form a defensive perimeter. Something drops a metacloak near her and triggers them almost immediately.

A ship. In quicktime, she has a brief flash of its shape, a blue, elongated droplet of smartmatter, like the petal of a flower. She fires her cannon at it.

The newcomer's EM field grabs her, hard. The 20G acceleration shakes her like a leaf in a hurricane. Prometheus becomes a pinpoint in an instant. *What is it doing?* Through the acceleration strain, she tries to scan the ship, target something she can hurt with the tiny antimatter payload in her cannon. It is pulling her in.

Wait. Wait. She tries to keep her weapon steady. The EM field pulls her closer. Her gogols are making sense of the ship's structure now, a strange zoku-Sobornost hybrid, high-end picotech and a micro-singularity somewhere inside. *Well, this should at least hurt.* She gets ready to fire the antimatter pellet, targets it to burrow into the ship's core. If the Hawking radiation containment breaks, it will take them both, but the fire in Mieli's mind wants something to burn.

Just before she presses the mind-trigger, a qupt comes.

Hello, Mieli. There is something familiar about this. Except this time, you were the one in a prison.

She hesitates for an instant. The EM field pulls her in, and the midnight skin of the ship swallows her.

16

THE THIEF AND MIELI

Mieli appears in the pilot's cabin of the *Leblanc*, just like she does in my fondest memories: wearing a furious expression.

'*You*,' she hisses. She is how I remember her from *Perhonen*, a compact woman in a black toga, her only ornament the jewelled chain around her ankle, a gift from an Oortian lover. The sudden rush of familiarity almost makes me embrace her. Still, I keep my distance: we may be in a Realm under my control, and I was prudent enough to delete her weapons when qupting her into the virtual space inside the ship, but Mieli is still one of the most dangerous individuals I know.

I grin. 'Me. Welcome aboard the *Leblanc*. As you have probably figured out by now, I didn't come here to steal Saturn's ring. I came here to steal *you*. I have a small Great Game jewel, and managed to slip some ideas into the zoku volition, so I could make sure you were somewhere I could find you. In case you had any ideas from someone called Lenormand, that was me. I had a strangelet bomb set up on Pandora as a distraction. Turns out I didn't have to use it, thanks to the exceedingly well-timed Sobornost invasion. Tell me, how does it feel to be free?'

Her hands clench and unclench. Then she moves faster than I can react. A silver filigreed blade shimmers into being in her hand, and then its point is inches away from my eyeball, her other hand firmly around my throat. *Of course. Zoku enhancements. Adapt to Realms. How silly of me to overlook that.*

'Wait,' I gasp.

'What makes you think I want to hear what you have to say? Get me back out there. Right now. I have a war to fight.'

This is going better than I thought. At least I still have a tongue.

'What did they tell you? That you would be free to leave any time? They lie about that, you know. I had to help you. The only way to do it was to break the whole system, to give you back your free will.' My eyes widen. 'Or … don't tell me you are still working for the pellegrini? I didn't see *that* one coming. What happened to the copy in your head, by the way?'

She throws me to the floor. I sit up slowly, massaging my throat.

'She is gone,' Mieli hisses. 'Just like the entire Supra City will be soon. What in the Dark Man's name did you do to the volition system?'

I smile sadly. 'The Spooky-zoku and the Great Game have known about this for some time, but they have worked very hard to keep it a secret. It's the reason why they destroyed Mars. I'll give you the crib notes: the Collapse was caused by quantum mechanics breaking down. It turns out there is a bound for the size of entangled quantum states: create anything bigger than that, and things get even more crazy than usual. The whole zoku quantum jewel system has been teetering close to the boundary a while. So I just gave it a little push.

'You may have noticed that there has been an increase in

the number of spam zokus recently. I have been generating them algorithmically, with Sobornost-derived gogol minds. It's amazing what you can do if you look past ideological differences and combine technologies in creative ways.'

I stagger upright. Mieli is standing with her back turned to me, still opening and closing the fingers of one hand, rotating the Realm-knife in the other.

'As I said, I did not anticipate the invasion. But Mieli, it will be fine, the zoku have dealt with Sobornost before, this is some power move in the civil war, Joséphine getting desperate since her scheme with the jewel went wrong, surely. The zoku are always at their best when pushed into a corner. And what do you care, anyway? Have you gone native? Don't tell me you have. I was going to take you home. They've done too good a job on you, Mieli. We are on our way to Oort, I thought that's what you wanted, *Perhonen* said you missed it.' My voice breaks.

'Shut up, Jean. Don't you *dare* to speak my ship's name,' she says in a thin voice, without turning around. 'And it's not some expeditionary force from a civil war, you idiot. It's the *entire Sobornost*. It's your All-Defector, controlling all of them. It has come for the Kaminari jewel. And you have just served the prize on a platter.'

I feel hollow and fragile, as if I was made of glass. Somewhere, I can hear my other self from the Gallery, laughing. *We are not that different.*

Mieli turns to look at me.

'Why couldn't you die with *her*, you bastard!'

My head spins. *The All-Defector.* I was wondering what Joséphine's backup plan was. I remember facing it in the glass cell of the Dilemma Prison. *The thing that never cooperates and gets away with it.* An anomaly forged in the crucible of endless Dilemma iterations, something the Archons never expected, not so much a gogol as a viral algorithm. It pretended to me, and I trusted it. In a *guberniya*, it would go through Sobornost minds like a scythe through wheat. *And it wants the Kaminari jewel?*

My mistake is so deep I can't even see the bottom.

The Sobornost is going to wipe out Supra City. I took away their only advantage. I remember Sirr, blue and golden, freshly reborn on the Irem Plate. I remember kissing the sisters' hands, how they smelled of henna and perfume. *I betrayed them, again. I broke my promise.*

Am I going to destroy everything I touch?

'No, this not my fault, it must have done something to me, planted an idea about the Wei bound.' I know it's nonsense, but the words come out, and I can't stop. 'It planned everything, ever since we met in the Prison, I could see it in its eyes, like a thinking mirror, it knew I would try to free you.'

The words bounce and shatter in my head, and for the first time in my life I know what it is like to want for the silence and the black that only truedeath brings.

She slaps me. Even in the Realm, it stings. I lean on the control organ of the ship to keep upright. The knife gleams in her other hand, like a promise.

'That's a Realm-knife, Mieli,' I whisper. 'It will work even here. It will hurt me. Why don't you just do it? I deserve it. Come on. It was my fault *Perhonen* died.'

She drops the knife. It bounces off the crystal of the round observation window and makes a tinkling sound.

'No,' she says. 'It was mine.'

*

Mieli stares at the thief. He is pale and shaking. There is grief in his eyes, and a death wish. She has seen that look before, in the mirror.

'I could have stopped all this,' she says slowly. 'If I had let you and the pellegrini go ahead.'

'I doubt it,' the thief says. 'And you were right. We need to draw lines somewhere. The jewel was a fake, and I think All-D would have gotten out anyway. You did the only thing you could.' He sighs. 'Matjek is here. The child chen gogol from the desert. If we survive this, maybe you'd like to meet him.'

She closes her eyes. 'Maybe. I only wish I could have been there, with her, in the end.'

The thief takes a faltering step forward. 'This was the last thing I saw,' he says. 'Please don't kill me yet. She sent you this.'

He kisses her forehead. She sees butterflies, burning, swirling in the form of a face, the ship's face she only saw in the *alinen. Tell her that I love her. Look after her. For me. Promise.*

There is a memory of a kiss on her lips. It tastes of fire and ashes. And then there is only black.

It is the first time I see Mieli cry. I don't dare to touch her. I sit with my hands in my lap.

The abyss in me is still hungry, but at least for a moment, I manage to hang on to its edge.

I summon the cat avatar of the ship and tell it to start decelerating. It's going to take a while: I've engaged the ship's Hawking drive, and we are already well out of Saturnian space. Then I qupt a self-destruct order to my zoku botnet. It may be too late to form a new war zoku, but it won't hurt. Finally, I order the cat to start gathering all the sensory data and chatter it can from the ongoing battle around Saturn.

When I'm done, I realise that Mieli is quiet again.

'We are on our way back,' I say. 'And once my signal gets there, the volition system should be coming back online, too. It will take time: I just hope it's not too late.' I pause. 'I guess we both know what she would say about this.' *That we are both fools. And we need to fix the mistakes we have made.*

Mieli nods and gets up.

'Come on,' I say and offer her my hand. 'We can't do anything more right now. I have a fast-time Realm, so we are not in a hurry. And I think we could both use a drink.'

The thief takes Mieli through a silver gate to a Realm that is a ship – a real ship, an ancient, sea-going vessel, with people in elaborate, heavy clothing. It is the first time she has been in an ocean-going vessel. Usually, planetary surfaces disturb her, but the fresh sea air clears her head a little, and the sound of the sea is soothing. She looks at the foamy line the ship draws in the dark surface of the sea. It is night, and the ship's lights make blurry reflections in the dark water, mirroring the round yellow moon in the velvety sky.

They sit in deck chairs by the railing in the bow of the ship. A man in a white uniform brings them two glasses.

'The best single malt in the Universe, or so I'm told,' the thief says. 'To your health.' His hand is still shaking. He downs half of his drink with one gulp and closes his eyes. Mieli tastes hers carefully. At first, it's just liquor with a smoky overtone, but as she holds it in her mouth, it blooms into something warm, soft and gentle, with a final endnote of a spice she does not recognise.

It mingles with the lingering taste of *Perhonen*'s last kiss.

They drink in silence for a while.

Only an echo of Mieli's anger remains. She feels tired and helpless. She grits her teeth. The thief was right. Supra City may be fighting, but why should she care? She fought the zoku herself, in the past. Surely, it is just the tugging of the quantum chains of the zoku jewels, wrapped around her mind. She sips the strange liquor again.

Zinda didn't have to tell me the truth. But she did. Everyone else has always lied to me.

'So, is this who Jean le Flambeur is, now?' she says aloud, just to brush away the thought. She pauses. 'Did you really truekill someone to steal this ship?'

'What? No! You have been listening to Barbicane, haven't you? There may have been some property damage, but that's all. It was *he* who did it, to protect his cover. He's a callous bastard. I've never been very fond of killing, true or temporary. It's not very elegant.' He looks at Mieli curiously. 'You *have* been busy.'

Mieli shrugs.

'To be honest, I have been thinking of retiring,' the thief says. 'For real, this time. Getting you out was going to be my last job. But it sounds like we are going to have to think of something else now.' He leans forward in his chair. 'What about you? What have you been doing since you fed me to the Hunter?'

Between careful tastes of her drink, Mieli tells the thief her story. When she describes her encounter with the All-Defector and Joséphine's sacrifice, the thief's eyes widen.

'Why would she do that? I know her pretty well, and I would have thought she considers you more expendable than even a low-level gogol of herself.' He looks at Mieli. 'But if she was more afraid of you being taken by All-D than of a copydeath—' He squeezes the bridge of his nose.

'*Perhonen* did tell me your story, you know. No offence, but to me, there was always something strange about the way Sydän led you to Venus, and how you found the pellegrini. As if it was *meant* to happen.

'You see, Joséphine doesn't just find people, she *makes* them. She did that to me, when I was young. She needed an agent she could trust, so she got me out of Santé Prison and moulded me into one.' He looks at the sky and smiles at a distant memory. 'Of course, it did not exactly work out like that, but that's how it started, between us.

'I recently … learned a little about the Kaminari jewel. To get it to accept you, you need to wish for something altruistic *and* something that is constant across your possible future selves. A singular drive, perhaps. Something all-consuming. Like saving someone from a black hole's event horizon.' The thief looks at Mieli. His eyes are bright.

'I think Joséphine needed me to steal the jewel. But she needed you to *use* it. She needed someone who wanted, wanted in a way that the Kaminari jewel would accept. And she did not want her instrument to fall into All-D's hands.'

Mieli stares at the thief.

'That's insane!'

'Is it? But it does lead to conclusions that you might not like. Can I see that chain you wear, the one that your friend Sydän gave you?' He smiles sheepishly. 'I promise not to steal it, this time.'

Frowning, Mieli whispers to her ankle chain, opens it and hands it to the thief. It spirals into the air from his hand and rotates, like the DNA of some strange crystal animal.

'Now, the nice thing about Realms is that they try to

preserve the quantum information contained in anything that's brought in here. It's a good way to study things. I should have had a closer look at this before, but you always made it clear it would not be good for my health.'

A spime opens around the chain, a digital shadow flickering with annotations. The stones in it are simple Oortian smartcoral, made with whispers to resemble the Great Work Mieli and Sydän built, a long time ago. The thief frowns and zooms in. The jewels become first a crystal mountain range, then a grid of interlocking molecules. It looks familiar, and it takes a moment for Mieli to realise why. *Prometheus. It's like the surface of Prometheus. Too regular.*

'Hidden picotech,' the thief says. 'Probably something Joséphine stole from the zoku: she was never too concerned with remaining ideologically pure. Now, you would have to ask your zoku friends what this thing does, but my guess would be that it is some sort of volition analysis engine, like the zoku jewels. *What makes Mieli, daughter of Karhu tick? What does she want?*' The thief sighs. 'Mieli, I hate to say it, but I think your Sydän was working for Joséphine from the day you met her.'

Mieli stands up and grabs the chain. She stares down at the thief, who leans back in his chair, a sad smile on his face. A part of her wants to strike him again, but she has no rage, no strength left.

'You are lying,' she whispers. 'This is a trick. You are trying to—'

'Mieli,' the thief says softly, 'what do you think I am trying to do, exactly? I have nothing to gain from this.' He pauses. 'I'm trying to keep a promise. I'm trying to tell you things you need to hear.'

He looks at his empty glass and gets up. 'Not exactly my strong suit, I know. I'll leave you alone for a while. Come find me in the pilot's cabin when you are done. I'm going to check on how things are going in Supra City.'

Mieli watches him walk away and disappear in a swirl of silver dust. She wraps her toga tighter around her and walks to the railing. The wind has picked up, and jagged glassy waves crash against the ship's sides. She holds the jewelled chain in her hand. *It can't be true.* But a part of her knows it is, a pattern that is as inevitable as the next note in a song. She tries to think of Sydän, but can't hold on to her face. Mieli's thoughts of her dissolve like Sydän's face, erased by the data wind from the singularity on Venus.

Made for a purpose, Zinda said. She thinks of the glowing jewels the zoku girl laid down onto the grass, for Mieli, pieces of herself, one by one. *What a fool I have been.* A sudden longing blooms in her chest. And fear, a memory of the horror on Hektor, the non-face. She imagines it swallowing Saturn.

She squeezes Sydän's chain in her hand so hard the edges of the stones dig into her flesh.

'Kuutar and Ilmatar, not this one,' she whispers, looking at the yellow moon. 'Give me the strength to save her.'

Mieli replaces the chain around her ankle. It is cold from the sea air. *It is good to keep reminders of your mistakes.*

She stands in the bow of the ship for a moment, looking at the horizon. White waves rise and fall against the hull, like beating wings.

It is also good to finally know where she is going.

She whispers one last prayer to the moon and goes to find the thief.

*

I recognise a certain look on Mieli's face when she returns. The last time I saw it was on Earth, when she fought a mercenary army and the wildcode desert by herself.

She says nothing, simply stands next to me and studies the spimescape, the hopeless tangle trying to represent millions of raions and zoku ships around Saturn. At least the *guberniyas* are obvious: all seven of them, positioned in Lagrange points, armed and dangerous, as only planet-sized zeusbrains can be.

'It is difficult to tell what is going on. The particle storm is too dense, and I can't access the Great Game intelligence network. But there is a lot of structural damage to Supra City.' I swallow, thinking of Sirr on Irem. 'A lot of strangelet events, a couple of Hawking blasts, nothing bigger than that yet. But it's only a matter of time.'

Mieli narrows her eyes.

'Here is what we are going to do,' she says. 'We are going to get to the Kaminari jewel before the All-Defector does. We are going to steal it from the Great Game Zoku. And then we are going to put things right.'

I smile. 'Well, that's a thought.' *Stealing the fire of the gods, that sort of thing.* 'Are you sure the Great Game won't use it?'

'I'm sure.'

'Do you know where it is?'

Mieli frowns. 'I … heard something in the Great Game's Realm. They talked about a Planck brane.'

I take a deep breath. 'Oh my. They've hidden it in *a parallel universe.*'

I should have let my other self tell me his plan. Mental note: never interrupt a villain who is monologuing.

I grit my teeth. If he could come up with it, so can I. I massage my temples.

The Planck brane. Of course. The ekpyrotic cannon. The idea leads to others, like dominoes falling.

I turn to Mieli. 'All right, I have a plan. Step one is to persuade the Father of Dragons to stop sulking.'

Mieli raises her eyebrows. 'And step two?'

'You'll see. We may have to destroy Saturn in order to save it.' I get up. 'Come on. I'm going to introduce you to Matjek Chen. You've already met, of course, but he has grown up quite a bit since then.'

I take a deep breath in the main corridor. I have been putting of talking to Matjek for a while, but the time has come. And finally, I actually know what to say to him. This time, the bookshop vir opens easily as Mieli and I walk through the gate.

The boy is not sitting in his usual spot. The vir is silent, except for the quiet whisperings of the stories of Sirr.

'Matjek! Where are you? I've brought an old friend to see you.'

There is no answer. I open the admin interface to the vir, make it transparent to my gaze. He is nowhere to be found.

I summon the cat avatar. It appears obediently.

'Where is Matjek Chen?' I ask. It cocks its head and looks at me with its glassy eyes.

'Young Master ran away,' it says in its whirring voice. 'He said to tell you he's gone to find himself.'

I can't suppress a groan. *So, it's Young Master now, is it? I should have kept a closer eye on him.* I access the ship's records of our passage past the F-ring and in the vicinity of the Sobornost fleet. They confirm my suspicions: a thoughtwisp was launched without my knowledge when we were passing the orbit of Rhea.

'Is the copy of the Kaminari jewel the previous Prime acquired still on board?'

'Negative,' the cat says. 'The Young Master took it with him.'

I close my eyes and press both fists against my forehead, hard. 'Shit. Shit. Shit.'

'What is it?' Mieli asks.

'Matjek has gone to kill the Chen-Prime.'

For the past weeks, Matjek has been moving through the *Leblanc*'s systems like a ghost. I review spimescape snapshots, watch him work his way up in the privilege hierarchy, until he has access to the small space where the few physical objects onboard the ship are stored, wrapped in q-dot gel. I watch a smartmatter shell form around the fake Kaminari jewel. He fuses it with a thoughtwisp and launches it – and himself – at just the right moment, when the *Leblanc* is carrying out the high-G manoeuvre of grabbing Mieli.

'Why in the Dark Man's name would he do that?' Mieli asks.

'He found out about what he became when he grew up,' I say. 'Doesn't matter how.' I tell her about the weapon the Great Game planned to use on the chens. 'He has gone to detonate it under Matjek Chen-Prime's ass.'

Mieli shrugs. 'I'm sorry for the boy,' she says. 'But this is war, and if it works, he could save us all a lot of trouble.'

'Except that as you found out, all the higher chens are now infected with All-D. Matjek doesn't know that. And he is just a boy. He is not ready for this.' I close my eyes. 'I'm going after him.'

'What?'

'You are the one who almost got us both killed to protect

245

this boy's innocence, remember?' I try to keep my voice cold. 'Besides, we need him.'

As we speak, I track the trajectory of the thoughtwisp. It went straight at the main body of the Sobornost fleet. Right at the chen *guberniya*. I can launch a faster wisp: I don't have to worry about extra payloads like the fake jewel. Still, he will get there a few seconds before I do. That might as well be an eternity. Even the microseconds in the *Leblanc*'s fast-time vir might make a difference.

'Need him for what?' Mieli asks.

I take a deep breath. 'We need two things to qupt to the Planck brane. One: matter that is entangled with something over there. That will have to be your department. By the sound of it, the Spooky-zoku have something like it. Two: we need a modulated gravitational wave source. We are made of stuff that is stuck on this brane, but gravity sees the higher bulk dimensions. Make a big enough bang and its gravitational echo will carry there.

'The Gun Club Zoku have a device called an ekpyrotic cannon, Matjek and I saw it when we stole the *Leblanc*. Assuming Iapetus is still intact, we will need it. Matjek got into their gunscape virs last time, and I'm certain he left back doors. I don't think we can get in without him, not this time. I managed to piss Barbicane off pretty royally.'

Mieli raises an eyebrow. 'I can relate,' she says, dryly. Then she grows serious. 'Jean, this is the worst plan I have ever heard. You can't go up against the chens and the All-Defector alone. The last time you tried, they caught you. I'll come with you.'

'No,' I say firmly. 'If we don't make it, you will at least have a chance with the zoku. And I have more tricks up my sleeve than last time. You take the *Leblanc* to Saturn, and try to get us some Planck brane entanglement. Matjek and I will meet you there.'

'Very well.' Mieli looks down. 'But how in Dark Man's name am I supposed to get the stuff? I can't just go knocking on the Spooky-Zoku's door.'

I think for a moment. 'I trust you, Mieli. You will find a way. But maybe this will help.' I pass her Isidore's last qupt that contains the Kaminari's message. 'This is the last mystery that Isidore Beautrelet solved. It shows you how to make a viral zoku. Maybe it will help.'

Mieli accepts it, her mouth a line of grim resolve.

'Kuutar and Ilmatar go with you,' she says quietly. 'And Jean? Try to come back. I'm tired of losing friends. And I can't find the words for death-songs anymore.'

I stare at her, astonished. Then I give her a grin. 'I know what you mean. Don't worry. I have a feeling it will be a high roll, this time.'

I take her strong, small hand and squeeze it hard. Her fingers are cold. 'I have been many things, but I have never been an Oortian's friend before. It makes me proud. Take care of yourself, Mieli. It's been fun.'

With that, I pass the admin rights of the *Leblanc* over to her, think a thoughtwisp into being in the ship's mass driver, and launch myself at the Sobornost fleet.

Interlude

THE GODDESS AND THE DEMON

Joséphine waits, sitting on the sand. She lets her metaself soothe her into a timeless state of readiness. Eventually, the pale morning comes, and the All-Defector returns.

She gets up. There are butterflies in in her belly.

The All-Defector is still wearing Matjek's shape, but the grown-up one, now, the monkish countenance and the grey hair. She imagines it striding through the *guberniya* in the glory of its Prime aspect, devouring high-ranking gogols with its mirror maw, sating its appetite.

She smiles at it.

'I am ready,' she says, looking at it like a lover after a long absence. 'You can take me now.'

For a moment, the All-Defector hesitates, looking into her eyes, as if wanting to say something. Then it whispers the Founder Code of Matjek Chen. It rings in the dream-vir like a thunderclap. The demiurges scream and scatter. Briefly, there is a glimpse of the All-Defector's Prime aspect, towering over the vir, seeing everything. The Joséphine-partial crumbles like dry sand and is no more.

'You can come out now, Joséphine,' the All-Defector says.

Joséphine gets up from her hiding place. Her bones feel fragile. Her legs shake.

'A partial with a self-destruct loop hidden inside,' the All-Defector says chidingly. 'That was never going to work.'

'How did you know?'

'Another pellegrini tried a similar trick. You are very predictable, Joséphine. You all are. And that is the problem.'

For a moment, he is her Jean, in a white suit and blue glasses, the one she made the partial to love and adore, and in spite of herself, her breath catches in her throat.

'This is what you wanted, isn't it? A mirror that reflects you perfectly. Well, I am the mirror that becomes. I look at you and make myself into you, know you better than you know yourself.'

'If you are going to torture me,' Joséphine says, 'please do not use philosophy. I thought there was something of him left in you, and I was right. You really are a terrible poet.'

'It's not poetry. It's what I am.'

'Sasha told me what you are,' Joséphine sneers. She imitates the Engineer-of-Souls' lecturing tone of voice. 'A game-theoretic anomaly, a zero-determinant strategy in the Prisoner's Dilemma, an agent that extorts others to do what it wants with a superior theory of mind. Like the Predictor in Newcomb's Paradox. You are running simulations of me, to see what works best.'

'And how do you know you are not one of those simulations? How do you know that anything you do here makes any difference?'

'How do *you* know, you bastard?' she screams at the thing that looks like her Jean but isn't.

The demon tells her. It all seems perfectly rational, perfectly inevitable, as if there was never any choice at all.

17

THE THIEF IN THE GUBERNIYA

In the thoughtwisp, the Universe is tinged with blue. The relativistic distortions turn the unaugmented view of the Sobornost fleet into a tunnel of elongated, azure sparks. I hurtle into it at nearly the speed of light, a mirror flake of thought, pushed by the *Leblanc*'s lasers.

The fleet is vast. Raions fall on Saturn, wave after wave, arranged in perfect crystalline formations that only shatter when they hit the upper reaches of Supra City. Kilometre-long oblast ships engage zoku fleets in fierce combat in the orbit of Phoebe.

A colossal system of mirrors, three million kilometres in diameter – dwarfing the solettas of Supra City – shadows the fleet, manoeuvring into position where it can redirect a beam from the Sobornost's stellar lasers in the Sun. There are Founder faces drawn on the reflector surfaces, larger than even *guberniyas*, watching the battle of Saturn with cold mirror eyes. Another tendril of the zoku fleet is attempting to take them out, but without quantum coordination, they are too slow and clumsy for the nimble raions. I watch them carefully: if the Sobornost can bring the sunbeams into play, the battle could be over very quickly. But at this rate, the mirror deployment will take hours, and by then, I'm hoping the Planck job will be well underway.

And then there are the seven *guberniyas*, the seven devils of the Inner System. Each a diamond sphere ten thousand kilometres in diameter, they are the ultimate embodiments of Sobornost might and technology. As far as I can tell, so far they are sitting still in the Saturnian system's Lagrange points, waiting. *Good. Watch the entertainment. Stay arrogant. We are going to steal the fire of the gods, and then you will burn.*

As I get closer to the core of the fleet, the wisp is bombarded with protocol requests and combat crypto. I brush them aside with my stolen Sumanguru Founder codes, gritting my dream-teeth in the wisp's bodiless vir at the memories of death and decay they bring. The presence of the warlord creates a satisfying ripple of fear in the raion formations I pass through.

I enhance the image of Saturn itself, trying to get a glimpse of the Plate of Irem, but it is a blur through the wisp's feeble optics. The mass streams that support Supra City's structures are being diverted as improvised weapons, lashing at the raion formations. *Hold on a while longer.* I wish I had gods or goddesses left to pray to.

It is not difficult to recognise the Chen *guberniya*: it is adorned with his face. I wonder what Matjek felt when he saw it. As I approach, it is blueshifted into an ovoid that swallows the sky in the thoughtwisp view. The artificial world grabs me with EM fields, decelerates the wisp, allows me a brief glimpse of the godscape of its surface, an endless frieze of Founder sculptures size of mountains, a raion mist pouring from endless fabber pits, a living, shifting, fractal skin of smartmatter, an unliving, immortal ecosystem where every dust particle and raindrop is a gogol.

Then a scan beam flashes, and I'm in.

A bare vir. A white room with a gogol with a barely sketched face, merely a gogol implementation of a communications protocol, meant to filter the contents of an incoming thought-wisp and pass it on to the deeper layers of the *guberniya*.

Today, I have no patience for automated bureaucracy. I flaunt my Sumanguru mindshell, and tear the whole thing down all the way to the firmament, sending the poor gogol scuttering away. I make my own path from there, flattening virs into a long glass-walled corridor, striding onwards, deeper into the guts of the god-world. The trick is to attract just enough attention, but not too much. I can feel countless lower-level non-Founder gogols swarming around me like insects. I raise my voice into Sumanguru's roar.

'The Great Common Task has been compromised! A quantum filth weapon has struck the *guberniya*! Find the impact point and report to me!' Contemptuously, I toss them a spime of Matjek's vessel. They obey instantly, driven by *xiao*, the instinctive respect of Sobornost gogols towards Founders, a metaself that rewrites their perception of reality. I even authorise branching of gogols for this particular task, and in a moment, there are thousands of them, travelling in all directions of the virtual pathways of the *guberniya*.

I find a deeper layer and create a fast-time vir where I can wait. I use just enough cycles to be slightly conspicuous: a grand Sumanguru vir, a simulated continent of Africa fighting the first Fedorovist War. In my warlord form, I smoke a cigar on top of a skyscraper in burning Nairobi, watching my gogol-piloted tiny drone troops rain death down onto the militia below. I flinch at the smell of burning flesh, gun oil and black smoke, but my normally buried Sumanguru part enjoys it. I let a touch of his rage filter through. It will serve me well in the next part.

I do not have to wait for long. The vir freezes, and a chen descends into it. Even my Sumanguru-self feels a flash of *xiao*. *Good*. This one is from Deep Time, from the millennia-old simulations from the deepest layers of the *guberniya*, where time runs fast, no doubt brought closer to the filthy flesh-world for the war effort. He wears the universal monk-ish chen face in a lithe, centipede-like body. What strange evolutionary path has produced it in the deep virs, I don't even want to imagine.

'Brother,' he says, in a voice of irrefutable authority. 'You are violating the Plan. These cycles are better spent to pro-duce further iterations of our brave warminds. The Great Common Task does not tolerate waste.'

I throw my frozen cigar away and grin. 'The Plan has changed. Didn't you get the memo? I am here to carry out my own part of the Task: to find a chen who has been com-promised by a viral invader from the outside.'

A nervous ripple goes through his segmented body.

'Counterintelligence in this layer is my responsibility. There are no compromised gogols here.'

I think carefully at the firmament. When I'm ready, I smile at him, my own grin this time. 'There are now.'

Then I wrap him in the story I got from Axolotl the body thief, and make his mind mine.

I bloom in the chen's mind and discard the Sumanguru mindshell. Fourth generation, Keeper-of-the-August-Dragon branch. *Good*. This gogol is senior enough to have a

Founder aspect. I step into a higher-order vir, look down at the seething fabric of the *guberniya* virs of this layer like god, and speak to their gogols with a divine voice. *Find the impact point of an anomalous thoughtwisp.* Millions of candidate answers come in seconds. I create a vir and evolve a small gogol population to sift through the data according to the parameters I give them. I also lay down the foundations of an escape route. It is always good to have a way out.

Finally, the answer comes. Matjek has been subtle: the wisp has come in as a sample from a science gogol, analysing structure of the F-ring to improve the nanomissile pilot gogols' abilities in the ongoing battle above Saturn. Together with thousands of others, the sample has been physically stored in the upper layers of the *guberniya*, in a smartmatter chamber with an attached vir that allows it to be manipulated. It is a good sign: it means that Matjek hasn't completely figured out how the false jewel works, and needs to study it.

Good. I am not too late.

I step into the firmament and tell it to carry me there.

'Matjek.'

The vir is a stark black space, with the jewel in the middle. It looks like a pair of folded, glowing hands. Matjek is surrounded by a flurry of partials of himself, all manipulating tactile software constructs and networks of graphical zoku language in the air.

For a moment, he stares at me in horror. I realise my mistake and let my features melt back into my own.

'Matjek, this isn't right.'

'What are you doing here?'

'I came to stop you. You don't have to do this. Whatever you are trying to do, it won't even work. Mieli told me—'

'Who cares what she told you! I never wanted to be *this*! Have you seen this place? It's like a giant cancer wearing my face.' His eyes are bright and hard. 'I've almost got this thing figured out. It's meant to be opened by a chen. There is a recursively self-improving algorithm inside. It's meant to overwrite all the data it finds with zeroes. I just need a remote trigger so I can open it from afar.'

I swallow. *A recursively self-improving algorithm.* It sounds an awful lot like a Dragon, only a Dragon that does not recognise a chen as its daddy. I remember that poor Chekhova was working on weapons like that. *Barbicane, what have you done?* There is no telling what the thing will do if Matjek or anybody else lets it loose.

'Matjek, give it to me.'

I search for words. What can I possibly tell him to make him understand?

'No! Get out of here, or you can die with them!'

I take a step forward and grab him by both shoulders. His partials back off. He blurs in my grasp for a moment, trying his time-speedup trick, but this time, I'm ready, and I have a Chen Founder code. He stares at my face, defiantly. *He has never grown up. His parents were a distracted quantum trader and a beemee star. He was so lonely that his only friends were imaginary, and he made them real.*

And he is being an insufferable brat.

'Matjek Chen!' I say firmly. 'You stop playing with that doomsday weapon *right now* and listen to me!'

He blinks, astonished, and suddenly I'm sure that no one has ever used that tone with him before.

'You don't have a right to hurt people just because you don't *like* them. Not even if they are you. I know you don't really know what truedeath is, and I hope you don't have to find out very soon. But you don't want to inflict that on anybody, not unless there is no other way to protect others. Like your mum and dad wanted to protect you. But if you do this, you become the opposite of that. Something much worse than this evil Matjek Chen of the future you hate so much.

'Trust me, I know about hating myself. But this is not going to fix things. It won't make you feel better. You want to hurt the other Matjek, the old Matjek?' I let my face flicker into his stern visage for a moment. '*Do something he would never do.* Help me to help people who are dying out there, dying truedeaths, not like in your games, dying and never coming back. Help me to take away what he wants. It's not *dying* that hurts him, Matjek. It's *losing.*'

He looks up at me. There are tears streaming down his face.

'I just want my mum and dad,' he says in a small, choked voice.

I squeeze him tight for a moment, unsure what to do. He grabs my neck with surprisingly strong arms and clings onto me. It takes a while before he lets go.

I smile at him, and suddenly I'm all out of words.

'Can we go home now?' he asks.

I take the false jewel spime carefully.

'Yes,' I say. 'But we still have work to do, and I will need your help.'

'All right,' he says, and takes my hand.

'He is lying to you, Matjek,' says a female voice. 'It's not losing that hurts the most, it's losing *people*. And Jean should know all about that. Isn't that right, Jean?'

Joséphine. I hurl my mind at the firmament to trigger the escape route I prepared, but something is locking the vir's structure, trapping us inside, a higher-generation Founder code. *A Prime.* Despair tears at my chest. The ground sinks beneath my feet.

And then we are standing on a beach of soft sand, looking at a clear blue sea. There are footprints on it, small ones, and far away, a little boy is making wild splashes in the waves. When he sees us, he stops to look, and comes up running.

Joséphine Pellegrini smiles a serpent smile at me and Matjek both.

'Don't worry,' she says softly. 'We are going to make sure that no one loses anyone, ever again.'

Joséphine looks *old*. It is a cruel joke to force her into such a mindshell, all bones, and strained, stretched skin. She plays with her diamond necklace with dark, mottled fingers.

'You were a fool to come here, Jean,' she whispers.

Matjek is staring at the other Matjek, the smaller one from the sea. The new boy has an aura that betrays him as the Prime here. But in his eyes, there is an infinite hunger that does not belong to Matjek Chen. The last time I saw it was in the Dilemma Prison, and the eyes were my own.

I lay a hand on my Matjek's shoulder.

'You are not me,' Matjek says. 'What are you?'

'All-Defector,' I say, nodding. 'It's been a while.' I squeeze the false jewel in my hand, mind racing. I know only fragments of Prison legend about its true nature. A game-theoretic anomaly that becomes you, that predicts what you are going to do and always wins. And I am in a vir it controls: it can probably see every neuron firing in my brain. Fear makes my chest heavy. It is difficult to breathe.

'Thank you, Jean le Flambeur,' All-D says. 'You have played your part well, better than I could have ever expected.

I have enjoyed being you. Without you, this conflict with the zoku would have been prolonged and tiresome.'

'Let the boy go,' I say. 'He does not understand what is happening here.'

My Matjek gives me a dark look, but does not say anything. Joséphine smiles at him. 'Dear Matjek,' she says. 'You don't have to be afraid. You said you wanted to see your mum and dad again. Well, in just a little while, we are going to bring them back.'

Matjek frowns. 'I don't believe you,' he says. 'I know liars, and you are one.'

There is mock shock on Joséphine's face. 'How rude! But then you have been spending time in *very* bad company! Jean, you have been a terrible influence on the boy.' She looks at me, and for the first time, I see a plea for help flash in her eyes, just for an instant. *She is a prisoner here, too.*

'I don't think you are much better, Joséphine,' I say, holding her gaze. 'I see you have graduated from thieves to monsters.'

'I don't think you understand either, Jean,' the All-Defector says. 'There are no monsters here. It is not easy to explain what I am – but I have noticed that whatever I become leaves … traces. I spent a long time inside you. So I find that I want to explain. I want to be liked. I suspect that comes from you.'

'And how is that working out for you?'

A smile flickers on All-D's lips, a smile that has just a hint of my own.

'Well. In a few moments, in the frame of this vir, I am going to find the zoku Elders, eat them, take their Kaminari jewel, and remake the Universe.'

I frown. 'And why do you think the jewel will accept you?'

'Because my goals are *rational*. It will be in the best

interests of everybody and everything to join me. In most games, defecting is rational.' It looks at the sky. 'It's about survival, you see. Existence is fragile. We live on an island of stability, but it is an illusion.

'The achievement of the Kaminari-zoku implies that there are other spacetimes. Certainly other regions of the Universe beyond our causal horizon. If rational actors have evolved in them, they will have broken their Planck locks – or worse, evolved natively in an environment with no restrictions on computational complexity. If so, it is likely that they will have optimised the expansion rate of their spacetime, turned into an expanding bubble of thought.

'If so, such a bubble of viral spacetime could erase ours at any moment. It would propagate at the speed of light, giving no warning. Things would simply end.'

All-D smiles. 'So, the rational thing to do is to do it *first*. We need to turn our Universe into a perfect replicating strategy to survive. We need to turn it into me.

'It is nothing to be feared. I will retain all information within me. I will complete the Great Common Task.'

He turns to look at the sea.

'Now, would you like to see how the war is going?'

Without waiting for an answer, he makes a small gesture. As we watch in hushed silence, the vir paints a burning Saturn against the gentle evening sky.

18

MIELI AND THE JEWELLED CHAIN

Mieli pilots the *Leblanc* to Saturn through a Sobornost storm.

The ship is an extension of her mind, and flying it is like soaring in a dream. The EM spectrum is a warm glow on her skin. The engines are her blazing wings.

In a boiling space of gamma ray lasers and raion swarms, it is almost not enough.

With a relentless burn of the Hawking drive, she swings the ship in a trajectory orthogonal to the giant planet's orbital plane, away from where the hottest battle rages. But the Sobornost are everywhere. In an eyeblink, she passes through a metacloaked raion grid, lying in wait like a fishing net in water. They shoot after her, short-lived strangelet engines firing, a hundred war raions made to survive the duration of the battle and no longer. She screams Sobornost Friend-or-Foe protocols at them at the top of her EM lungs, but it does not fool them: they know her ship, and want to taste it.

She gives her gogols access to the *Leblanc*'s picotech processors. They grind possible trajectories through Nash engines, and come up with nothing that leads out of the tight cone of raion vectors around her.

Nanomissiles hit, a tingle on her skin, dump their viral code payloads into the *Leblanc*'s systems. She sheds the outer layer of the ship's armour to get rid of them: it feels like tearing off a scab. It floats around the ship, an expanding cloud of dust. A bigger target: another volley of Gödel bombs and kinetic needles flashes through it. One hyperdense projectile passes right through the ship, uncomfortably close to the Hawking containment sphere.

She catalogues the ship's weapons. Anti-meteorite lasers, thoughtwisp launchers, q-dot emitters. No antimatter, strangelets or nanomissiles. Mieli imagines new weapons, tells the ship to grow them, but it is going to take too long. The heaviest armament she has is the micro-singularity of the engine and its needle of gamma rays, but it's no good against the raions: it's too slow to aim, and using it would introduce a new constraint into the optimisation problem of escaping. The *Leblanc* is built for speed, not for battle, and even that is not enough.

Another volley comes, but this time, she is ready: a delicate flick of the Hawking drive diverts the ship slightly in the microsecond before they hit. *Still not fast enough.*

She runs a mass reduction scenario, stripping the ship down to essentials, into barely more than the drive sphere itself. Even so, Saturn is too far. There is no escape from the cold hand of Newton. She could take them with her, detonate the Hawking drive. But that would serve no purpose at all.

Then it hits her. *I'm still thinking like the Mieli who flew* Perhonen. *But I am not her. The atoms of my body were disassembled by a picotech gate, duplicated as qubits inside the* Leblanc's *Realm. My thoughts are quantum information in a photonic crystal made of artificial atoms.*

I need to be someone else.

'Nearest router,' she hisses at the ship's cat. 'Now.'

A lone zoku router near the orbit of Phoebe has survived the invasion unscathed, a kilometre-long glass wedding bouquet, glinting and spinning in the reflected light of the war of the gods. When the *Leblanc* reaches it, it is barely more than an eggshell around the Hawking drive. To avoid the third barrage of missiles, she transforms the ship into a distributed configuration, free-floating modules tethered to the drive. She derives some pleasure from ejecting the thief's treasures into the void. *He can always steal new ones.*

The Sobornost squadron knows what she is doing now. Another shoal of raions is coming. They twinkle like meteors in the night sky: the flashes of a nanomissile cloud, firing.

She takes a deep breath and sends a command to the router, praying that the zoku volition system is working again. The router responds and unfolds, revealing the giant Realmgate within, like the stamen of a flower.

'You have served your master well,' she tells the cat. 'Die with honour.'

The cat bows and tips its feathered hat at her.

Then she thinks a zoku trueform for herself, shapes it into a foglet wedge with her jewels nested inside, and fires it at the Realmgate.

Behind her, the Hawking containment sphere collapses. A black hole turns white. With one hot photon breath, it burns the raions, the router, the *Leblanc* – and all the secrets of Jean le Flambeur.

Mieli races through Realms. The volition system is back online, and she feels the gentle pull of the Great Game jewel again, even if nearly all her carefully won entanglement within has evaporated with the mini-Collapse that the thief created.

There is war in the Realms, too. Weaponised gogols in hated quantum shells invade the zokus' imaginary realities in waves, each generation spawned by a *guberniya*, trying to adapt to the counterintuitive rules of the virtual battlefields. There, at least, the zoku are holding their own. But it cannot be long before the physical infrastructure of the Realms is compromised.

She joins the battle, briefly, under the red sky of an ancient imaginary planet where green men wielding blades with four arms try to hold the tide of buzzing gogols in the form of great white apes. As they fall beneath her Realm-knife, her Great Game jewel starts to fill and hum with entanglement again. She levels up again, and then again, into a Level Six Man In Black. Then she forms a wish and casts it at the jewel. Another gate opens and takes her into the Invisible Realm.

The Great Game Realm is in chaos. The thought-threads are a tangled web, and each bead burns with images of death. The zoku voices are a chorus of panic that is so dense Mieli has to shut them out.

She turns away from the thought labyrinth and qupts Zinda, heart pounding. **Where are you?**

Even in the quicktime of the Invisible Realm, the next moments feel like an eternity. The furious qupts of the thought-game around her blend into a distant thunder. *Let her be safe.*

When the answer comes, it feels like summer rain.

Mieli?

Zinda? Where are you?

Again, a few heartbeats of agonising delay.

In a Realm running on reversible computation near the metallic hydrogen layer inside Saturn. It's very slow here. We are trying to set up a guerrilla operation.

There is not going to be an occupation! I told you, the All-Defector is coming.

What happened to you?

There is no time to explain. Mieli pauses. I need you. She lets her fear and longing from the deck of the *Provence* to filter down the qupt, and feels a sudden stab of anxiety, as if something precious just slipped through her fingers.

And then Zinda is there, in her green dress, beautiful against the labyrinth of the thought-web, smiling a little sadly.

'What do you want me to do, Mieli?'

'What you did on the mountain. I want you to save me.' She kisses the zoku girl fiercely, until neither of them can breathe. Finally, Mieli lets go.

'And to forgive me,' she says.

They find one of the meeting rooms, away from the frantic qupt chatter. Mieli explains the thief's plan to Zinda.

She frowns. 'I don't know anything about the Planck brane, or how to get entangled with it. It would have to be something only the Elders know about. My level is simply not high enough. The only one I know is Barbicane, and I doubt he would be willing to help you, even now. All the entanglement I have is yours, but it's not going to help you very much. I lost most of it when the volition system collapsed, like everybody else.'

Mieli frowns. 'Can you have a look at this?' She hands Zinda the huge complex qupt the thief gave her. The zoku girl's eyes widen as she takes it all in.

'Mieli, do you know what this is?' she says. 'It's a viral zoku. It's a giant twinking machine.'

Then she grins. 'If there is ever a time to do forbidden things, it's at the end of the world!'

It is Zinda who sends out the qupt, carefully crafted according to the Kaminari template, with the precision and speed of an experienced party organiser.

Twink the Liquorice-zoku if you want to save Supra City and to slay the Sleeper.

It spreads from Great Game member to Great Game member, even through the chaos of battle.

'We have to be fast,' Zinda says. 'The Elders are going to notice, and reset everybody's entanglement. But we might have time for one quick volition request, so be ready.'

It starts slowly. But little by little, the twinks start coming in, all the EPR qubits the zoku armies are earning by slaying the enemies of Supra City. In a few moments, the trickle is a flood. The connection to the zoku hums inside Mieli's mind, and suddenly the Great Game jewel feels like a part of her brain, something that has always been there, a true q-self.

'Now!' Zinda breathes. 'Do it quickly!'

Mieli casts the thought they crafted together at the Great Game jewel. **Give me Planck tanglematter from the Spooky-zoku.** The entire zoku rings with her volition. 'I bet they are going to notice *that*,' Mieli says. And sure enough, a moment later, the feeling of omnipotence disappears, replaced by a sense of almost complete emptiness.

Twinking is against the zoku rules, an angry qupt comes through her jewel. **You are now back at Level One.** Mieli's heart sinks, but then she catches herself. *It's just a game,* she thinks, smiling to herself.

Then the tanglematter package arrives with a pop, carried to their small corner of the Invisible Realm by quantum teleportation protocols. A grey dull sphere with a simple volition interface, a dense data spime wrapped around it. Mieli glances at it, but is immediately lost – *EPR states distilled from neutralinos using the entire mass of Saturn as a detector, entangled with supersymmetric matter on the Planck brane.* Whatever it is, it is the key to sending her and the thief to the hiding place of the Kaminari jewel.

'It looks terribly boring!' Zinda says. 'Are you sure this is what we need?'

Mieli smiles. 'No. But I … trust the man who said it is.'

Mieli frowns, looking at the Great Game intel spime. With the sudden drop in her entanglement level, she can't see most of the battle anymore. But she can monitor the specific vectors that the thief said he and Matjek would use when escaping the *guberniya* in a thoughtwisp. *Where are they? It should have only taken them minutes in our frame.*

'What do we do now?' Zinda asks.

'The only thing there is to do before the last battle,' Mieli says. 'We wait.'

19

THE THIEF AND THE ALL-DEFECTOR

I look at the flaming sky and the All-Defector, squeeze the jewel of judgment in my hand and try to think. There is always a way out.

Or is there?

The vir shows us a painfully detailed view of the battle of Saturn. The supramundane world-shell is unravelling. There is a swirling boil on the side of the giant planet that can only be a black hole, shooting up a fountain of X-rays.

Plates have shattered, Strips broken. On the ground, botlets and combat alters pour from Realmgates to resist von Neumann beasts, slow-moving but tenacious creatures that turn any matter into copies of themselves.

The zoku are redirecting mass streams from the undone structures towards the sky as improvised defensive weapons, weaving a dense sheet of iron pellets, each tiny metal flake carrying the kinetic energy of a train. Raions shatter against them like bugs on a windscreen.

Above the Plate of Irem, something strange is happening. There is a raion formation above it – but they seem to be defending the Plate from other Sobornost craft. *The Aun are still fighting. But it won't be enough.* All-D is not using Dragons yet, but he will, if he has to.

I look at the Saturnian space beyond the torn fragments of the planet's rings. The zoku ships have been decimated. The battle for the sunbeam mirrors is almost over, and the perfectly reflective quantum dot structures are aligning to burn away the rest of zoku resistance.

Finally, I can't take it anymore.

I take a step forward. 'Hey,' I say. 'Aren't you forgetting something?' I hold up the trap jewel. 'You let me and Matjek go, or I open this, and we find out if you can outplay a Dragon.'

He smiles contemptuously, a cruel expression on a little boy's face.

'I know you too well, Jean,' he says. 'I can predict your every move. The moment you decide to do it, I will know. Why do you think I let you keep it? I can't touch it, but I can touch *you*. The moment you decide to open it, I will erase you. And you would not risk the boy, not now. You have to lie to me much better than that.' He sits down on the sand and looks up at the battle in the sky again. 'Not much longer,' he says.

I look at Joséphine. *A prison door, opening.* We have danced a long dance, she and I.

'He is me, isn't he?' I say. 'A Dilemma Prison anomaly, but from a le Flambeur seed. Do you want to lose to *me*?'

'I'm not losing, Jean,' she says. 'I am winning. You were never the enemy, death was.' *Help me*, her eyes say.

'Matjek,' I whisper. 'Do you remember that game we played, back in the *Leblanc*? The game with time?'

He nods, eyes wide.

It's worth a try. All-D may control our surroundings, but this vir does come from Matjek's memories, very close to something he spent centuries in on Earth. And I only need a moment.

'Let's play it now.'

Matjek closes his eyes. The air around us becomes viscous and thick. It is difficult to talk.

'It won't help,' Joséphine whispers. 'It knows you were going to do this. It knows what you are going to do next. It knows everything.' She smiles, sadly. 'I'm sorry, Jean. If I had won, I would have wanted you by my side. But it is too late now.'

'We both know that would never have worked out. But you opened a door for me once, and that buys you a lot of forgiveness.' I lean closer to her. 'But if you really want me to forgive you, get the boy out of here. If you get him to Mieli, we may still have a chance.' I pass her the escape protocol I planted in the *guberniya*'s firmament. 'If we could get him to lose control of the vir for just one moment—'

She shakes her head. 'I'm sorry, Jean. I can't. I can't fight him. It's not even like fighting myself, I've done that many times, it's like fighting a god who sees what you are going to do and is never wrong, who makes moves that *force* you to do things you don't want—'

He must have a weakness. *Traces*, he said. I remember far too well how the Dilemma Prison shaped my mind, made me see the world in a grid of cooperations and defections.

'What is he? How do I beat him? Give me something I can use!'

Joséphine swallows.

'He sees what I'm doing,' Matjek says, his voice strained. 'He's breaking through.'

Joséphine runs a shaking hand across the diamonds in her necklace, frantically touching each one. 'Simulations,' she says. 'The All-Defector said it runs simulations to predict what we do, that we can't even know if we *are* those simulations.'

I remember the gun, pointed at my head, my double image in the All-Defector's mirrorshades, just before he pulled the trigger. *Always mirrors.* And in the small and naked reflection of my memory, there is the faintest glimmer of an idea.

I grab Joséphine's hand, hard. 'Remember,' I tell her. 'If you have a chance, get out. Promise me you will get him to Mieli.'

'I promise,' she whispers.

Time lurches into its normal course. Suddenly, All-D is facing us, looking at Matjek curiously.

'That was interesting,' he says. 'I would like to know how you did that.'

'Ask your mum,' Matjek says tartly.

All-D takes a step forward and stretches out a small hand towards Matjek.

'I think I will take you now,' he says. 'It will be interesting to see if you and the Prime are any different.'

I shove Matjek behind me and raise the fake jewel.

'No,' I say. 'If you want to play, play with me.'

The All-Defector looks at me curiously.

'You know,' I say, 'something I often thought about while in the Prison. What would it *truly* be like to play Prisoner's Dilemma with myself? Not just a copy, but *me*. A perfect predictor of what I am going to do. What should I do? Obviously, I should cooperate, since we are going to think of the same things, and make the same decisions. Obviously,

I should defect, since no matter what I do, it's not going to affect what you do. But you will have thought of that as well.

'Why don't we find out? Put your money where your mouth is. Let's make it a formal game.' I make the jewel dance between my fingers. 'It should be more or less equivalent to the Dilemma. I decide when and if to open the jewel, and you try to predict it. If you can really be me, the moment I decide to open it, you erase me. Perfect correlation. And if I don't – well, we are back to where we started.'

'And what if I just erase you anyway?'

I raise my eyebrows. 'Well, then you will have been *wrong*. Surely, that's a smaller payoff. What do you say?'

'All right,' he says. 'One more Dilemma, for old times' sake.'

He stretches and blurs and becomes me, in a white tennis shirt, shorts and mirrorshades. 'All right, loser.' There is a gun in his hand, a sleek silver automatic pistol. 'Would you like a gun, too? Or are you happy with your toy?'

Carefully, I summon the chen-gogol whose mind I stole earlier closer to the surface, close enough that I can become it with a simple mental trigger, open the fake jewel with a mental command and unleash the Dragon-thing within.

'I'm good, thanks.'

'It would have given you some extra points for style.'

'Look who's talking. You lose style points for threatening little boys.'

He raises the gun. 'I think you and I are playing different games, Jean.'

'Oh yes. So we are. Boom boom.'

'Very funny.'

'Déjà vu.'

I stare at my reflection in his mirrorshades, and think about opening the jewel.

I look for a trigger in my memories.

A boy in the desert, getting caught.

When the first blow lands, I will open it.

The man with the silver watch raises his hand. All-D's gun hand twitches.

I smile. *No.* Sitting in a cell, reading a book. *When the door opens, I will open the jewel.*

No, not that.

Another Prison. Another me. The mirror image of a mirror image. When he pulls the trigger, I will open the jewel.

I can tell he doesn't like that. His finger tightens on the trigger.

Well. Plenty of memories left. He is caught in the game now, back in the frame of the Prison. *Good. Need to keep moving.*

I'll do it

when Mieli breaks the wall of my cell.

when I push the sapphire shard through my hand.

when Raymonde, sitting naked at the piano, plays the first note.

when Isaac shatters the third bottle.

when I reach the end of the Corridor of Birth and Death.

On and on it goes, a thief's life, random memories and associations. The All-Defector is very still. I can tell it's working. *Theory of mind.* Modelling the behaviour of others. I'm trying to create a problem that is Jean le Flambeur-complete, that will require him to run a full simulation of me, not just one, but many and many and many.

The jewel opens

when Xuexue stops smiling.
when I hatch from Sumanguru's mind.
when the story Tawaddud is telling ends.
when the Collapse begins.

I can't defeat him alone, but those simulations have to run somewhere in the *guberniya*, and there is a way out of every box, an escape from every prison. If I do this right, I'll have a billion chances, and I only need one.

when the first star falls above Noctis Labyrinthus.
when Matjek closes his book.
when the Cannon of the Jannah booms.
when the warmind pulls the trigger—

The All-Defector fires.

Time slows down. The muzzle flash is a flaming flower. The bullet is a slow train, first stop my head, travelling on invisible rails. *Is it Matjek? Is he trying to buy me time?* But it is too late. The bullet does not matter, it is just the vir's shorthand for All-D reaching out to end me.

Cracks appear in the All-Defector's mirrorshades. They spread down to his face. His mindshell shatters, turns into a hole in the vir. He is swallowed by the blind-spot blankness of the firmament beneath.

And replaced by another me, young, dark-haired, grinning.

He reaches out and catches the bullet in mid-air.

The other me holds the bullet up, like a magician.

'That was quite a gamble,' he says.

'Hey. If you can't trust yourself, who can you trust?'

'We still needed a high roll.'

There are other firmament flashes along the beach. More Jean le Flambeurs are arriving. Their faces are all mine, but different, a gallery of past lives and moments. I smile. It is good to see them, for one last time.

I turn to Joséphine and Matjek. 'Go,' I tell her. 'That trick will only work once.'

The other Jeans are doing something to the vir, creating encrypted firmament layers to keep the vir under our control. It's not going to help us for long: All-D has the entire *guberniya* under its control.

Time is running out.

'Jean, you don't have to—' Joséphine begins. I cut her off. 'Yes, I do.'

I kneel and hug Matjek, hard. His hair smells of the sea.

'Be good, okay? Tell Mieli I said goodbye.' I squeeze his shoulders, and run out of words again.

I turn to Joséphine. 'And you. You stay away from Mieli. Leave her alone? Do you understand?'

She nods. I kiss her. Her lips are papery and dry, but there are other kisses beneath them, serpent lips of a goddess that taste of roses and open doors and beginnings. It is hard to let go.

'He's coming,' one Jean says. 'He is in us,' the other whispers.

'*Now*,' I tell Joséphine. She and Matjek raise their hands in a silent goodbye, and then they are gone, in a firmament blink.

I turn to the assembled ranks of Jean le Flambeur.

'How much time do we have?'

The dark-haired young Jean looks at his pocket watch. 'Twenty seconds,' he says.

I nod. I don't have to say anything to them. They already know.

I walk down to the waterline and dig my toes in the warm

sand. I cradle the dragon jewel in my hands. I never realised how beautiful it is, shaped like a butterfly, made of liquid light.

The sea sighs and the water pulls back, leaving behind a dark grin of wet sand.

I close my eyes.

When the wave reaches my feet, I will open the jewel.

20

MIELI AND THE KAMINARI JEWEL

In the Invisible Realm, Mieli and Zinda watch the chen *guberniya* die.

It begins with a sudden confusion among the raion clouds around the Sobornost diamond world, like a shift in weather. Sobornost ship formations near the *guberniya* lose cohesion and break before smaller zoku forces. A ripple goes through its surface. At first, Mieli thinks it is an optical illusion, but a touch of the spime shows them the proud statues and thoughtwisp fountains and antimatter furnaces of the diamond sphere's surface.

A wave is travelling across the adamantine vastness. Where it passes, only a smooth, featureless surface remains, an endless, shining plain, a nothingness. The constant neutrino roar of the *guberniya* is silent, suddenly.

The dragon jewel, Mieli thinks. *Did the boy Matjek open it? Did the thief fail?*

Kuutar and Ilmatar. Killing one guberniya *won't be enough. We need the Kaminari jewel.*

The ragged remnants of the zoku fleet gain a brief respite as the Sobornost forces deal with the *guberniya*'s death. But it does not take long for the other Founders to regroup, and soon, whatever power struggle the chens' sudden departure caused is over.

And the sunbeam mirrors are still moving.

Mieli looks at the spime and thinks of giving in to the battle call of the Great Game jewel. The dull eye of the brane tanglematter sphere stares at her, mockingly. She takes Zinda's hand. The zoku girl squeezes her fingers.

An alarm rings in her mind. There is a thoughtwisp in the approach vector the thief gave her, with the signature of a qupt data package. It is escorted by three pellegrini oblasts, three killer whales guarding a fleck of plankton. They are transmitting declarations of neutrality, announcing that the pellegrini *guberniya* will withdraw from battle, on the condition that the contents of the thoughtwisp are routed to—

A Realmgate opens, and a boy of twelve steps out. He has just a hint of grey in his hair. He has grown since the last time Mieli saw him, on a beach, in the Lost Jannah of the Cannon, on Earth.

A tall woman with auburn hair follows him.

'Hello, Mieli,' the pellegrini says.

Mieli ignores her. She looks at the boy. 'Matjek,' she says. 'Do you remember me? We met on a beach, once.'

Matjek nods. 'I remember you.' His mouth is a straight, serious line. 'Jean says goodbye.' His voice breaks, but he presses a fist against his mouth, refusing to cry.

Mieli offers him her hand, thinking of little Varpu, her *koto* sister. 'Ssh,' she says. 'It will be all right.'

Then she turns to the pellegrini. The scar on her cheek burns.

'I suppose you are here to tell me that Sydän still wants me back, and that you will give her to me in exchange for the Kaminari jewel,' Mieli says.

A faint smile flickers across the pellegrini's rouge lips. 'No, Mieli,' she says. 'I am here to say goodbye, and to thank you for your service. I made a promise to Jean to leave you alone, and I plan to keep it.' She sighs. 'A pity. You were just beginning to show potential.

'Now, I suppose I will have to watch as my brothers and sisters destroy you. Jean hurt the All-Defector, but it is still in many gogols across Sobornost, not as high-ranking as Matjek-Prime was, but it hasn't given up. But by all means, give a quick truedeath to as many of them as you can. It will make things easier for me, afterwards.'

'Perhaps I will surprise you,' Mieli says.

'Nothing would please me more, Mieli, daughter of Karhu. Good luck, and goodbye. I release you from your oath to me. Go free.' She turns and takes a step towards the Realmgate.

'Wait,' Mieli says. The pellegrini looks at her over her shoulder.

'Did you ever love him, truly?' Mieli asks. 'The thief. Or was he just a tool?'

The pellegrini closes her eyes. A veil of sadness passes across her face.

'Of course I loved him, Mieli. There is no greater love than a maker's for the things she makes. Especially when they grow to be something she never imagined.'

She blows Mieli a kiss and walks through the silver gate. Mieli feels something on her face, a touch of lips. She touches her cheek. It tingles under her fingers.

'Mieli?' Zinda says.

'What is it?'

'Your scar is gone.'

*

The *Zweihänder* takes the Liquorice-zoku and Matjek to the yin-yang moon of Iapetus, taking advantage of the disorder caused by the withdrawal of the pellegrini fleet. On the way, Mieli has to convince Sir Mik that engaging the four oblasts that are exchanging fire with Gun Club holeships is not a good idea.

'ButMyladyMieli!' the diminutive warrior protests. 'NoGreaterHonourForKnightThanFightingGiants!'

Mieli sighs. *What would the thief tell him?*

'Except a sacred quest,' Matjek says. 'We seek the Holy Grail!' Zinda has taken the boy under her wing, and one of the first things she did was to make the young chen a member of the Liquorice-zoku.

'WhyDidn'tYouSayFirst?'

Wearing a heavy metacloak, the ship takes them down near the equatorial ridge. Mieli wears the body and the weaponry she created for her mission to Prometheus. In spite of her claims of having a combat alter, Zinda is unarmed, in a simple q-suit. Anti-de-Sitter-times-a-Sphere wears her incomprehensible four-dimensional form. Sir Mik, of course, is armed to the teeth. Matjek carries the tanglematter sphere, guarded by heavy botlets under Mieli's control.

The lightning flashes of the battle above make their long, sharp shadows flicker as Matjek leads them to a sheer face of the colossal cylindrical mountain range. He touches the rock, and a disc-shaped area of it dissolves, revealing the eerie blue of the Arsenal's pseudomatter wall. The boy qupts a large quantum state at the impossibly smooth surface and it, too, opens, revealing shifting folds that part before them.

Zinda creates a q-dot bubble to carry them through, and then they are in the giant blue-green tunnel of the Arsenal.

It does not take them long to find the ekpyrotic cannon. Mieli stares at it: it reminds her of some monster of the void of Oortian tales, a thing with a four-lobed eye made of black holes.

'Algorithm termination: undecidable,' Anti-de-Sitter-times-a-Sphere says.

'Do you really have to do this, Mieli? How can you go inside that thing, and ask us to fire it into Saturn?' Zinda's eyes plead until Mieli has to look away.

Mieli smiles. 'I'm afraid that the waiting will be your job, this time,' she says. She turns to Matjek: the boy is already busy feeding the tanglematter sphere's contents to the mon-strous weapon. 'Matjek, can you—'

A lightning bolt strikes at her through her Great Game jewel, like the All-Defector's blow on Hektor, only inside her mind. Around her, she sees the other Liquorice-zoku members shimmer into their trueforms, frozen in place like huge snowflakes.

'This is not how the Great Game is played,' Barbicane says, shaking his head.

The Great Game Elder is alone, wearing his brass cyborg form. His Game jewel shimmers in his hand: the others orbit his stovepipe hat in a dimly glowing halo.

'We don't take the easy way out! We don't use cheat codes! Would you risk all of reality for one insignificant war?' Barbicane gestures at Zinda with her gun hand, exasperated. 'And you, little girl! I made you to keep her sane! What were you thinking?'

Barbicane winks. 'My apologies. I am being facetious! You are all doing exactly what I wanted you to do. Sobornost infiltrators who broke into our most secure fortress during a time of crisis, and destroyed the Kaminari jewel! That's the official version! Why do you think I let you know where it was, pretended to overlook Zinda's twinking?

'I always wanted to do it myself, but the volition of the Great Game would not let me. It was too tempting for too many. I kept a balance of indecision for a long time, managed at least to hide it on another brane.

'But now, our mutual friend Jean has set us all free! It has been forever since I did not feel the volition of the zoku in my head. It is like playing a new game! I am finally free to do what the zoku *needs*, not what it *wants*!'

He gestures at an iridescent cube floating behind him. 'A strangelet device. It will go with you all into the cannon. It should cause a Big Crunch on the Planck brane. Ah! A grand truedeath for all of you! I almost wish I could share it!'

Mieli, comes a quiet qupt from Mieli's Liquorice jewel. It's Matjek. **I can move. And I still have access to the gunscape. I don't think he knows I'm not Great Game. Can you keep him talking?**

'There won't be anyone to remember our deaths,' Mieli says. 'The Sobornost is about to wipe out Supra City if we don't use the jewel.'

'Oh, there will be survivors, my dear! Like I said, it is time to start a new game, and I look forward to the challenge! We had grown too powerful. But being the underdog again, a rebel, one of the few ragged survivors of a great empire, fighting a vastly superior force. What a jolly Great Game that will be!'

I'm almost ready, Mieli, Matjek says. He pauses. **Are you?**

Mieli casts a quick glance at Barbicane, hovering in front of the ekpyrotic cannon.

You can't be serious, she qupts.

The entire Arsenal is a linear accelerator. I will fire you at Saturn. The rest of us will be fine. Just promise that you will come back.

'We could end that game, here and now, if you just let me,' Mieli shouts.

Ten seconds.

'And are you so arrogant that you think the jewel will accept you, Oortian?' Barbicane growls. 'You are nothing special, no matter what le Flambeur thinks. I had to dangle you in front of him to goad him into desperation, into breaking the volition system. I even filled his ship with tools! I suppose I should thank him. After all, it was his Collapse that created the Great Game Zoku in the first place, to make sure it would never happen again!'

His face darkens. 'Then again, there are parts of me that remember what I lost on the day it rained fire. So I must admit it gives me some pleasure to think that his attempt to rescue you was in vain.

'Perhaps I will allow myself the indulgence of taking care of you personally. It will not make a difference in the end, after all, and may teach a lesson to incompetent little Zinda here. Discipline amongst the newbies is far too lax these days, that's what I always say!'

He presses the cold mouth of his gun arm against Mieli's head.

Do it! Mieli qupts at Matjek. She casts one more look at Zinda. The zoku girl's eyes flash with understanding. The metal against Mieli's flesh grows hot.

Done. Mieli is qupted into the gunscape, her mind encoded into the quantum states of the tanglematter sphere. She is inside a tiny Realm, bodiless, only dimly aware of the

Arsenal around her, of the minuscule shape of Barbicane right in front of the ekpyrotic weapon.

Matjek fires. The Arsenal walls come alive with energy. An EM field pushes the ekpyrotic shell to an enormous velocity in seconds. It flashes through chamber after chamber, spinning faster and faster, erasing every gun in the Gun Club's collection in its path.

Even inside her cocooned Realm, Mieli feels the impact on Saturn's south pole, of the shell pushing deep into the metallic hydrogen core. Then the four black holes of the ekpyrotic shell come together.

The entire giant planet pulses like a heart, pumps gravitational waves across the space between universes. They carry Mieli with them, a message in a bottle, washing onto an alien shore.

Everything is soft. Everything is liquid.

Mieli does not see or feel as much as *perceives*, does not move as much as *flows*. There is only a bubble-thin boundary between her and Other, inside and outside. It is like a dream where you dive and start breathing underwater.

She has a vague sense of up and down, and of infinite depths below her. Something huge passes beneath, moving with slow strokes, and her fragile bubble-self wavers in its wake. For a moment, she stays very still, fear spilling out of her in ripples.

How did the zoku build this place? Solitonic states, governed by alien physics, just about complex enough to compute, to provide a platform for thought, here on the Planck brane. *Did they build it or find it?*

Slowly, carefully, she lets herself expand, reaches out with her awareness, feeling for things that are not her. After a while, she starts to sense a knotted flow, something warm in the liquid other, something shaped like hands, folded together, or a sleeping butterfly.

The Kaminari jewel.

Here, touching is a metaphor, and when Mieli reaches for it, its flow lines pull her essence in, make her a part of it, create a knot in what she thinks of as her chest.

Then the jewel opens.

At first, there is only a cool presence, filling her, spreading to her every cell. Then the jewel *is* her, and she is *it*, and they are all possible Mielis at once.

An old winged woman dying of a smartcoral growth in Oort, telling a story to her great-grandchildren.

A Sobornost goddess whose wings spread over the Solar System.

A zoku trueform with a halo of jewels, like a tarot card.

A story told by a jinn in the wildcode desert.

A caleidoscope of images, a superposition, many things all at once. And yet they have one thing in common.

Softly, note by note, Mieli starts singing, as if she was filled with *väki* of Oort, ready to shape itself to her/their will. The chorus of angels rises together, and sings a last song for the ship *Perhonen*.

She sings of *alinen* and the dark, and of another song that made a ship like a butterfly of the void. She sings of advice and love. Of fear of goodbyes, of closing doors. Of a thief in a prison. Of an ending, of wings burning against a sphere of blue and white. Of a last butterfly kiss.

Of all the lives around her, entangled in not a jewelled chain, but a spiderweb.

She sings of a new beginning.

In between the notes of the song, there is a Universe.

The jewel listens. The wish is granted.

A pattern emerges in the weave of quantum threads, in the emptiness of the Planck brane. The perfect symmetry of nothing shatters into the imperfect order of gauge fields, quarks and gluons.

Many things are born from one. A path is chosen through a forest of possible orderings. Chaos crystallises into a diamond of causality.

Mieli's song begins to sing, and there is a flash of light.

Epilogue

Joséphine Pellegrini the Prime watches the war from her *guberniya*, drinking wine. She misses her temple on Venus. That seems like a more appropriate distance from these messy proceedings, in any case.

And she has many rediscovered emotions to file away in her Library. Like grief. She raises a lonely glass to Jean le Flambeur. *Still, there are many more where that one came from. Perhaps it is time to ask Sasha for a favour and visit the Dilemma Prison again.*

Joséphine sighs. It is almost time to get ready for another war. Her brothers and sisters are about to wipe out Supra City with their shiny sunbeam. Shame, really. They will have to come up with a new and better common enemy. Something less risky than the All-Defector.

Something outside the Solar System, perhaps? She will have to branch gogols to think about it.

There are still things to settle with the hsien-kus and the vasilevs: the cooperation the All-Defector forced upon them did not help them to put aside their grievances with her. But they have expended far more of their forces against the zokus than she did, and even without Chen support, she has a much better chance against them, this time. The others will be distracted. Chitragupta will spend millennia combing through the remains of the zoku Realms. Sasha will play with his new toys. And sumangurus are little more than weapons, just asking for targets to be pointed at.

She sips her perfect chardonnay, the product of millions of iterated worlds and taster gogols. *Perfection. So hard to come by, so hard to make.*

Oh, yes, the future looks bright.

Saturn flashes white, a tear in the skin of reality, the lightning wingbeat of an angel. *The sunbeam,* she begins to think, before the frantic cries from her gogols come in.

Saturn is gone. A strange gravitational shadow remains, holding the Sobornost fleet in orbit around empty space. But the planet itself and Supra City are nowhere to be seen.

Joséphine stands up in her Prime aspect, steps into the minds of a billion gogols, replays the event from every possible angle. *Gravitational anomalies. Dense radiation, scattered all over the System. Quantum disturbances in brains and hardware.*

The Spike. It was just like the Spike.

All the gogols in her *guberniya* sense her rising emotion, and cower in fear, gripped by the iron fingers of *xiao*.

Then Joséphine Pellegrini starts laughing, laughing in a chorus of billions: a thundering sound, full of joy and pride.

The sky of the new world is endless, as is everything else, but Mieli does not mind. The suns are warm, and she is eating a peach. Or a half of it: Zinda is nibbling at the other.

'To be completely honest,' the zoku girl says, 'I don't

see the attraction.' She looks at the stone in her hand with puzzled distaste.

'Paris the man gave it to the prettiest goddess, I was once told,' Mieli says. 'It's a compliment.'

'Oh!' Zinda says, and kisses her. 'A story is always better than a piece of fruit!'

Mieli smiles to herself.

For a while, they lie side by side. Supra City is in the sky, healing, but they are in a small world of their own. Here, reality is like *väki*, more malleable, and you don't need machines to make Realms. Yet, it holds surprises, just enough so you don't forget the razor blade within.

'Do you think they will follow us?' Zinda asks.

'Why would they? They have a Universe of their own now,' Mieli says. Another smile rises to her lips, unbidden. 'Besides, I have a feeling they are going to be busy.'

She gets up and takes Zinda's hand.

'Come on,' she says. 'I want to fly.'

The Archon is happy.

It has been guarding the Dilemma Prison for a long time, but there are always new patterns in the infinite grid of co-operation and defection, always new flavours to discover. Its most recent hobby is looking for a Prison-complete pattern that would allow it to build the Prison itself out of flashes of the prisoners' guns. Finding the right Eden state should only take a few subjective millennia.

Thus, the Archon does not care much for the distant wars of the Founders, and when the radiation burst comes from Saturn, it merely changes the error correction schemes of the Prison's computronium to compensate. To pay attention to the inner workings of subatomic particles would be to follow the teachings of the quantum filth.

Inside one of the Prison's many, many cells of glass, a man sits, reading a book, or trying to. His body dreads the next game with guns. His mind drifts to memories of a boy in a desert, to a choice he made, to the paths he did not take. They are the kinds of thoughts that come to you in a prison where nothing ever changes.

Harsh, sudden sunlight falls on a blank page of the book. The glare hurts his eyes. He takes blue sunglasses from his pocket, puts them on and looks up.

There is a door, open, white and bright.

He puts down the book, gets up and walks through it, whistling as he goes. He is surprised, but only a little. For in the end, there is always a way out.

Acknowledgements

It has been a long journey, and it would not have even started without two people: Simon Spanton at Gollancz, and my agent John Jarrold. So many thanks to them for their trust, advice and companionship along the way. I am looking forward to travelling on to new lands with them, beyond those of the *Quantum Thief* books.

Deep heartfelt thanks also go to:

All you readers who decided to come along and stick with it – there are more of you than I ever dared to imagine!

All those who provided feedback on the early drafts of this book, in particular Sam Halliday, Mark Harding, Esa Hilli, Lauri Lovén, Kathryn Myronuk, Ramez Naam, Phil Raines, Brad Templeton, Stuart Wallace, as well as the usual Writers' Bloc suspects: Halsted M. Bernard, Morag Edward, Andrew Ferguson, Bram Gieben, Gavin Inglis, Helen Jackson, Jane McKie, Andrew Wilson and Kirsti Wishart. Also thanks to Antti Autio for going above and beyond his translating duties and asking all the right questions.

Hugh Hancock, Martin Page and Charlie Stross for all those creativity-enhancing espressos.

My fellow GSP13 students at the Singularity University for injecting some exponential weirdness into the writing process – especially the amazing HelixNano team: Carina, Geoffrey and Kat.

The sadly absent Iain Banks, with a quiet toast, for showing me and an entire generation of writers the way.

My parents for continuing to show me what courage means.

And finally Zuzana, who appeared one Halloween night five years ago, just as the last words of *The Quantum Thief* were being written, and changed everything.

— Hannu Rajaniemi
In Edinburgh, 2008–2014.